Where the Road Ends

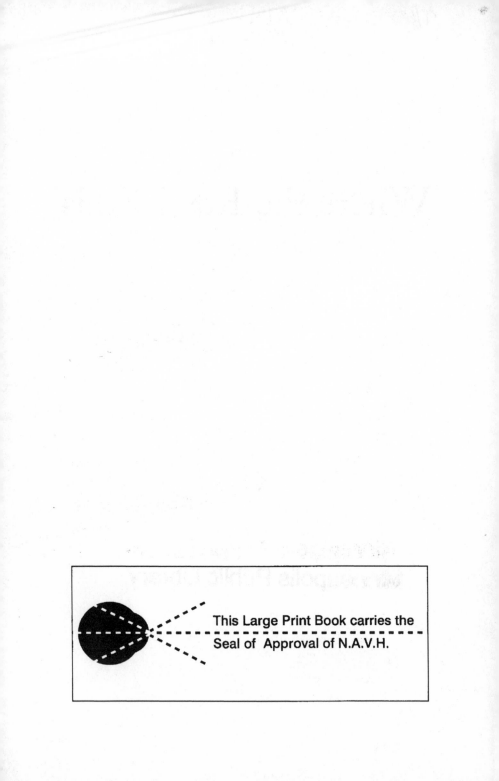

This Large Print Book carries the
Seal of Approval of N.A.V.H.

Where the Road Ends

Tara Taylor Quinn

Published in 2005 by arrangement with Harlequin Books S.A.

Wheeler Large Print Softcover.

The text of this Large Print edition is unabridged.
Other aspects of the book may vary from the original edition.

Set in 16 pt. Plantin by Christina S. Huff.

Printed in the United States on permanent paper.

Library of Congress Cataloging-in-Publication Data

Quinn, Tara Taylor.
    Where the road ends / by Tara Taylor Quinn.
      p. cm.
    ISBN 1-59722-024-8 (lg. print : sc : alk. paper)
    1. Single mothers — Fiction. 2. Missing children —
Fiction. 3. Large type books. I. Title.
PS3617.U586W47 2005
  813'.6—dc22   2005008810

For Kevin, who has to endure far too many challenges for the honor of being my spouse, but who approaches every step of the journey as if it's a privilege.

And

For Rachel, whose childhood has been unique but who doesn't seem to resent that fact.

I love both of you with all my heart.

As the Founder/CEO of NAVH, the only national health agency solely devoted to those who, although not totally blind, have an eye disease which could lead to serious visual impairment, I am pleased to recognize Thorndike Press* as one of the leading publishers in the large print field.

Founded in 1954 in San Francisco to prepare large print textbooks for partially seeing children, NAVH became the pioneer and standard setting agency in the preparation of large type.

Today, those publishers who meet our standards carry the prestigious "Seal of Approval" indicating high quality large print. We are delighted that Thorndike Press is one of the publishers whose titles meet these standards. We are also pleased to recognize the significant contribution Thorndike Press is making in this important and growing field.

Lorraine H. Marchi, L.H.D.
Founder/CEO
NAVH

* Thorndike Press encompasses the following imprints: Thorndike, Wheeler, Walker and Large Print Press.

Acknowledgments

Special thanks to my "Michigan Research Family" — Alyson Hamacher, videographer extraordinaire and special vacuum coordinator; Rachel Reames, videographer, entertainer and owner of the disfigured finger; Patricia Bodell, for her notes; Kevin Reames, chauffeur, and Steve Meredith, navigator. As far as I'm concerned, the road never ends.

Thanks also to all the owners and employees of the many, many establishments we visited, some of which appear in this book. Without fail, everyone we approached was gracious, helpful and kind, from people we stopped on the street to the UPS delivery lady. Please note: while most of the places mentioned in this book are real, there were times I needed to use less-than-appealing establishments, and they are fictitious. The school in Lowell, Michigan, is also fictitious. Thanks to my in-laws, Deanna Reames and David

Reames, and to Julie Greer for jumping in to help with last-minute location glitches.

And one more thank-you to all of those who supported me through this exciting opportunity: my agent, Irene Goodman; my editor, Paula Eykelhof; Debbie Macomber; Lee Anne Vangarderen for her nightly e-mails of encouragement; my many friends in Romance Writers of America; my mother and brother, Penny and Scott Gumser. Any time I started to doubt, one of you was there.

Dear Reader,

I'm excited to bring you this novel, which is very special to me. It's one of those stories that had a life of its own from the beginning, taking me places I would never have dared to go before this. It first came about in a darkened and mostly empty theater as I sat through several nights of dance rehearsal with my daughter. I was entertaining myself, not working. I wasn't plotting or developing characters. I never intended a book to be born. When I sat down at the computer one midnight after rehearsal, it was only to play around a little bit. How twelve pages appeared in less than an hour, I still don't know. But they were the beginning of something that had more power over me than I could ever have imagined.

I'm partial to this story for another reason, as well. It's set in Michigan — which I've always considered home. Though I've lived all over the country, most of my family — and my husband's family — is still in Michigan. We own seventeen acres there, just outside of Baldwin. You'll see it about halfway through the book. And no, the owners don't want to sell.

One more thing. I said this book took

me places I wouldn't choose to go. One of those was the world of child abduction. During the months I spent writing *Where the Road Ends*, researching procedures and statistics, I became concerned about my own daughter's safety. Until I stumbled on a fairly new program sponsored by the National Center for Missing and Exploited Children — Know the Rules. Know the Rules is a public-awareness campaign designed to educate and empower teens and their parents, and to help in the prevention of child abduction. I found that in educating myself about some simple rules, I could alleviate a lot of the fears I had. I was able to allow myself and my daughter to live not in fear but with confidence, because my child knew what to do if danger presented itself. You can receive a Know the Rules publication free of charge through my new Web site, www.tarataylorquinn.com, or by contacting the National Center for Missing and Exploited Children at www. missingkids.com.

My hope is that, empowered with knowledge, we all continue to live happy and healthy.

I love to hear from readers! You can reach me at ttquinn@tarataylorquinn.com or at P.O. Box 15065, Scottsdale, AZ

85267. You're also invited to check out my Web site. With trivia contests, prizes, free giveaways, message boards and more, we have a lot of fun there! Come join us.

Tara

Prologue

She was going to have to let the nanny go.

Staring out the front-room window, taking in the beautiful rolling grounds of the Wainscoat estate, Amelia reined in emotion, trading its insidious confusion for logical thought.

Would it *always* feel as if her life was out of control?

Or was letting Kathy go the first step toward taking charge? The beginning of a new existence for herself and her son?

Fingers trembling uncharacteristically, Amelia pushed her dark hair over her shoulders, ruining the effect Donald, her hairdresser of ten years, had so painstakingly created. And if the tears that were threatening actually fell, the time she'd spent on her artfully applied makeup would be wasted, too.

As she stood there in her slim-fitting, dove-gray designer suit waiting for Kathy to appear, Amelia tried to focus on the facts. And she remembered the last conversation — almost a year earlier — she'd had with her husband.

They'd been in her suite in the high-rise building that was home to the head office of Wainscoat Construction. After a short day at his current construction site, Johnny had come to drop off Charles before going to the dock to take the new boat for a trial run, prior to teaching Charles to water ski the following day.

"I'm a little uncomfortable with how possessive of Charles Kathy's getting," he'd said slowly. "It's almost like she's jealous of your place in his life."

"I've had to remind her once or twice that as his mother, I make the decisions," she replied. "Kathy's very involved with him, but that's natural, don't you think? They spend a lot of time together."

He'd nodded, but hadn't looked convinced.

"Do you think there's a problem?" she'd asked Johnny. "More than just two women being territorial?" She'd studied his face, usually able to read his thoughts.

His broad shoulders square, Johnny had shrugged. "I think it's possible. Which is why I wanted to talk to you."

Amelia's stomach had started to hurt

then — just as it hurt now. "So what do we do about her? It's not like we can fire her, Johnny. She's part of the family."

"Well —" Johnny had drawn out the word meaningfully "— no, she's not."

"She's been living with us since Charles was born."

"She's an employee."

He'd been right, of course, but . . .

"One we've trusted with our son's life," Amelia said.

"And I think we still can, to a point."

"To what point?"

Johnny's eyes had been warm, concerned, as they met hers. He'd suggested they keep an eye on things. Listen carefully to everything their four-year-old son had to say.

And with that warning, she'd wanted to get rid of Kathy then and there.

"Don't overreact, Amelia," Johnny had said.

Her heart missed a beat now as she remembered the grin he'd given her. The one that had always melted her heart.

"I'm not suggesting anything drastic here," he'd continued. "I don't think it's gotten out of hand. . . ."

She remembered thinking, that Johnny was right. As usual.

Things hadn't been bad enough to warrant firing Kathy. Not then.

But this past year, since Johnny's death, the situation had changed.

At least Amelia thought it had.

Thinking back over the past months, she made a mental list of times she'd been concerned about Kathy's actions and was surprised — and a little frightened — by how extensive the list had grown.

Most recently with Kathy's insistence that Amelia not change the school her son was attending.

Johnny had been worried that Kathy was overstepping her boundaries.

And she had been; there was no longer any doubt of it. Amelia reviewed her list.

And then her mind switched back to Johnny that day in her office. Bruising her with memories of the husband she'd lost . . .

He'd reached for the door.

"Johnny?"

"Yeah?"

She hadn't known why she'd called out to him. She'd just wished things had been different, that he'd kissed her while they'd had that moment alone. That she'd said, "I love you."

"You'll be home for dinner?" she'd asked.

"I always am," he'd said, heading back to the outer office.

He *was* always home for dinner. It was she — CEO of the multibillion dollar company for which Johnny was a construction worker — who missed out on family dinners. But what else could she do?

She'd met Johnny on a job site. He was a master carpenter and project supervisor for Wainscoat Construction. She'd known there would be some challenges in their relationship, but they'd loved each other passionately and she'd been certain that would be enough. She'd had no way of knowing, when she'd married Johnny and had Charles so soon afterward, that her father would die suddenly. Hadn't realized that while Johnny's pride demanded he continue to work, he had no intention of stepping into her father's shoes, of working a desk job. Ever.

"Hey."

She'd jumped, hitting her elbow on the doorjamb. Johnny had come back.

"What?"

"Just wanted to make sure *you'd* be home for dinner."

"Yeah," she'd said softly, very glad he'd asked.

"Good."

He'd kissed her then, deeply, intimately, exploring her mouth with his tongue in ways that left her feeling, as his touch always did, more like a giddy teenager than the boss of an internationally known company.

It had been the last time she'd ever felt his lips on hers.

Kathy's voice interrupted Amelia's memories. "This might have to wait until tonight, I really can't talk long." Kathy had come into the room so quietly Amelia hadn't realized she was there. "Charles's swimming lesson starts in half an hour and I like to let him warm up first."

Kathy's once-forthright gaze was elusive. And Amelia's resolve, along with her stomachache, deepened.

Sometime over the past year, the pretty woman who'd been living with them since Charles's birth had stopped wearing makeup — and her fashionably attractive clothes were hanging on her slight frame. Things Amelia had noticed, yet not really acknowledged. She'd been too overwhelmed with grief and trying to get on with life.

She took a deep breath. "I'm going to be making some changes around here."

The nanny's gaze shot up, her brows straight beneath cocoa-brown bangs, her face a mask. "What kind of changes?"

In that second Amelia was certain about a decision she hadn't even thought she'd made.

"Since Johnny died I've been forced to consider what's important to me," she began.

"Your company is important to you."

"My son is important to me."

"Of course he is, which is why I'm here to look after him for you."

"But what about *you?*" Amelia asked, forcing her trembling hands to remain by her sides. "Your personal life has slowly dwindled down to nothing. You've not only tried to take Johnny's place in Charles's life, but you're trying to make up for his absence in mine, as well."

Cloyingly so.

Amelia hated herself for that reaction. Almost buckled under the guilt. *Was* she doing the right thing?

Because if she was letting fear or insecurity take over, she had to stop. Now. She needed to make rational decisions based solely on what was best for her son; she couldn't afford to lose emotional control. She had to be strong for Charles.

And she wasn't going to let Johnny down, either.

For a moment, silence filled the space between the two women, and Amelia remembered the history they'd shared. The years. The celebrations. The grief.

Kathy's stoicism slid away into the silence, leaving a lonely woman with slumped shoulders. "My heart is here," she said softly, as though that explained everything. Tears welled in her eyes.

Amelia almost hugged her. This was the woman she'd entrusted with her son's life. The only family she and Charles had left in the world.

How could she fire her? What was she thinking?

Could she even manage without Kathy? Could Charles?

There was Cara, of course, Amelia's best friend since childhood. But as Amelia's right hand at Wainscoat, Cara was needed at work.

And what about Kathy? Was it fair to let her go after she'd dedicated five years of her life to them?

"You're only twenty-eight, Kath," she said, taking a step closer to the woman. The two of them were standing in the middle of the elegant front room.

Facing off or moving together?

"Until this past year, you've always had a lot of boyfriends. You wanted to get married and have children of your own, but you haven't been away from Charles or me in months. And talk of any life outside this house doesn't even exist anymore."

Kathy's eyes darted around the room, her forearm jerking up and then back to her side as though signaling an end. "Charles is my child." The words were sharp.

Where was the woman Amelia had wanted to hug just seconds before?

Suddenly, Johnny's warning was all she could hear, all she could think about. Her husband had been observant, intuitive about people, and the most dedicated father she'd ever known. She remembered the immediate reason for this meeting, Kathy's remark, in front of Charles, that Amelia did not have the right to make important decisions regarding her son's life.

How had it come to this? At one time, it had been a blessing just to have Kathy around. Amelia and Johnny had often marveled at how lucky they'd been to find her. They'd been so thankful.

"You know he's not really your child," Amelia said softly, treading carefully in territory she neither recognized nor understood. "He's *my* son, Kathy. Mine and Johnny's."

Kathy motioned awkwardly again, her entire body jerking slightly, as though she'd been hit and was trying to hide the impact.

"Johnny's dead."

Amelia couldn't argue with that. They'd brought her the shirt he'd been wearing that last day. Pulled out of the ocean almost a mile from the initial explosion. It was little more than shreds.

"In body, not in spirit."

Kathy's fingers fidgeted almost imperceptibly at her sides, then stopped and her chin rose belligerently. "You hired me to love Charles."

"To care for him, yes," Amelia admitted. And of course she'd been gratified, and greatly relieved, to leave Charles in the hands of someone who not only kept him safe, but loved him. Kathy had been young and inventive; she'd entertained Charles, made his life fun. Made all their lives fun with her impromptu games and celebrations.

"That love gives me rights." There was no mistaking the challenge in the nanny's tone.

"Some."

"Do you love Charles?"

"Of course! And because he's my son, he's my responsibility."

"He's my responsibility, too. And I love him every bit as much as you do."

Amelia sighed. "Kathy, I'm his mother."

They stood there on the plushest of carpets, and continued to confront each other, one in business clothes, the other in capri pants and a pastel, button-down blouse.

"But, I've raised him."

Amelia's throat closed as she faced Kathy's hard-eyed stare. The younger woman still maintained an outward calm. But she was way out of line. In her thinking. In her attitude.

Just as Johnny had suspected.

"You've helped, yes," Amelia murmured, not at all sure how to proceed. "Tremendously. But that doesn't change the fact that he's my son and you should have sons of your own."

Kathy started — not trembling, nothing so uncontrolled as that. "Charles is as much my son as he is yours, Amelia," she said in an odd, faraway voice. "Being a mother is more than a biological function. We both know I've filled that role for Charles much more than you have."

Oh, God. Who *was* this woman?

Fear rose within Amelia as she accepted

that her deceased husband's fears had been realized. On the verge of losing what little breakfast she'd eaten, she stood straight, strong, in control.

"Which is why I've decided it's time to change some things," Amelia said, calmed by her own voice, her ability to sound as though she could handle anything.

She didn't know whether she was having any effect on Kathy, but she was convincing herself.

"What things?"

Was that panic she read in Kathy's eyes?

Could the bravado be just that, then — a brave front Kathy erected as a way to deal with the pain and tragedy that had been crippling this household for the past year? Amelia could certainly understand that. Some days it felt as if bravado was the only glue holding *her* together.

So was Kathy's behavior merely her attempt to achieve a sense of control over uncontrollable circumstances?

Amelia just didn't know.

"You're never going to find a husband or a life of your own as long as you're tied to Charles."

"I have plenty of time to find a husband, to start a family. Right now Charles needs me."

"It's not good for a little boy to have someone who's dedicated her entire life to him," Amelia said, certain of that much at least. "He'll be spoiled, growing up to expect his relationships to be centered on him. He'll expect to be waited on, to have whoever's in his life there for him whenever he deems it necessary or desirable."

"He's just going on five, Amelia. He's *supposed* to be able to count on having someone there for him."

"There for him, yes, but he also needs to be aware that those around him have their own lives. He sees me go to work, sees me with Cara. Johnny worked, went out with his friends. Charles sees you go nowhere. He sees you loving no one but him. You're always here, always available. Your existence has no purpose other than him." Amelia broke off.

The nanny was silent for so long Amelia started to sweat. She was completely unsure of Kathy's mental state these days and couldn't begin to predict what the woman was thinking. Or how she might react.

"It's not healthy for you, Charles or even me to have you so completely dedicated to us," she added, hoping that Kathy wasn't too hurt by her words.

When Kathy moved suddenly, Amelia barely stopped herself from throwing up her arms in defense. She was taller and stronger than the nanny, but . . .

Kathy dropped onto one of the sofas, resting her forearms on her knees, head bent.

"You may be right." The words were soft but clear. "I guess I didn't realize how much I've closed myself off." She glanced up at Amelia. "There always seemed to be . . . so much need here, and I need to be needed."

"You *are* needed, Kath," Amelia said, coming to sit beside the younger woman, taking her hand. "It's just that I think we've fallen into a co-dependency that's dangerous for all of us." She winced at using a term she considered psychobabble, but couldn't come up with a better one.

"Dangerous?" Kathy pulled her hand away, clasping it with her other one in front of her. "I don't like the way that sounds," she said, staring at her clasped hands.

Standing, Amelia crossed the room to look out at the expanse of green lawn she'd once taken such pride in. "I'm sorry," she said. "I've been forced to face a lot of truths this past year. About my life. My marriage. Myself. And I'm finding that while there are some things I can't control, there are other things I can — and I've let them slip out of my control."

Kathy was silent. Neither friend nor employee. Or family member. Glancing at the bent head, Amelia wasn't sure who Kathy was, what she needed.

So Amelia continued with what she did know.

"I've done a lot of searching since Johnny died, trying to find my identity, a new course for the rest of my life. Trying to find out what really matters."

"Wainscoat Construction matters," Kathy said, looking up. "It always has."

"But my son matters more," Amelia replied. Yes, the company meant the world to her, but Charles was life itself. And what good was a world without life?

"From now on, I'm a mother. First and foremost. I'm going to be delegating many of my day-to-day responsibilities at the office," she said now, imagining Cara's reaction when she heard Amelia's decision. Would her best friend think she'd lost her mind?

Somehow Amelia doubted it.

This was right.

"I'm going to spend the next fifteen years here at home, raising my son. Caring for him, practicing the piano with him. Encouraging him. Teaching him."

Kathy paled. "And where does that leave me?"

Amelia almost caved then. Almost.

"Finding the life that's out there waiting for you . . ."

"You're letting me . . . go?"

Amelia nodded.

The nanny looked as though she might faint.

Once the decision had been made — and delivered — Amelia wanted to get Kathy out of her home immediately. Safely away from Charles.

There was no justification for the urgency.

Still, the urgency drove her.

While Kathy was packing her essentials, Amelia called Cara at the office and then her secretary to have all her morning appointments rescheduled. She also arranged for Celeste and Clifford Smith — the couple who'd been looking after the Wainscoats for thirty years — to have the remainder of Kathy's things packed up and sent to her. And she canceled Charles's morning swim lesson.

Then she escorted Kathy into Charles's

playroom, where the little boy was painstakingly drawing a picture with a big purple crayon clutched in his left hand. Left-handed like his father. The picture was for "Daddy's grave to leave when they had the annivers'y day" the following week.

As they filed slowly into the room, Charles looked up from his child-size wooden table, pushing his glasses up his nose with the side of the hand still holding the crayon.

He didn't say a word, but Amelia's heart lurched at the expression on her son's face as he saw the two of them together. He knew something was up.

What was she doing?

Charles had already lost so much. Far too much.

She couldn't meet Kathy's eyes as the woman hesitated at the door.

"Charles . . ." Both women spoke at once.

Kathy approached the little table, kneeling down until she was nose to nose with Amelia's son.

"Charles," she said, a forced smile stretching her unnaturally taut lips, "I just came in to say goodbye."

His feet stopped swinging beneath the table. "Where ya' goin'?"

"To my mother's," Kathy said. "I spoke to her a little while ago and she asked me to come for a visit."

Charles wrinkled his nose. "I thought you said she's not good at games."

Kathy shrugged. "So I'll teach her." She ran a finger lightly down his nose. "Before I go, though, I want you to promise me you'll be a good boy."

"Uh-huh."

"You know it's what your daddy would want."

Amelia didn't miss the nanny's lack of reference to *her.*

Charles nodded, picked up his picture of four square-bodied people standing in the air above what could have been a grove of purple trees or a crowd of very sunburned people at a baseball game. "You think he'll like my picture?" he asked Kathy, the need for his nanny's approval evident.

"Oh, yeah, buddy, he's gonna love it," she said, real warmth in her voice.

Charles sat up a little straighter, grinning at Kathy. His denim-clad legs were swinging again. "I know he will."

Throat tight, Amelia was tempted just to call it off. Kathy's love for Charles was so obvious — as obvious as Charles's was for her. How could Amelia rob them of something so precious? What kind of mother did that make her?

Just as she was about to change her mind, a mental flashback to the scene in her living room half an hour ago held Amelia rigid. There'd never been any doubt that Kathy loved Charles. The doubt lay in whether or not that love was healthy.

Charles grew still again, his brows drawn together beneath those black frames that made him look too serious sometimes. His dark hair skimmed the collar of his polo shirt when he tilted his head back slightly to peer at Kathy. "Will you be done visiting to come home for the annivers'y party? That's what Daddy would want, right?"

"My mom's pretty lonely, Charles," Kathy said. "I'm going to be living with her for now and then probably getting a little house of my own."

"You don't like our house?"

"Of course I do!" Kathy said, moving a little closer to the boy. "I love your house! But I've been here a long time and everybody needs a house of their own when they're grown up."

"Is that why Daddy went to live in heaven? To have a house of his own?"

"I don't think so, Charles," Kathy said.

"This is your daddy's house. He didn't choose to go away from you. It was an accident."

Feeling completely ineffective, Amelia simply stood there. Kathy was handling things so well — and deserved the chance to handle them.

Kathy knew exactly what to say to Charles. How to say it. And she was, even now, putting all her effort into making her departure something Charles could accept.

She had been a remarkable nurturer from the very beginning. It was one of the qualities that had made her such a great addition to their home.

Still frowning, so serious for his five years, Charles asked, "But you're choosing to go away from me?"

"Oh, sweetie, no!" Kathy shot Amelia a half gloating, half lethal glance. "I don't really have a choice, either, just in a different way." Amelia was poised and ready to discontinue the conversation before anything damaging was said. Only the loving tone of Kathy's voice as she spoke to Charles gave her pause.

"I'm a daughter," the nanny said softly, "just like you're a son. And as a daughter, I don't have any choice but to mind my

32

mother, who told me this morning that I should come home."

"Like we do what Daddy would want?"

"Just like that." And then, with another glance over her shoulder, "and what Mommy wants, too."

Charles was silent, his legs swinging slowly, as he seemed to ponder his nanny's words. At last he spoke.

"But if you go make your mom not lonely, doesn't that make me be lonely?"

Tears sprang to Amelia's eyes.

"Oh, buddy, come here," Kathy said, pulling Charles onto her lap. She hugged him tightly, rocking back and forth slowly. "No matter where I go, I'll always be loving you," she said. Charles's chubby little face was visible over the nanny's shoulder. His eyes were squeezed shut.

"You only have to think of me and you'll be able to feel me loving you, okay?"

" 'Kay."

Amelia started to panic. Wondering what had ever made her think she could cope without Kathy's help.

Kathy set Charles back enough to gaze into his eyes. "Promise me you'll remember that? That you'll think of me?"

The little boy hesitated and then slowly nodded. "I promise."

Amelia might as well not have been in the room.

She cleared her throat.

Kathy slowly set Charles back in his chair, straightening. "And besides," she added, "I won't be far away. My mom lives right here in Chicago. I can still visit you."

Amelia had already established that much. She had no intention of robbing them of the right to care about each other, to see each other.

The visits would be supervised, of course, but Charles didn't have to know that.

Charles was staring down at the table. "Will you come back to see my pictures when you're visiting your mom's? And take me to swimming lessons?"

Kathy's shoulders stiffened. "I don't think your mom —"

"It's Kathy's turn to be busy with other things in her life right now, Charles, just like Mommy's been busy at work," Amelia interjected quickly. "And now I'm through with that." She crossed the room, kneeling to put an arm around Charles's shoulders. "I'm going to be here from now on to take you to all your lessons and play ball with you and everything else. But I've invited Kathy to have dinner with us as soon as she can."

She let go of a very tightly held breath when Charles's face cleared. "Just don't come on the meat night when it's hard to chew and gets stuck in your teeth," he said to Kathy before returning his attention to the box people he was coloring red.

"He doesn't like roast tenderloin," Kathy told Amelia.

Amelia nodded. She knew that.

"Okay, well, I'll see you soon, buddy," Kathy said, heading toward the door.

The little boy looked up briefly and then resumed coloring. " 'Kay. Bye."

Kathy turned for one last glance at that bent head before she left.

Her eyes clouded with pain.

Trying perhaps a little too hard, Amelia filled the days immediately following Kathy's departure with far more activity than Charles was used to.

She broke the rules she and Johnny had established together during those long hours late at night when they'd lain awake in bed, her head on his chest, his hand on her belly, and planned how it would be once their baby was born. She knowingly spoiled Charles. Despite her certainty about the rightness of what she'd done, she overcompensated in her attempt to divert his affection away from the young woman with whom he'd spent most of his waking hours.

She told herself that *wasn't* why she and Cara were standing in line with Charles at Six Flags amusement park that August afternoon. The park was one of Charles's favorite places; they had season passes and more hours to fill than Amelia and Charles had ever had before. The park had been one of Kathy's favorite places, too.

The park was crowded, surprising, since it was only Thursday. As soon as they entered, Charles's brows came together in a considering look that was familiar to his mother and her redheaded manager of operations and best friend, Cara Carson. "I think we should do the Looney Tooter first," he said, the barely contained excitement in his voice making it an octave higher than normal. " 'Cause it goes everywhere around and then after that, we can remember what we should do next."

"Looney Tooter it is," Amelia said, grinning at her friend as Charles pulled at them, eager to get on with his afternoon. He was making it a little difficult for her and Cara, one on either side of him, to keep a firm grip on his hands.

In deference to the ninety-degree weather, or maybe more to fit in with the crowd, all three of them were wearing shorts, thin cotton shirts and tennis shoes. Amelia also had on a floppy straw hat and sunglasses that she hoped would disguise her. Her face would be recognizable to anyone who read the business section of any Chicago paper.

"We're going to be there pretty soon," Charles informed her with an extra tug. Amelia felt a pang as she noticed how Charles was starting to show promise of having his father's tall, muscled body. She wondered if Johnny was watching over them. If he approved of her decision to dismiss Kathy. If he thought she'd waited too long to do so. If he disapproved of her bringing Charles to the amusement park for no special reason on a weekday afternoon.

And then it was time to ride. The Looney Tooter. Waddaview Charter Service, Porky and Petunia's Lady Bugz and Buzzy Beez . . .

"It's been two weeks since Kathy left, and he doesn't seem to have suffered any great damage," Cara said as the two leaned on the wrought-iron fence surrounding one of the kiddie rides Charles had insisted on riding alone. He'd had his fifth birthday, he'd reminded them, and was now officially "a big boy."

"He misses her," Amelia murmured, eyes on Charles's bright-green shirt going around and around. "But right now, the novelty of having Mommy home more often — and of having his own little office at Wainscoat — has been a good distraction."

Cara was frowning, although when Charles passed them and waved, she bestowed a huge, engaging grin on him.

"Isn't it possible that having you around now has made her expendable to him?"

"I guess."

"How are *you* doing without her?" The words were spoken softly, both women looking straight ahead.

Amelia didn't even think about prevaricating. Not with Cara. There was no point. "The evenings are hard once Charles goes to bed." Shifting her weight from her right foot to her left, Amelia rested her elbows on the fence. "You know, after my dad died, things weren't great between Johnny and me, but I never realized how much I still relied on his companionship at night."

"You were out a lot."

"Yeah." At the business functions Cara had been attending for her since Johnny's death. While she wouldn't trade her time with Charles for anything, Amelia yearned for the days when everything was clear — or she was too busy to notice that it wasn't. "I shouldn't ask this, Cara," she said now, "but you've been talking about getting out of your neighborhood, selling the condo. And with Kathy's apartment vacant . . ."

"You're asking me to move out to the estate?"

"You don't have to. It's just an idea."

"A great one," Cara said, elbowing Amelia in the ribs. "I've always loved your house, you know that. But I'd insist on paying rent."

"No way." Amelia shook her head. "Consider it a well-deserved raise." Each time Charles passed them, he waved. God, she loved that kid.

"We always talked about living together when we were young, remember?" Cara was smiling.

Cara had been raised by her aunt — her father's older sister — after losing both of her parents in a car accident when she was five. Amy's mother had been killed by a drunk driver before Amy's first birthday. It was something that had drawn her and Cara together from the very beginning, losing a parent that way, and kept them together during all the years of their growing up.

And while Amelia had adored her father and Cara her aunt, they'd both thought that somehow the void in their hearts would be filled if they could live together. A childish dream but one that still meant something.

Amelia couldn't help smiling at her friend's reaction. "Kathy's apartment has its own entrance and kitchen," she said. "You'd have as much privacy as you wanted."

"It would sure be convenient for me to be out there on the days you don't come in to the office," Cara said. "I could just bring stuff home and we could work at night after Charles is asleep."

For the first time in weeks, Amelia felt a lessening of the dreadful loneliness that had been gripping her.

"You'll tell me if you're not happy with that arrangement?" she asked, shifting to meet her friend's eyes.

"I will." Cara's gaze was as forthright as always.

"Okay."

Amelia turned as Charles came barreling

over to the Buzzy Beez exit. She grabbed the back pocket of his shorts before he could get swept up in the crowd.

"Oh, Mom, that was so cool! Did you see me go faster and faster, maybe sixty-four miles an hour, and no hands or anything?" The little boy pushed his glasses back up his nose.

"We sure did, Charles! You're going to be as big and brave as your dad was pretty soon." Amelia grinned.

"Yeah," Charles said solemnly. "Next week, pro'bly."

After an ice-cream bar, a ride on the Ferris wheel and an encounter with Elmer Fudd that included, on Charles's insistence, a hug for each of them, the trio started on their second go-round of Charles's favorite rides.

"I'm going to make a dash for the ladies' room," Cara said when Amelia rejoined her on the sidelines after buckling Charles into Lady Bugz.

Nodding, Amelia continued to watch her son and he want around and around. His grin pulled at her, reminding her of his dad. It had been a year, and the pain of his loss hadn't diminished at all. Johnny had been a great father. The best.

And as a husband —

41

Amelia couldn't see Charles.

The ride came to a stop with the little boy on the opposite side of the enclosure, the machinery between them. She moved quickly, vaulting over the rail. She braced herself, expecting him to barrel into her as she dashed around the ride.

Charles wasn't there.

In the couple of seconds it had taken Amelia to get to the other side, he'd disappeared.

Impossible.

Looking around frantically, trying to calm her frenzied heart, telling herself Charles had to be there, that panic was ridiculous, Amelia panicked.

"Charles?" she called, her heart pumping so fast she could hardly breathe.

He had to be there.

"Charles?" she called again, more loudly, weaving through the masses of kids exiting the ride, searching for a glimpse of that bright-green shirt. He'd just gone around the other way. She was sure of it.

He knew the rules. She'd tested him just a minute or two before he'd boarded Lady Bugz.

"Don't ever be alone," he'd recited. "Always hold hands when we're walking. Don't talk to anyone but the exact ones I came with today and if I have to throw up, tell you . . ."

Charles Wainscoat Dunn was worth a lot of money.

The rules were what kept him safe.

"Charles!" she shrieked, consumed by terror as she reached her original vantage point and her son was nowhere to be seen.

"God, no." Tears sprang to her eyes and she angrily blinked them away. She had to find him. This wasn't happening.

"Charles!" She hollered again and again, running around the entire ride, which was now being invaded by a new mass of children who'd been waiting for their turn.

A couple of little girls looked scared as she ran past. People were starting to stare.

"Can I help you, ma'am?" A ride attendant appeared. "You really can't be in here."

"My son," Amelia panted, half-hysterical with fright. "He was just on this ride and now he's gone."

"The exit's that way," the young man said, pointing in the direction Amelia had just come from.

"I know that!" she snapped. "He's not there!"

"Have you looked outside the fence? He

probably just wandered out with the rest of the kids."

"Charles wouldn't do that. He knows the rules." Amelia continued to scour the area, certain her son had to be there someplace.

Oh. God.

She choked back blinding tears. *Johnny. I need you.*

The skinny young man looked around at the restless kids now buckled in and waiting impatiently for the Lady Bugz to start moving.

"Sometimes kids get excited and take off for the next ride," he said, his tone reassuring. "Don't worry, he'll turn up. If he's not right here or in the vicinity, then head over to Lost Parents in Hometown Park. It's across from The Orbit. That's where whoever finds him will take him."

"You don't understand . . ." Amelia started to explain, and then stopped.

If Charles wasn't here, he was someplace else. And she was wasting precious time.

Stumbling in her haste, Amelia tore around the outside of the ride, hardly seeing anything, searching only for that bright-green shirt.

Her worst nightmare was coming true and she was helpless. Helpless!

"Charles!" she screamed, desperate, her entire body shaking.

"Amelia!" Cara's familiar voice, her touch on Amelia's shoulder, slowed her panic, but only for a moment. "What's wrong?" Cara was asking urgently. "Where's Charles?"

"I don't know!" Amelia cried, the last of her composure disappearing. "When the ride stopped, he was gone!"

"He's got to be here, honey," Cara said, her calm voice belying the worried look in her eyes as she twisted her head. "He knows the rules. He'd never let someone haul him off without a helluva lot of hollering, and you were standing right here. You would've heard him."

Cara was right, of course. Amelia straightened. Shoulders back, she looked over the heads of the people passing in front of her. "Where is he?" she demanded, autocratic, commanding, in an odd parody of leadership. "Where is he, dammit?" The bravado ended abruptly with a gulping sob.

Cara's arm slid around Amelia just as she might have fallen to her knees. "Come on, sweetie, we'll take one more walk around the immediate vicinity and then go to Lost Parents. Charles knows where it is, and even if he doesn't, anyone who finds him will take him there."

Amelia nodded, allowing herself to be led as they walked around the ride one more time, checked behind trees, under benches and behind a vendor's cart.

"He's gone," she whispered, desperation making her light-headed even while something inside her was pushing her to be strong.

"Let's go to Lost Parents," Cara said, right beside her. "He'll get scared if he has to wait there too long."

Adrenaline propelled Amelia through the park faster than she'd ever traveled it before, guiding her as she ducked around and through people. Her straw hat was knocked off and she hardly noticed, leaving it to be trampled. She could feel Cara right behind her, but wouldn't have slowed if the other woman got held up.

Charles needed her.

And she needed him. More than anyone knew.

She and Cara burst through the entrance to Lost Parents together. And somehow were standing there hand in hand when an attendant told Amelia that Charles wasn't there.

"He *has* to be here!" She heard herself

screaming as if she was somewhere outside, watching the whole horrible incident
from a safe place.

"What's our next move?"

She heard Cara ask the question, grateful on some level for her friend's strength,
her ability to think when Amelia couldn't.

"We'll search the park, put everyone on
immediate alert. I'm sure he'll turn up.
They always do . . ."

Sometime over the next grueling hours,
while park security, the police and eventually — as dusk and then darkness fell —
the FBI conducted searches, Amelia
slipped into shock.

Cara was holding her when the park finally closed, was cleared out, thoroughly
searched a final time — and the official
word came in.

Charles was not in the park. He might
have wandered away. Might be in the vicinity. But no one seemed to think that.
They were going under the assumption that
the Wainscoat heir had been abducted.

Cara was holding Amelia when the
wrenching sobs wracked her friend's body.

And was still holding her when, so lost in
her fear and grief Amelia didn't even know
where she was, they were escorted out of
the park.

1

Five months later . . .
Another town.

There'd been so many.

But this town, on this cold January day, was the one. It had to be.

She didn't even glance at the dirty snow-banks, the barren trees.

Her dark hair pulled back into a ponytail, Amy Wayne, as she called herself on the road, couldn't take the time to care which fast-food places were being advertised on the billboards she whizzed past, or what the economic atmosphere in this particular Michigan town seemed to be. Depressed. Run-down. Thriving. Prosperous. Gray and broken. Beautiful. She'd seen them all.

She'd come to Lawrence, Michigan, to find her son. Nothing else mattered.

Without taking her gaze from the road, Amy reached for the thermostat, flipping it on defrost to clear gathering condensation from the windows.

A few minutes ago she'd lost sight of the car she'd been tracking all day, but she was intimately acquainted with the fact that county roads went in only two directions. To the next town. Or back.

Her ex-nanny's vehicle was a spruce green, four-door Pontiac Grand Am — purchased after she'd been exonerated, at least by the law, of any suspicion in Charles's disappearance. The car hadn't passed in the other direction, so it had to be up ahead.

And almost out of gas.

As far as Amy could tell, that sedan hadn't stopped for several hours. Which meant its driver would probably be forced to stop in Lawrence.

And Amy was going to be right there when it did.

After almost five months on the road alone, chasing down every hint of hope while the officials investigated everyone Amelia Wainscoat had ever known, Amy would see her son again. To fill her aching arms with his sweet, robust little body.

She'd made only occasional visits home, primarily to deal with business matters. The few people who knew what she was doing, who knew she'd undertaken this search a few weeks after her son's disappearance, wondered about her sanity. But no one had been able to stop her.

Amy could hardly remember what it felt like to be the confident, in-control woman who'd accompanied her son to the amusement park that afternoon so many months before. Some days she could hardly remember what it was like to feel at all.

How much did five-year-olds grow in five months? she wondered, her eyes alert, darting here, there, everywhere at once, ensuring that nothing — no one — got by her. Had he lost that baby fat she and Johnny had loved so much?

The multimillionaire mother might not look so powerful in her department-store clothes and polyester-filled parka, with her barely made-up face, as she drove the ordinary black Thunderbird she'd purchased to replace the chauffeur-driven limo she'd left at home. But her slender appearance, still sporting remnants of the sleekness she'd once worn so naturally, was as deceptive as the car she was driving. Over the past months of searching for her abducted son, she and her car had proved just how high performance they were.

They were going to win this one. Johnny had always said she could do anything she put her mind to. He'd told her many times, usually while shaking that gorgeous blond head of his, that he'd never met anyone who could make things happen the way she could.

Of course, that had been B.A. Before the accident. Before she'd known she could take nothing in life for granted. That all the money in the world did nothing for her at all. Bought nothing that mattered.

Her stomach in knots, Amy pressed a little harder on the accelerator, the eight-cylinder coupe sliding only slightly when she rounded the next bend. Where was that green car?

She'd lost it twice that day and each time had found it again within minutes. The Fates were with her now.

And maybe Johnny was, too. In the past months, Amy had felt an odd closeness to the husband she'd lost. Odd because, in some ways, she felt closer to Johnny after his death than she had during the last few years of their marriage. As though he was watching over her.

In those last years, the one thing that had bound them together was Charles. No wonder she felt his presence, his support, as she dedicated every ounce of energy to finding their son and returning him safely home.

And Johnny had warned her about Kathy. He'd understand why she'd undertaken this search, which others considered a complete dead end.

He'd also understand that she couldn't just sit at home, waiting for the professionals to do their jobs. He'd share her uncompromising need to be out here on the road.

What would her little boy be wearing? He'd always preferred denim. And baseball jerseys. But of course Kathy knew that . . . if Kathy was the abductor, as Amy firmly believed.

Did Charles have a winter coat?

She should call Brad Dorchester. Let him know she was so close. She was paying the private investigator an exorbitant amount of money for a reason. She'd hired him — a Denver resident — over the perfectly competent detectives in Chicago because he was reputed to be the best in the country.

And she'd promised to keep him informed of her whereabouts.

While the renowned P.I. did not approve of Amy's active participation in the hunt for her son — especially as she was working independently of the official search, driven by her own instincts — he was seriously engaged in keeping track of her and her progress.

And he followed up on every hint, every lead, she might find.

Eyeing her cell phone in the console, she continued to drive.

Dorchester, an ex-FBI agent, and the FBI, along with various local police forces, had been working around the clock for months. In the beginning, they'd received about a call a minute from people reporting sightings. None of them had turned out to be accurate, but they'd had to check them all.

The past five months, they'd investigated Wainscoat business associates, both in the company and outside it, gardeners, repairmen, even her mailman. They'd talked to every single employee of the amusement park, but no one remembered seeing anything unusual. Some had remembered Charles, but no one had noticed him with anyone in particular.

The Chicago police had even had her and Cara, Celeste and Clifford Smith, the chauffeur and a few other key people take lie-detector tests. To no avail.

Kathy had been among those tested; she'd been questioned repeatedly. The police had concluded she wasn't guilty —

and then she'd vanished without a trace. Until recently, when there'd been sightings in or near various Michigan towns.

Charles's picture had been everywhere. On television, posted around the country at police stations, schools, churches. Even in the tabloids.

She'd given them the picture of Charles that had been taken at his fifth birthday party, less than two weeks before his disappearance. The pitcher for the Chicago White Sox had been there. In the photo he'd been ruffling Charles's hair.

And what about that hair, dark and thick like hers? She and Johnny had kept their son's hair just long enough to be untraditional. Had his abductor cut it short?

Another bend in the road.

Still no green sedan.

The town was just ahead. Instead of billboards, she could see buildings. The green sedan might be just around that curve. Amy pressed the gas a little harder.

Where would she and her son stay that evening? Grand Rapids, maybe? Or Kalamazoo? Someplace far from the dusty little towns she assumed Charles had been dragged through all through the fall and into the winter. Someplace where she could get them a penthouse suite and they could order room service and play video games until her little boy fell asleep at the controls and she could pull him onto her lap and never let him go.

Another curve. No car.

Hands trembling, Amy wondered what she'd do if she didn't find him that night.

How could she possibly take this for another day? Or week. Or month.

An insidious burning crawled through the lining of her stomach, settling just beneath her rib cage. Hands clenched around the steering wheel, shoulders hunched in her parka, she admonished herself to stay focused. On the road. On what mattered. She wasn't going to allow doubts. Wasn't going to get discouraged. Charles needed her.

And she needed him, too.

This was the day. The town. She could feel it. She'd never been this close. Never had a lead that lasted longer than the minutes it took to check it out.

Wiping the sweat from her upper lip, she slowed as she approached the town. One motel, a diner, some shops, scattered homes — nothing as formal as a neighborhood — a school that looked a little shabby . . . Occasional piles of dirty, melting snow.

And a green Grand Am. It turned the corner in front of her.

Thank God.

Giddy with renewed confidence, Amy ignored the twenty-five-mile-an-hour speed limit, ignored the grumbling in her stomach, pressed her foot to the floor — and caught the glimpse of taillights as the green car turned again. And then again. It was winding over roads that looked as if they'd been forgotten in the previous century. Cracked, graying pavement. Potholes. No sign of human life on either side.

Kathy Stead — the brunette driving that car *had* to be Kathy — was traveling away from the county road that led out of town. And turning without hesitation, as though she knew where she was going. But Amy couldn't remember the nanny ever mentioning the town of Lawrence.

There were no taillights at the next turn. Head snapping from left to right, Amy peered intently. The car had to be up there; she just wasn't seeing it. Had it turned into a drive? Or a street that she'd missed?

Fighting the nausea that would only slow her down, she drove the stretch of road twice more, slowing at every slight break in the overgrown brush. Cars didn't simply disappear into thin air.

Five-year-old boys, yes, that happened, but not three-thousand-pound cars.

Still, there was no sign of it.

A huge, wrenching sob filled the Thunderbird. She'd never heard herself make such a sound until the night Johnny died. It didn't surprise her anymore. Mostly she just gave in to it. Let it twist her ribs painfully, ripping her throat as it exploded out of her. Sometimes she hurt so badly she couldn't help herself.

All day she'd been chasing this car. Daring, after so many months of emotional torment, to hold on to some minuscule thread of hope. And now the car had been out of her sight for longer than it'd been since she'd first spotted it coming out of the motel drive early that afternoon.

Yesterday she'd been in Flint, showing around a picture of her ex-nanny. The cashier in a gas-station food mart had recognized Kathy, said she'd been in the evening before. She thought Kathy had said she was staying at the motel down the street.

Damning the dusk that was falling in spite of every effort she'd made to outrun it, Amy choked back more tears.

Please. Please don't let me lose him again, she silently begged.

Back at the intersection where she'd last seen the sedan, Amy turned abruptly and sent gravel flying.

She pictured Charles as he'd been that day at Six Flags, prancing along beside her. His sweet eyes had shone with joy behind those dark frames.

She wasn't going to fail. She couldn't.

She retraced her path again. And again. Nothing.

And then she took every side road, private drive and turnoff that bisected the forsaken stretch of old blacktop.

An hour later found her once more at the main road, staring out into the blackness that was a perfect cover for secrets. Was Charles out there in the darkness? Crying for her?

Was the world making any sense at all to the small son she and Johnny had tried so hard to protect?

"No!" Amy cried aloud, slamming the palm of her hand on her steering wheel. "No! No! No . . ."

Cotton pants sweaty and wrinkled, her face stiff with tears and a day's worth of highway grime, Amelia Wainscoat, CEO and principal stockholder of a nationally famous billion-dollar construction firm,

58

wearily slid the big metal key into the lock on the motel room's discolored door.

She didn't have to stay in Lawrence. Could have gone on to Grand Rapids or Kalamazoo, supplied herself with the comforts and amenities of a five-star hotel, but she hadn't been able to make herself leave this nondescript town — not while there was still a chance that her son was here.

She'd barely dropped her leather bag on the bed before she was stripping down on her way to a bathroom that would only be passable at best, to stand in a skinny and cracked tub the likes of which, until nine months ago, she'd only seen in movies.

There were no bugs. That was good enough for her.

Careful not to let the suspiciously stained plastic curtain touch her more than she could help, Amy stepped into the tub. The towel provided for her use — a threadbare piece of terry cloth barely big enough to cover her shoulders — was hanging in close proximity. And the complimentary shampoo was a brand she'd at least heard of.

It was her lucky day.

Or so she tried to convince herself until she turned on the shower — and discovered that calling it a shower was far too generous. And no matter how far to the left she twisted the faucet handle, the temperature was tepid at best.

Amy burst into tears. She cried until her head ached. Her hair, cut straight and just to her shoulders, hung wet and limp around her face.

Maybe she was going crazy. What on earth was she, Amelia Wainscoat, only child of the once-prominent, now-deceased William George Wainscoat, doing in a tiny depressed town, standing in a shower with who knew what growing in the drain at her feet? And all because she'd seen a car that had looked like Kathy Stead's. And a woman driving it who — judging by the glimpses she'd had — could have been her former nanny.

"But what else can I do?" She asked the question aloud, no longer uncomfortable with hearing her own voice. She wasn't sure when, during the past months, the habit of talking to herself had started.

"You're losing it, Wainscoat, if you really believed you were going to be holding your baby tonight." There'd been no sign of a child in that green sedan.

"Why do you do this to yourself?"

Of course, Charles had always slept in the car. He could have been lying down, either in the seat beside Kathy or on the back seat — depending on how much he'd grown, how much space he'd need for legs that weren't going to be as short and stout as she remembered them.

She hoped he'd been strapped in.

If Kathy wanted Charles badly enough to have kidnapped him, surely she'd be seeing to his safety.

Johnny had warned her about Kathy that day in her office, but even he had been certain that Charles was not in any physical danger. Of course, that had been before last year, before Kathy had become almost insanely possessive.

Amy had to struggle not to lean against the mildewed tile wall beside her. To lean, and slide right down with the minimal stream of water to the dirty tub and then slowly down the drain.

2

"Brad Dorchester."

It was almost ten o'clock at night. Didn't the man ever go off duty and just say hello?

"It's Amy."

"I've been expecting your call."

"Why?" They'd had no specific arrangement.

"Because it's been three days."

Dressed in the white flannel pajamas she'd bought the previous week, Amy methodically arranged the pillows against the nailed-down headboard and dropped to the mattress, clutching her cell phone.

"Do you have any news?" she asked.

"Nothing significant. I'd have called if I did."

She nodded. Brad was very good at keeping her informed.

Forcing the desperate, grieving woman deep inside, Amy escaped into the nonchalant manner she'd developed somewhere between Kenosha and La Crosse, Wisconsin, the previous fall.

"I think I found Kathy today."

There was a pause on the other end of the line. She shouldn't have bothered calling. She knew that Brad agreed with the police. They'd run a thorough investigation on Kathy, on her bank account, her habits, her home. Questioned her intensively. Administered two lie-detector tests. Watched her carefully. After which they'd absolved her of any suspicion of wrongdoing. That was the reason Amy was out on the road; she still suspected that Kathy had taken Charles. She believed the nanny was guilty because nothing else made sense. There'd been no ransom demands, no communiqués, no threats.

And if *she* didn't look for Kathy, no one would, considering the official verdict that the nanny wasn't involved.

She wouldn't have called except that she wanted Brad armed with every possible piece of information, no matter how small, insignificant, inconsequential or unnecessary it might be. Regardless of what Brad believed about Kathy, Amy had all her hopes wrapped up in him.

If anyone could put seemingly random pieces together, it was Brad Dorchester. He wouldn't be working for her otherwise.

"You're out on the road again." His no-nonsense tone was resigned, disapproving.

"Of course."

"When did you leave Chicago?"

"Two days ago."

"You were only home twenty-four hours this time."

"I can't just sit there and wait. You have no idea the toll it takes on me."

"Traveling incognito from town to town is taking its toll, Amelia."

"He's got to be going to school somewhere, or having his teeth cleaned, visiting a doctor, playing a video game or eating a fast-food hamburger. Someplace, someone's going to have seen him."

"Every law officer in that part of the country is looking for those leads."

"The abductors know that. They'll be on guard. But they won't be guarding against an unremarkable woman who's just moving to town. There's nothing threatening about that. And townspeople talk. All I have to do is be in the right place at the right time, get to know the right person, and I'm going to find my son."

"Or make yourself ill."

She wasn't paying him to look out for her health. "I know it was Kathy I was following today."

"Kathy was cleared of any suspicion months ago."

"And afterward she buys a new car and leaves town."

"Wouldn't *you* have needed a new life after all that publicity? Being questioned in connection with kidnapping a child is a little hard on the reputation. Especially in her line of work."

"She was unbalanced and had a motive."

Charles had disappeared less then two weeks after Amy had let Kathy go. Kathy had tried to visit the boy twice during that time — without Amy's approval — but Celeste and Clifford had denied her entrance to the Chicago Heights mansion.

"I followed her myself for those first weeks after the abduction," Brad said. "She never left Chicago. She neither had Charles, nor made contact with anyone else who showed any evidence of having a newly acquired child. Her alibi was solid, Amelia."

They'd had this conversation before. Countless times.

Kathy's claim that she'd been at the mall shopping had been confirmed by two different sales clerks who remembered seeing her. Still, Amy wasn't convinced. The clerks might have been mistaken. Or friends of Kathy's. Or . . .

Amy rubbed the bridge of her nose, trying to remember if she'd eaten anything that day.

"Your resources work very well in the big city. But if we're going to turn over every stone, we need infiltration in the small towns, too."

"Small towns have police departments, Amelia."

"But they aren't all that practiced at handling big cases. They give speeding tickets, sponsor the local baseball team and drink bad coffee."

"You've been watching too much television."

"Some of these towns don't even *have* their own police departments."

He didn't answer. She'd scored.

"Why do you think Kathy would be moving from small town to small town, instead of trying to get lost in a big city?" he asked easily, as though doing nothing more than making conversation.

Brad Dorchester never just made conversation.

"I don't, necessarily." She studied the faux quilted stitching in the patterned bedspread. "You and your men are more effective in the big city. I'm more effective in small towns. And it seems to me that if I

66

were on the run from negative publicity in a big city, I'd try to find a hole in a small town. One that's mostly oblivious to the rest of the world so I could cuddle up, wait it out. And if I had a little boy to hide, I'd find some obscure place where his picture hadn't been plastered all over every public building within miles."

"You've given this a lot of thought."

"You already know that."

"I also know that Kathy Stead does not have your son."

The room's earth tones — medium brown and a dark rusty orange — were suddenly cloying. They were everywhere she looked. The carpet, the bedding, the chair and walls. And when she closed her eyes — more earth tones. She couldn't escape.

Her stomach churned with nausea.

"Then tell me why, if a perfect stranger took him, there's been no ransom note," she said when she could.

"Children are taken for any number of reasons," Brad told her patiently. "Some crazy woman who can't have a kid sees one standing alone and figures she can do a better job of keeping him safe than whoever left him standing there."

"But if some sicko just wanted a child,

why take one with such a high profile, one whose mother can afford to go to the ends of the earth looking for him?"

"It's possible the abductors had no idea who they were taking that day. You and Johnny were pretty careful about keeping the press away from your son."

Amy traced the pattern in the cheap bedspread with one finger. "Tell me something, Brad."

A pause, then, "What?"

One part of her, perhaps the tiny part that was still completely rational, didn't blame him for that hesitation.

"With all the publicity that's been out about Charles's disappearance, the abductors surely know his identity by now."

"One would assume so."

"So how's that knowledge going to affect them if they really *hadn't* known who he was before they took him?"

It wasn't a question she'd needed to ask before. Kathy had Charles; she was certain of it.

But there'd been no sign of a child in that car today. . . .

"Scare the shit out of them, I'd imagine."

"Beyond that."

"Make them nervous."

"And more apt to do something drastic?"

"Kidnapping a child's pretty damn drastic."

Sweat gathered between her palm and the little black cell phone.

"But if they thought they were taking just any kid, a kid whose parents couldn't afford to hire private help, who had to rely solely on the limited resources of public law enforcement, their risk of getting caught was much smaller. Now that they know who they've got, they must realize that their chances of getting caught have become greater — and that the repercussions will be greater, too, because I have clout and the case has been so publicized. Suddenly the game is much more dangerous."

"Yes."

His bedside manner left a lot to be desired. Yet, while he might resent her insistence on joining the search, he always gave her straight answers. Over the past months, that fact alone had earned him her respect.

"At this point, even if the kidnappers wanted to give him back, they'd be afraid to because they know I have the money to overturn every stone until I find them and bring them to justice."

"Yes."

"And after this long on the run, they have to be getting desperate."

"If they *are* on the run."

She ignored that and continued with her thought. "Desperate people do desperate things."

"Yes, Amelia, they do."

She was suffocating. She laid her head back against the thin pillows. "They might be driven to . . . get rid of the evidence."

"There's always been that possibility."

And others, as well. Charles might have been taken by another kind of crazy. The kind that liked little boy's bodies. Her son's body might be nothing more than decaying bones in a ditch somewhere.

Hand over her mouth, Amy choked back bile.

"He's alive and well, Brad," she managed to whisper.

"We have no reason to believe otherwise."

Except possibly the fact that, in five long months, they'd found no concrete evidence to support that belief.

"He is, isn't he?" Her voice broke.

"Don't do this to yourself, Amelia. You have no business being there in some motel room by yourself. You should be home with Cara, seeing your counselor regularly."

"I don't need a counselor. I need my son."

"You've been all over the state of Wisconsin chasing inconsequential leads. Don't spend the next few months getting to know Michigan the same way. Go home. Let me do my job."

"If you'd done your job, *I'd* be home — with my son."

No one knew more than she how dedicated Brad was to this case — how many hours he put in, how frustrated and disturbed he felt at times when the clock kept ticking and leads turned up nothing.

"I'm sorry," she said, all too aware that her apology was inadequate.

"Tell me about today."

"A woman in a gas station recognized Kathy's picture lat night," Amy said softly. "She said Kathy was staying at a motel down the road. There was no sign of her, but when I went by this afternoon for another look at the parking lot, a green Grand Am with a brunette at the wheel pulled out in front of me. Her shoulders were slight, like Kathy's. She seemed the same height. I'm sure it was her."

"Did you get the license plate?"

"It was a Michigan plate, not the Illinois one we knew about, but that doesn't mean

71

anything. If she's capable of taking a child, she certainly wouldn't have a problem switching plates."

"*If* she'd taken a child, I'd agree with you."

She gave him the plate number, then said, "I followed her all afternoon, Brad. She led me to this little town, Lawrence. You know where it is?"

"Vaguely. Is that where you are?"

"Yes."

"I take it you lost the car you were following?"

"She turned off onto a series of old roads that looked like they hadn't been used in years. There were no streetlights, no houses around to light the area. It got dark and all I had to go by were her taillights."

"Which, if she knew she was being followed, she could have turned off."

"She'd still have had brake lights."

"Not if she slowed down enough not to need her brakes."

"I went back and took every turnoff," Amy told him, frustrated and confused all over again. "Even private drives. I don't know how she could've disappeared into thin air like that."

"You drove, by yourself, in the dark, on deserted private roads."

"Of course. I didn't want to lose her."

"What about losing *yourself?*" he asked, real anger in his voice. "Do you have any idea how stupid that was? Who knows what might've happened to you?"

"I'd have handled it," Amy said. "I had my cell phone."

"Which you didn't use."

"I was looking for Charles. Nothing else mattered."

"And what if you'd found him and ended up getting abducted yourself?"

Then at least she'd be spending this night with her son in her arms.

"If, and I'm not saying it's so, but *if* these people are dangerous, Amelia, they wouldn't be averse to hurting you in front of Charles just to get his cooperation."

She was getting dizzy. Light-headed. Nauseous again.

"It would be so much easier if they'd just wanted money," Brad continued, "but with no ransom requests, absolutely everything about this case is random."

Another given that had been discussed too many times.

"I'm taking another look at some of your competitors, Amelia," he said when she was thinking about disconnecting the call.

"Okay."

"We might notice something — some big projects that have been awarded with you out of the picture, a sudden influx of cash . . ."

"Wainscoat hasn't lost any work."

"And you have your finger on the pulse of the construction business these days? You know what projects are up for bid and who they're going to? You know what people in the industry are saying about Wainscoat? About you?"

Longing for the sleeping pills that had been prescribed for her the previous August — which she'd never used — Amy turned her head on the pillow.

"You think someone could be slowly sabotaging me, insinuating doubt about Wainscoat's reliability, trying to undermine the years of trust we've built?"

"It's possible."

"Wouldn't Cara know?"

"That depends on how talented the culprit is."

God, she was tired. Too tired to care if she lost her business. "How valid is your theory?" she asked.

"Valid enough to warrant a check, Amelia."

"On a scale of one to ten."

"Four to five."

Amy hooked a pillow with one arm, hugging it to her. She took an odd and immediate comfort from the soft worn cotton and flattened foam. A feeling similar to the reassurance brought about by Brad Dorchester's thoroughness.

"Can you please call me Amy?"

"If you'd prefer."

"I would."

"If you won't go home, at least give me your word that, in the future, you'll call me before taking off on a chase."

"You won't stop me."

"I'm aware of that."

"Then yes, I'll call you." She'd at least try.

"Good. Now get some rest . . . Amy."

As if she could.

She didn't know how much more of this she could take.

The kid was crying again. She hadn't been prepared for that. Never thought that a kid who was five years old would still cry.

But this one did. All the time — or so it seemed to her. He didn't cry when she was pulling him along and he fell down and skinned his knee so bad there was blood all over. That she could've understood. Nor any of the times she'd slapped him. Not

75

even when she'd made him throw his ice-cream cone away the day she'd seen a dress in a store window that she wanted to try on and there'd been a No Food Allowed sign posted at the front door.

She would've understood that, too. Probably would have yelled at him to shut up. But she'd have understood.

But no — she pulled one of her fluffy feather pillows over her head to drown out the pathetic sound before it pissed her off enough to make her get up and do something about it — this kid only cried for one reason.

The one reason she absolutely could not forgive.

The fucking kid was crying for his mother.

Needed ASAP, Blade, Loader & Scraper operators . . .

How did one operate a Scraper? For that matter, what *was* a Scraper?

Printing pressman, exp. only . . .

That left her out.

ADULT NEWSPAPER CARRIERS WANTED. Immediate openings. Must be 18 or older. Call . . .

Amy circled it.

Janitor needed, Lawrence Elementary

School. No experience necessary. FT position. Salary commensurate w/exp. Apply M-F, 8-3, at Lawrence Elementary main office.

Perfect.

"Can I get you more coffee, ma'am?"

"What?" Amy looked up from the newspaper want ads. "Oh, no, thank you, I've had enough."

"You sure I can't get you something else to eat?"

"No thanks." She smiled at the friendly girl dressed in an old-fashioned waitress uniform with big front pockets. "The toast was fine."

"You hardly ate any of it."

"I wasn't hungry." Amy glanced back at the paper. "Listen, you wouldn't happen to know where the elementary school is, would you?"

"Sure, it's just down this road." She pointed out the window to the road Amy had taken into town the night before. "Go right at the corner. It's about half a mile down the street. There're some swings in the side yard. You can't miss it."

"Thanks." Amy smiled again.

Coffeepot in hand, the girl continued on to the next table, and Amy read the ad one more time. Infiltrating towns had become a way of life for her. Plans formed naturally, as though she'd been living this way forever.

Sometimes that was how it seemed.

She hardly gave a thought anymore to what her shareholders would think of their CEO cleaning toilets.

Or sitting here, dressed in a pair of cheap jeans, a polyester orange sweater and tennis shoes, in this sticky-tabled restaurant with black scuff marks all over the floor.

Remembering Brad's theory that someone might be out to destroy her professional reputation, Amy still didn't care. She'd sacrificed so much for Wainscoat Construction, and in the end, all that money hadn't been enough to buy her the one thing that mattered. Her son's safety.

Which was why she was sitting in a greasy spoon in a town that would never be able to afford the services of a nationally renowned group of builders. And it was why she belonged there.

Each of the small towns was a bit different, yet her goal was completely the same. Get into the schools, scour records. Of course, Charles wouldn't be registered under his own name, but maybe, being the boy's mother, she'd recognize some hint. Some clue, however slight. Maybe a new student who chose chocolate milk on the lunch plan . . .

And outside of school, her aim was to get to know the townspeople enough to win their trust — and their confidences. Be an ordinary woman getting to know other ordinary people. Put herself in the various places where she might hear talk of children. And maybe the mention of one child.

The goal was to find Charles.

But never had a plan fallen into her lap as easily as it had today. It must mean something.

The job was made for her. She had to get to the school, show Amy Wayne's fake ID she'd found frighteningly easy to obtain using her own social security number, give Cara as her reference and secure the position before it was given to someone else.

She should have asked for the check.

Where was that girl?

Amy glanced around — and noticed a car pulling out of the gas station/convenience store across the street. A green Grand Am.

Throwing a twenty-dollar bill on the tabletop, she grabbed her purse and the cheap navy parka and ran — across four lanes of traffic. Glad of the tennis shoes that were a regular part of her wardrobe now, Amy was only vaguely aware of the honking horns.

Yanking her picture of Kathy out of the back pocket of her bag, Amy cut in front of a man wearing overalls, buying a pack of cigarettes at the counter.

"Have you seen this woman?" she asked addressing both the bearded customer and the middle-aged female clerk.

"Yeah, she was just in here," the clerk said. "Wearing a pretty fancy white ski jacket and expensive-looking black pants."

"She left in that green Pontiac," the man added. "She was real nice-looking in a natural sort of way." And then, "You know her?"

Amy didn't bother to answer, just ran to the door.

Her car was across the street. She was losing valuable time.

Hand on the door, she stopped. "You didn't happen to notice if she had a small boy with her, did you?"

"Nope, she was by herself," the clerk said.

"She bought animal crackers, though," the man, a friendly sort, told her. "And two ice-cream bars. I noticed mostly because she cut in front of me and then I couldn't figure out why a woman all by herself needed two of 'em at once. It wasn't like she could save one for later. . . ."

The door closed behind Amy, who was already halfway across the parking lot. Animal crackers were Charles's favorite — next to ice-cream bars. Johnny had bought both for him regularly. To go with the brie and filet mignon her little boy more commonly got at home.

Amy's son might not have been at the store, but Kathy had to be going to him.

And he had to be close. That extra ice-cream bar wasn't going to last long.

Holding up her hand to stop traffic, Amy ran back across the street, ignoring the angry honking. The Thunderbird purred instantly to life and Amy threw it in reverse, blinking away tears as she backed out of the parking space.

Kathy had at least five minutes on her.

They seemed like five years.

3

Squealing out onto County Road 215, gravel flying behind her, Amy choked back emotion until she could no longer feel the acidic burning inside her. She was going to get this woman.

Kathy had taken Charles. Amy knew it as surely as if Johnny were speaking to her from heaven. Knew it despite what Brad and the police had said. The feeling was stronger than intuition. Stronger than desperation.

The first bend didn't faze her. She leaned to the right as the powerful car took the curve, her eyes intent on the road unfolding before her. A straight stretch. But the two-lane road gave her nothing she wanted. No green Grand Am. Only a slow-moving rusty blue pickup with two sheep in its bed, a bearded and bent old man at the wheel, and windows so clouded she could hardly see through them. It was blocking her view.

"Damn!"

Jerking the wheel to the left, Amy crossed the center yellow line far enough to see beyond the truck. A station wagon was coming from the opposite direction.

"Get out of my way," she growled at the driver of the pickup, which was only inches from her front bumper. Every second these people took from her gave Kathy an edge.

The station wagon passed. Amy crossed the center line again. A sport utility vehicle was coming at her now. And then another pickup truck.

The car's defrost was blowing at full speed. Every muscle in her body tense, Amy rode the back of the blue pickup, laying on her horn, willing the driver to get nervous and pull over. He was doing ten miles under the speed limit. It wasn't fair.

But then, life wasn't fair. Nothing had been made clearer to Amy these past months. Intellectually she'd always known that, but now she understood what it really meant, understood — viscerally, emotionally — how it felt to be the recipient of perpetual unfairness. Life had never been fair. Her privileged existence had simply made her unaware of it.

The pickup driver didn't slow down and pull over to let her pass. He didn't speed up. With nearly frozen fingers she pulled the cheap black gloves from her pocket and put them on.

It took her a precious ten minutes to finally get around the old man. Ten minutes that stretched her already dangerously taut nerves.

Engine roaring as it slipped into high gear, the Thunderbird sped up till the speedometer needle flew to the end of its range. The road continued straight for a mile or two. And there were no cars in sight. At least not on the side of the road that mattered to her. The damn blue pickup had given Kathy a chance to get away.

When Amy started to wonder if the driver of the pickup was an accomplice of Kathy's — perhaps he'd even hidden her the night before — she gave herself a mental shake. She couldn't afford this kind of paranoia; it only obscured her goal. Okay, she'd lost ten minutes. She'd find them. The roads were clear, the day crisp and sunny. At the rate she was driving, it shouldn't take more than half an hour to catch up with Kathy.

So she started to plan. How was she going to handle the apprehension? Call the police? They'd exonerated the younger woman.

She had to stay calm. Act precisely, correctly, to ensure that her new life with Charles began that day, immediately. There would be no further investigating. No charges filed against Kathy for illegal behavior. All Amy wanted was her son.

Glancing at her speedometer, she frowned. The illegal behavior in question might well be hers — a traffic violation. She kept her foot on the gas. So what if she got a speeding ticket?

She'd willingly pay.

"I need your help."

Clutching his cell phone — it was the number she always called — Brad Dorchester looked out at, but didn't see, the panoramic view of snowy Denver from the thirtieth-floor window of his office highrise.

"Amy," he said, the stiff muscles in his jaw making words difficult. "Where are you?"

Would there be time for him to save her pretty ass?

"On the road. It *was* Kathy I was following yesterday, Brad. I saw her again this morning — at a convenience store across the street. The clerk and a customer both ID'd her from her picture."

Brad's gaze returned to his office. To the mass of papers and photos and reports spread on the conference-size table across the room. He didn't have to look at them to know what they contained. He knew them all by rote, played them over and over in his mind like an irritatingly catchy tune.

The papers and photos represented hundreds of hours of work — all generated because of one very small boy. Charles Wainscoat Dunn.

Brad shook his head, then wrapped one hand around the back of his neck, which had taken on a habitual soreness. He had all the information. And it wasn't doing a damn bit of good.

Dared he hope that his second thorough investigation of the world of construction business would turn up something new?

"Did you follow her?" He hated to ask. Hated to give Amelia Wainscoat any encouragement in her current endeavor.

"I'm trying, Brad," she said now. His stomach sank at her eagerness. "I've been on 215 — you know one of those two-lane roads that —"

"— only go to one place," he finished for her. He knew. Not only had he been up and down them himself, he'd been hearing

86

her talk about them for months. Picturing her racing over them all alone in a vain search that was going to kill her sooner or later.

If not physically, then emotionally and mentally. He just wasn't sure which would come first.

"I haven't seen her since she left the convenience store. I'm approaching M-43, which ends in South Haven. She'd have to take the highway from there."

If anything happened to Amelia Wainscoat while she was out there trying to do his job, he was sure as hell going to end up carrying that guilt around forever. He didn't appreciate the burden.

Goddammit! If she'd just let him concentrate on doing his job, instead of making him waste time worrying about her.

"So should I stop in South Haven and risk letting her get farther ahead of me, or do I skip the town and risk the possibility that she might have stopped there?"

"I'd check the town. If she didn't stop, it won't take long to figure that out."

He couldn't believe he was giving her reinforcement to continue with this futile course.

"But what if she went on ahead?"

Phone lodged between his ear and his shoulder, Brad rolled up the sleeves of the white cotton shirt he'd tucked into his slacks at an ungodly hour that morning. "She'll only have an hour or so. It shouldn't be hard to follow her trail."

"Okay."

"Amy, I'm putting some of my men on this." Even though he knew the nanny was a dead end. He'd assigned two men to make absolutely certain of that. They'd checked every aspect of her background, spent weeks doing surveillance — and they'd come up with nothing.

"Good."

He'd already called in the license plate number. "Keep your phone on. I'll be checking in every hour. Call me sooner if you find anything."

"Okay."

He studied the table across the room again. He could rearrange the papers there. Stare at the photos until he went blind. And still, the facts weren't going to change.

"She was exonerated, Amy."

"I know."

"She's perfectly free to travel across the state of Michigan, or any other state, for that matter."

"She left town right after the police

dropped her as a suspect and she's been missing ever since."

"Who, besides you, is looking for her? The police aren't. And after all the negative publicity, who could blame her for starting over?"

Amy ignored his remark. "I'm going to spend the rest of my days hunting her down if that's what it takes."

"If you find her, don't do anything stupid."

"I won't."

Why didn't he feel confident about that?

"What *should* I do?" she asked. "If I find her, I mean."

Questions like that really scared him. She didn't even have a goddamned plan.

"Nothing," he said, his feet landing on the floor as he pushed away from his desk and stood. "You should go home and let my men take care of this."

"I'm going to question her, but what's the right tactic?" Amy continued, ignoring him. "Do I act friendly and pretend this is a great coincidence, try to reestablish some trust? Or do I try to bluff her with the idea of some new evidence, hoping I can scare her into a confession?"

Jaw so tight he couldn't speak, Brad wandered over to the conference table. With his free hand in the pocket of a pair of navy Dockers he stared down at the array of documents, picturing, instead, the beautiful and completely out-of-her-element heiress alone on a county road in Michigan.

"Come on, Brad, I don't have much time. I've just taken the South Haven turn-off."

"Stay out of this, Amy," he muttered, refusing to acknowledge the cold sweat slinking down his back. "If you do find her, and that's a big *if*, I don't want you going near her. Keep her in sight, call me immediately and don't do another damn thing."

"Okay."

"I mean it, Amy."

"I know. She bought animal crackers, Brad. And two ice-cream bars. Not one, two."

Animal crackers and ice-cream bars. Charles's favorite foods.

If Amelia Wainscoat really found her ex-nanny, she wasn't going to wait quietly on the sidelines. Kathy Stead would be lucky if she wasn't down at the first count.

And then Brad would be wasting time getting his client out of jail rather than doing what she was paying him to do. Find her missing son.

"Amy."

"Gotta go, Brad. I'm just getting into town. It's quaint. Quiet. Old-fashioned shops with angled curb parking. I don't see the Grand Am yet. . . ."

"Amy . . ." Men who'd been trained to kill were intimidated by that tone.

"I know, Brad." Her voice would have been weary if not for the excitement that tinged it. "I'll call you."

He said her name again, but was met with a click as she hung up.

Swearing, Brad started to count to ten to cool down before he talked to her again. He made it to three before hitting speed dial.

"Yeah?" She didn't conceal her irritation.

She was irritated?

"Don't bluff. You'll risk getting any ensuing confession thrown out of court."

This time it was Brad who disconnected. But only because he had some favors to call in. He wanted a man on Amelia Wainscoat's tail in the next half hour. Which meant finding an off-duty cop in the state of Michigan who'd be glad to make some extra money.

That done, satisfied that he'd hired a man he could trust, one who came with the highest recommendation from one of his ex-FBI buddies, Brad had a conference call with his Wainscoat team, Diane Smith and Doug Blyth, two of the country's best investigators, who each had another four or five legwork men reporting to them. Together they decided on a couple of guys they could pull from their current assignments. These two would be sent to Michigan on the next available flights.

His last call was to request that the plane Ms. Wainscoat had provided for his private use be gassed up and ready to go, just in case.

The only thing keeping him from heading straight to Michigan was that damn phone call he might or might not get. As much as he needed to do something besides stand in his office and stare at papers that led him nowhere, he couldn't risk being in the air — where he couldn't keep his cell on — if Amy called him.

Knowing her, she wouldn't try twice.

Clementine's was nice as far as bar-and-grill joints went. Its warmth was almost a shock after the bone-chilling January cold. With its long, historical bar and lots of tables and booths for friends and families to eat and enjoy themselves, the restaurant had a welcoming feel. But no one there had seen Kathy Stead. Nor had they seen her at the department store, a place whose wooden floors spoke of another era, a simpler time when kids could wander downtown by themselves. When parents didn't have to worry about some maniac stealing them away.

On her way out of town, Amy picked up her phone with fingers stiff from cold and hit redial. More because she couldn't stand to be alone with herself, with her disappointment, than because she had any real desire to speak with Brad Dorchester. The man depressed her.

Still, she'd told him she'd call. And there was a small but persistent part of her that trusted him implicitly, that wanted to feed him every single piece of knowledge she had in case it was the one thing he could use.

A part of her that needed to know she wasn't doing this alone.

He picked up in the middle of the first ring.

"She wasn't there. I'm on 196 heading north." The two-lane highway was only slightly easier to travel than M-43.

"I've got someone heading up M-43 into South Haven and beyond in case you missed something."

Amy nodded. Brad was taking her seriously.

Still, tension ate away at her regained sense of control.

"What's your man going to do if he finds her?" As she'd already revealed to Brad, she had no concrete plan for getting information from the woman who'd managed to dupe the Chicago police and FBI into thinking she was innocent. Up to this point, her plan had always been about finding Kathy. And nothing about what she'd do when she actually did.

"Ask questions," Brad said. "Try to get her to reveal something. It's all he *can* do."

"What kind of questions?"

A long pause. And then a sigh. "You're in way over your head, Amy. Go home."

The grassy median, brown now from the winter cold, sped by her window. Pine trees grew in the distance. "What kind of questions?" she asked again.

"Anything to keep her talking. Maybe ask her about a tire on her car needing air. Maybe about the food in the restaurant she stopped at. He'll know what to do. The idea is to get her to disclose anything at all about her life. Where she's been. Where she's going. Why. And hopefully, if he can keep her talking long enough, she'll give us a detail that'll crack this case."

He paused and she could hear him sigh a second time. "Details. It so often comes down to details."

Amy quickly cataloged his response. When she found Kathy, she'd be ready. While the car heater blew steadily, warming her skin, her heart remained completely unaffected.

"What if she won't tell me anything?" she asked, her mind already skipping ahead, playing out a full scenario. "I can't just let her walk away."

"She'd better not tell you anything because you'd better not be talking to her. My men will get her to talk, Amy. It's what they're trained to do. If not at first, they'll just happen to turn up wherever she stops next. Go home. Let us do our job."

Yeah, and if she'd done that, his men would still be in Wisconsin or Chicago or Washington, D.C., or wherever else they'd been looking. If not for her, they wouldn't have any idea that Kathy Stead was traveling on an innocuous strip of highway in western Michigan.

"I'm going to stop in every small town

along the way until I find someone who's seen her," she replied.

"Keep in mind that you're doing this against my advice."

"I know."

"Call every half hour." Brad's voice was gruff, impatient. He was obviously not prepared to entertain any arguments.

She might have argued, anyway, except that he hung up.

And the loneliness once again consumed her.

"No, ma'am, no one here's seen her." The middle-aged woman at Monroe's Café and Grill in Saugatuck handed the snapshot back to Amy with an odd, not quite suspicious but not entirely sympathetic look. "Is she your sister?"

"No." Amy took the photo, eager to move on. "Just an old high-school friend who used to live in these parts." She tried to deliver her spiel with some of the ease she usually exhibited. "She's remarried and I don't know her new name or I'd just look her up in the phone book."

Shoulders relaxing, the other woman nodded, her brown eyes warming. "I wish we could be more help," she said. "Have you tried the sheriff's office in Douglas?

It's over the bridge, a little past the Holiday Inn. They'd probably know if she
lived around here."

Amy nodded, tucked the picture into the
pocket of her parka, thanked the woman
and hurried back out into the cold.

Saugatuck appeared to be a tourist town,
judging by the marina, shops and bed-and-
breakfast places she passed. But it was a
small one, although it had its share of big
old aluminum-sided homes in pleasant,
shady neighborhoods. As quickly as possible, Amy perused as much of the town as
she could manage, stopping at Mario's
Pizza, a convenience store and a couple of
motels that weren't name brand. She gave
the artists' shops a miss. Something told
her Kathy would not be in the mood for
shopping.

And then, as she turned, looking beyond
the big trees that lined the town, her heart
stopped. Just for a moment. But it was
long enough to take her breath away. And
to let panic in. There, by the lake, was a
ferry. The perfect way for a woman — and
her car — to disappear. Amy swore. She
tried to take a deep breath to prevent the
tears that threatened from falling.

Kathy could already have left. Gone.
Missing again.

And if she had, Amy would have to wait who knew how long for the next ferry. By that time, her ex-nanny could be anywhere. Her hand came down hard on the steering wheel. Why the hell did this keep happening?

Johnny? Are you up there? Help.

The Butler served great steaks, a neon sign told her as she drove past to the ferry.

And the Bayside Inn had suites with fireplaces.

A worn wooden sign proclaimed the existence of the Singapore Yacht Club. The deserted facility did not deliver the promise of its expensive-sounding name.

The bandstand by the ferry was completely desolate. Forlorn-looking. Not even the ducks were venturing out in this cold.

Maybe the ferry would follow. Maybe it, too, would remain inactive, not operating on such a bone-chilling day.

Of course, Amy wasn't that lucky. As the cold seeped through her jeans, she stood by the dock and waited while the elderly ferry worker thought back over his morning.

"No, miss, we've only had a couple of families and a few business travelers today," he told her when she inquired about the day's passengers.

"You're sure you haven't seen a green Grand Am? Or a woman who looks like this?"

She showed him the weathered snapshot again, just to make sure his old eyes really saw the woman depicted there. Her fingers were shaking, though from the cold penetrating her body or the stress consuming it she had no idea.

He held the photo close to his face.

"I'm sure," he finally said, still studying Kathy's image. "I haven't seen her."

Amy's cheeks hurt as she broke into a grin. "Thank you, sir," she said, and half skipped back to her car. This time no was a good answer.

Brad called. Three of his investigators were covering western Michigan. One was behind her. One in front of her. And one was taking the off-shoot roads. Amy was relieved to hear the news, but she couldn't rest.

She did, however, take the time to scout out the elementary school in Saugatuck after her visit to the sheriff's office turned up nothing. Or rather, the elementary school in Douglas, Saugatuck's neighboring town. They split educational responsibilities; Saugatuck had the high school, Douglas, kindergarten to grade six.

If Kathy was living nearby with Charles, he might, at that very moment, be in Douglas Elementary. Learning to read. Or to do simple math.

Maybe playing in the schoolyard.

Amy hoped Charles had a warm coat with a hood. He'd always been prone to ear infections during the winter months.

But then, Kathy would know that. She was the one who'd taken Amy's son to the doctor, picked up his prescriptions and more often than not, administered them. It had usually been Kathy — or Johnny — who was up nights, walking with the crying toddler, soothing him, while Amy got a few hours sleep before having to face another day of high-pressure meetings with powerful men who frequently tried to get the best of the young woman doing a man's job.

Her father's job.

William they'd trusted. With Amy, during those first two years, they'd withheld judgment until she'd proved herself worthy of their confidence. William's Amelia had always been respected, but more because William thought the sun rose and set on her than because of her MBA.

From the time of her mother's death in a car accident when Amelia was less than a year old, the child had been a regular at the Wainscoat offices. She and William had been closer than most fathers and daughters, enjoying each other's company, sharing each other's vision of life, the world and, of course, the business. When he died so unexpectedly, Amelia might have died, too, if not for Charles. And Johnny. And the sudden responsibility that had been thrust on her — to run the company her father had spent his life building.

Amy looked at the Kid's Stuff Park across the street from Douglas Elementary. Not a soul in sight.

The school, a one-story brick building that took up almost an acre, was on Randolph, right off Blue Star Highway. Two white mobile units were the first thing she saw as she pulled into the almost full parking lot. Friday morning, nearly eleven. Too early for lunch. School would still be in session.

Cut-out snowflakes adorned the classroom windows. They upset her. She was missing out on all the art projects made by tiny hands.

Please, God, don't let Charles be missing out on them, too.

The playground behind the school was as empty as the bandstand had been. Empty, cold, unfriendly.

Hoping she wouldn't be stopped, Amy parked and headed into the building like the CEO she was. As though she had every right to be there. As though she'd never been told no in her life.

With a competence born of habit, she scanned the hallways, determined the school's layout and then quickly peeked into the classrooms on both sides of the corridor. It didn't take her long to locate the kindergarten. Or to see that her son was not among the children there.

It took her a lot longer to dispel the heavy darkness descending on her as she smiled at a passing administrator and made her way back to her car. Leaving her gloves off, she started the engine.

Why did she let her hopes rise every single damn time? Why couldn't she just wait until she found out the results before she even thought about celebrating? Why, whenever she came to a new town, did she have to envision her reunion with her son?

Play it out in glorious detail so that each time the dream died, it was that much more painful?

But Amy knew why she didn't stop, why she let her hopes build. Because as soon as she quit hoping, her life might as well be finished.

It was those images of Charles's little arms wrapped around her that got her out of bed every morning. That kept her eyes open and her mind clear while she continued, day after day, to venture into the unknown for something that might not be there.

She *had* to believe.

It was that or die.

4

She made it onto Randolph before she had to pull over. Cold though she was, her body was sweating, her head light. She found it hard to think. The cycle of hope and disappointment got to her sometimes, jeopardized her equilibrium, her ability to go on. Or at least, during moments like these, it seemed that way.

Where was her phone?

Amy looked down at the console, fumbling in the general vicinity of where she'd left her cell. Finally her little finger grazed the plastic.

With her head resting against the seat, she felt the keypad with her thumb, pushed a speed-dial key and hit the call button.

"Hi," she said softly when Cara answered.

"Amelia! Where are you, love? *How* are you? Do you have any news?"

If she'd had the energy, Amy would have smiled.

The vent was pointed directly at her

face, a blast of heat hitting her on the left cheek. Irritated and hot, she thought about moving her head, the vent, something.

"I'm in Douglas, Michigan," she said, thankful that she didn't have to hide the weariness that was swallowing her up. Cara would see past any attempt she made to pretend. Her friend had been there last month, when Amy was pretty much catatonic for the days it had taken to get through Christmas. Cara had tried, forcing Amy to go to Christmas Eve service, insisting on the traditional turkey dinner, buying Amy a gift — a beautiful, one-of-a-kind mohair coat from Amy's favorite designer.

The coat had brought tears to Amy's eyes, the only evidence of emotion she'd shown the entire five days she'd been home.

She thought of that coat, tucked away, unworn, in her closet at home. Amy Wayne had no use for a mohair coat. "I found Kathy this morning, but —"

"You what!"

Cara's shriek resounded in Amy's aching head.

"I saw her leave a parking lot this morning. I was in a diner and apparently all she needed was the five minutes she had on me. I haven't seen her since."

"Did you call Brad?"

"Yes." She hated it when Cara nagged. Especially when she was on Dorchester's side. "He's got three men on her."

"Oh, honey, I can't believe it!" Cara sounded so normal. Alive. Energetic. "You actually *saw* her!"

Though she'd seen her friend in Chicago just a few days before, Amy missed her terribly. "That's not all," Amy said now, sitting up. She noticed an art gallery on the corner.

Another time, another life, she'd have wanted to go there, adrenaline pumping at the thought of making a great find.

"She'd come from a convenience store. She'd just bought a box of animal crackers and two ice-cream bars."

"Charles's favorites." Cara's voice dropped in volume but seemed to gain emotional fervor.

"Yeah."

"I'll be damned."

"Yeah."

"You're still positive she took him?"

"Yeah." Amy's voice broke.

"We're going to get him back, you know that?"

"I know."

"I mean it. We really are."

Cara's conviction struck Amy.

"Haven't you always thought so?"

"I don't know. I did at first." Cara paused and Amy held her breath. She needed Cara on her side, believing enough for both of them. Needed Cara to see her through those times she was too exhausted to fight off the demons that stole her faith.

"Mostly, yeah. I've always at least hoped . . ."

"How you doin'?" Cara continued. Amy could picture her friend's gray-blue eyes, the compassion they held when they met Amy's, willing her to hang on.

"I'm fine," Amy said. "I passed this yacht club a little while ago," she said, rambling as she put the car in gear and pulled onto the road. "And it occurred to me that at another time, the only way I would ever have seen this town was if my yacht had docked at that club for lunch."

"Speaking of the yacht — I offered it to Hubbard for the week like you suggested," Cara said, her voice businesslike, devoid of the exuberance it had held only moments before. "It worked. He's ready to sign."

Her manager of operations had taken charge while Amy was out on the road. Cara was running Wainscoat Construction, handling it virtually alone while everyone thought she was getting all her orders from a CEO who was working at home during her time of mourning.

"He just needed to know that we value him more than the competition does. Everyone needs to feel valued."

"Everything else going okay?" The question was pure habit.

"Yes."

She thought of Brad Dorchester's newest theory. "Has there been any fallout from my absence? Any drop-off in contracts? Any derogatory comments?"

"Brad Dorchester asked me the same thing a few days ago. And there's nothing to worry about, Amelia. You were out of the office a lot before Charles went missing. You'd already established that Wainscoat quality and service were not going to suffer."

"Yeah." Amy almost wished there *had* been something, although it would in no way have indicated that one of her associates was behind the kidnapping. A drop-off in business could simply be a by-product of the hell her life had become, could have indicated a loss of confidence in company leadership.

But any lead was better than none.

"I had the team make the adjustments you suggested to the Anderson building plans. They passed inspection today."

"Good." She could barely remember what city the Anderson project was in.

She couldn't make herself care.

About anything. Except finding Charles.

She tried to take an interest in the company, tried to force herself to focus on business during her stops in Chicago . . .

"Life has changed so much, you know?" she said as she turned left onto 196. Holland was about twelve miles ahead. Surely Kathy would've had to stop there. She'd been driving most of the morning. Even if she'd gassed up in Lawrence, it must be almost time to do it again. Her Thunderbird had a larger tank than the Grand Am, and she was down to her last quarter.

Of course, she'd driven through town. More than once. More than one town.

"I know. But don't give up hope, Amelia. Before you know it, we'll have Charles home and things'll be good again."

"I've changed, Cara." Some days she didn't care. When she was in Chicago, she slipped back automatically into the role she'd played there. But today, during the split second she'd noticed that yacht club, her former identity had collided with the stripped-bare, current version — the frantic mother looking for her kid. The collision scared her.

"I know," Cara whispered.

"I never realized that every day, good, normal people are eating in restaurants with dirty floors and showering in hotels with rusted drains."

There was a cemetery on her left. Amy looked the other way. She only needed to concern herself with places Charles might be. "I pump my own gas now and I feel terrible about the fact that I used to expect people to do that for me, as though it were my due."

"There are only so many hours in a day, honey," Cara said, taking on the tone she'd used during those long-ago days in the office when Amy had forgotten to eat or was scheduling herself beyond human capacity. "You used every moment you had and then you hired people to do the things you didn't have time for."

"Like raise my son?" Guilt overwhelmed her. For five months now, she'd been torturing herself with the possibility that she'd lost Charles because she hadn't been a good mother to him. Hadn't deserved him.

"You provided for him. Johnny and

110

Kathy raised him," Cara said strongly. "How is that any different from the father who goes to work and leaves his wife home to tend to the children?"

Amy drove, took the turnoff for 196B. It merged with 31N to Holland — the next town. She hated the barren landscape on either side of the four-lane highway, the towering trees with their leafless branches.

"Besides, you spent a lot of time with Charles," Cara continued. "Maybe you weren't home for dinner every night, but you were there a lot. You played with him, took him places, had him up here at the office regularly. . . ."

Amy passed a sign for Muskegon. Kathy could have gone there.

"Thank you." Amy knew her friend would understand the real emotion attached to those simple words.

"Anytime, boss," Cara said lightly. "You take care of you, 'kay?"

"Yeah."

She pushed the button to end the call and put the phone back on the console. If Brad's men were going to find Kathy, they'd have to be everywhere. And that was impossible, even if Brad was one-hundred percent committed to the validity of this particular search.

★ ★ ★

Nondescript little strip malls dotted the road as she approached Holland. There were banks and car-repair garages. Two different submarine-sandwich shops. A dry cleaner and florist. A fast-food burger joint.

Amy swore as a passing truck blocked her view of the east side of the highway.

Head turning sharply to either side as she drove, she tried not to panic. This wasn't the usual small town she checked out. Kathy could be only feet away and she might miss her. There were too many buildings to hide behind, too many streets to turn into.

Enough gas stations to keep Amy busy for the rest of the day.

"You've faced huge projects before," she reminded herself sternly. "You've overseen the construction of skyscrapers, entire downtown areas, from dirt to completion. You can do this —" She interrupted herself to swear again, as traffic boxed her in. "One step at a time," she finished through gritted teeth.

Her stomach burned as she veered left at Holland Community Hospital. The big redbrick building was not a comfort. *Please, God, don't let Charles be there.*

Saying that prayer every time she saw a

hospital had become a ritual as the horrific months blurred into one another.

Still, Charles could be there under an assumed name and she'd never know. She'd just have to trust that personnel at all these county hospitals had paid attention to the descriptions Brad's team had sent.

Another side street — one neighborhood after another, each consisting of well-kept A-frame houses in various colors with covered porches. Green or black shutters, awnings and big bare trees. Like something on a postcard.

Embodying life. Dreams. She imagined the kids walking home from school in groups of two or three — boys on one side of the street, girls on the other. She saw them going trick-or-treating. Watching their fathers hang Christmas lights while fires crackled in the fireplaces in their living rooms. Playing catch in the street on a summer day.

Where the tears came from Amy didn't know. They were just there, rolling down her cheeks and dripping off her chin. She was imagining a life she'd never known. A warmth and security that would never be hers again.

And then she saw him.

She'd just crossed Seventeenth Street. Wondered why the town thought they needed a No Left Turn sign there. And glanced up to see a solid little boy in a zipped-up winter jacket coming out of the A&W, his nose buried in the whipped cream on the cup he was carrying. His thick, dark hair was short, but she'd know that body anywhere.

Running a red light, Amy squealed into the A&W. Her heart was pounding so hard she could barely breathe as she kept the boy in sight and tried, at the same time, to find the green Grand Am he must surely be heading toward.

Kathy must still be inside, paying. Amy felt a surge of anger that the woman had let Charles leave the building alone, but that reaction was quickly overshadowed by another. Amy's entire body was shaking with joy, shaking so fiercely she had to try more than once to hit the automatic window button.

Her little boy!

Pulling up alongside him, Amy called out before she'd even stopped the car. She was out the door without turning the ignition off or even putting the car in park.

"Charles!" she called a second time when the little boy didn't respond to her first attempt. Her tennis shoes thudded against the blacktop as she ran.

"Charles!" She reached him, sobbing, pulling him into her arms. "Oh, my God, Charles. I can't believe it's you! I've missed you so much." The thickness of her parka meant her hug wasn't as close as she'd intended.

"Let me go!"

Charles's hugs were usually as enthusiastic as everything else he did. It took her a couple of seconds to realize that had changed.

"Let me go!"

It wasn't the words so much as the desperation with which those little arms were pushing against her — or maybe it was the hard kick on her shin — that pierced the fog of near-insanity that held Amy in its grip.

Springing away from the little boy, she stared, horrified, trying to accept the fact that her son no longer welcomed her touch. She had no idea what to do.

And then, there was nothing she *could* do.

As soon as she'd freed him, the little boy had dropped his root-beer float and run, almost tripping over his own feet in his frantic haste to get away.

"Wait!" she called.

The boy glanced back and the fear in his eyes cut through her. Something else penetrated, as well. The boy wasn't wearing glasses. And he had freckles.

Amy's body convulsed with pent-up pain.

It wasn't Charles.

The boy she'd just accosted was a total stranger.

Amy wrapped both arms around her middle as she stumbled back to her car, bumping her hip on the steering wheel as she fell inside.

She couldn't get that little boy's frightened face out of her mind. "I'm sorry," she said over and over again. "I'm sorry."

Had Charles looked like that when his abductor snatched him from Lady Bugz at Six Flags?

With one last terrified glance, presumably to see if he was being followed, the little boy fled from sight.

Her apologies faded to a whisper. She wanted him to know there was no danger at his heels. That there'd been no danger in her embrace. That his world was still safe and secure.

But she had no way to tell him. He was gone.

★ ★ ★

Brad Dorchester hated failure. Twenty years ago, he'd gone on a three-day drinking binge when he'd failed to get into Harvard Law with his near-perfect grade-point average — simply because he'd lacked the civil-service experience his competitors had claimed. He'd added a day to that personal record after his first failed marriage.

When his second failed marriage was upon him, he'd grown up a bit. He'd put a hole in the drywall of his garage that time. And then gotten drunk while, with a bandaged hand, he repaired the damage for the new owners.

He'd long since accepted that he was an imperfect man living in a colossally imperfect world. Failure abounded. In society. In the FBI, with its many divisions, its checks and balances that didn't always check and balance. In churches, according to the news. And in himself.

But the one place he'd never failed, the one place he refused to accept failure, was his work. Brad always did whatever job he'd taken on — and did it right.

Standing, feet apart, hands in the pockets of his slacks, he looked past the half-empty cardboard carton of cold and abandoned fried rice to the papers spread on the table before him. The room had grown dark, the single lamp by the couch not really bright enough to do more than give an eerie glow to the forms and reports and photos.

The sleeves of his wrinkled white shirt were still rolled up. There was a coffee stain on the front, and he knew his hair must be disheveled, adding to the overall worn look he'd gradually assumed on this long and frustrating day.

He pinched the bridge of his nose and picked up the cell phone he'd tossed down, unused, moments before.

This time he punched the six key.

And waited.

"Hello?"

She picked up before the first ring finished.

"Do you sit on that thing?" he barked.

"Do you ever say hello?" she barked back.

Damn. This wasn't how the conversation should go. But then, the fucking conversation shouldn't be happening, period. He was calling her because he'd failed. Failure was not acceptable.

"Did they find her?" she asked now.

"No. Where are you?"

"Holland."

"You decided to stay put. Good."

"There are a lot of places to check. It's a college town. Lots of families. A variety of people coming and going. And since your men have better resources for tracking Kathy now that we've had a sighting, I figured I'd do more good here."

Yeah. He'd get to that in a minute. The part about his men and their resources. Brad sank into one of the blue upholstered chairs at his dining table and pulled a very used pocket-size spiral pad toward him.

"Where are you staying?"

"The Haworth Inn and Convention Center. It's across the street from Hope College, but more importantly, it's got a view of Centennial Park and is right by Lincoln Park and an elementary school. I spent a couple of hours in Lincoln Park late this afternoon watching little guys do amazing things on the skate ramps."

"Looking for Charles every second you were there."

"I look for Charles every second I'm alive."

They had that in common.

"Sounds like the Haworth might be a step up from your usual fleabag." He jotted down the name of the inn.

"I'm not planning on staying long," she said, sounding distracted. "If I was doing

119

my usual, I'd have to take a cheaper room. No one would believe that a woman new to town, looking for work as a cafeteria cook or a custodian or a day-care worker, could afford to spend a hundred dollars a night on lodging."

Brad grunted. It was the same explanation she'd given him a hundred times before. Every time he reproached her for not choosing safer accommodations.

"You'd approve of this place," she continued. Her voice was soft but had a sarcastic edge. "There're elevators to the rooms, vending machines and, downstairs, a gift shop and a ballroom. In case I get bored enough to shop or I find reason to dance."

Not bothering to comment, Brad twirled his pen between his fingers, a skill he'd perfected during unending hours of being cooped up in classrooms during college.

"Downtown Holland has several unique children's stores." Amy's tone had changed.

Brad stopped twirling his pen.

"Sandcastles is an upscale toy store. Then there's The Paper and Doll House and Hutchinson's Children's Store."

She was leading up to something she thought was important. Something she was afraid he was going to shoot down.

Experience told him that much. It also said he probably would. Damn, he hated this.

Sometimes he hated her, too. But not often enough.

"An older gentleman in Sandcastles recognized Charles. He said he was sure Charles was the little boy he'd seen."

"You've heard that before."

"And not once have we received any proof that these identifications *aren't* valid."

She had him there. Except that he couldn't allow her to have false hope. It just wasn't the way he operated. It wasn't even kind.

"You have absolutely no proof they were, either."

"This time was different."

He'd made her defensive.

Brad pinched the bridge of his nose again. Hard. "How was it different from the other eleven times?"

"He said all Charles wanted to talk about was baseball gloves."

"Lots of little boys are obsessed with baseball."

"He was with a woman."

Brad sat up straighter. "Did he give you a positive ID on Kathy, too?"

The pause was too long.

Goddammit.

The pen twirled back and forth between his fingers. His suspicion that he would only shoot down whatever hope she'd been drawing from the day's encounter had just been confirmed.

In their months of fighting with each other, he and Amelia had established their own, unspoken means of communication. Sometimes he felt as though they read each other's minds more effectively than they spoke.

"He thought she had the same body build," she said, her voice defensive. "But different hair."

Amy was a smart woman; he knew she'd already figured out where this was going.

Brad decided it was kindest to let her get there on her own. Or maybe just easier on him. He said nothing.

"I know the positive IDs on Kathy yesterday and today confirmed that her hair's the same as it was five months ago. But she could've been wearing a wig when the old man saw her."

She was still fighting. Brad hated what she was doing to herself.

"What about her face, Amy? Did he recognize that?"

"Hairstyles can sometimes change the shape of a face. . . ."

"And women who otherwise don't share any resemblance can have similar body builds."

"It's possible the woman wasn't Kathy, but you can't prove it," Amy said.

"How long ago did the old man see the boy that reminded him of Charles?"

"Three months."

He didn't even bother to reply. Amy knew as well as he did that a three-month-old flimsy lead was almost no lead at all.

Of course, almost was still better than no lead at all. Which was what he and his men had come up with recently. So far, even the newest construction-industry probe had yielded nothing.

This obsessed, intelligent and too-beautiful-for-her-own-good heiress was doing his job better than he was, despite his entire team of highly paid, highly respected professionals.

For the first time since he'd opened up shop, Brad considered getting out.

"My men found the Grand Am."

He'd spoken casually, but had no doubt Amy would understand the significance of that remark.

"She abandoned it?"

He'd known she'd catch on immediately. "Someone did, yes."

"Where?"

"In the parking lot of a shut-down restaurant on the road leading into Grand Junction, Michigan."

"That's just east of South Haven."

He could almost hear her thinking. "You've already checked all the car dealerships, new and used, in Grand Junction, haven't you?" she asked. In case Kathy had purchased a vehicle to replace the abandoned one.

"And in every other town on the western part of the state. We also heard back on the license plate. It was registered to an '88 Buick owned by an old woman who's been dead for months."

"So that lead is gone."

"Yes."

He held the phone away from his ear during the string of expletives he'd bet his last dollar Amy had never even heard, let alone said, before this nightmare began.

And then he sat there, listening to the dead silence that followed. He should probably say something to make her feel better. Give her hope. Some kind of reassurance — or platitude, such as tomorrow was another day.

But if he'd had a bedside manner, he would've been a doctor.

"She knew she was being followed," Amy said.

He didn't reply.

"Okay, that's good, then."

He frowned into the darkness. "How so?"

"I obviously scared her. And she wouldn't be scared if she didn't have something to hide."

Trust Amy to come up with some positive spin on a situation that was growing more hopeless with every day that passed without a real clue — without even a verifiable hint that the boy was still alive.

"And she's close," she added.

"Even if it was Kathy, she could be anywhere in the state — or in another state. It's been more than twelve hours since she pulled out of that convenience store this morning."

"Thanks one hell of a lot, Brad. I needed that reminder."

"You need to face facts and go home." Where her friend could comfort her. And her counselor could give her survival strategies.

Where she had a life waiting . . .

She needed to get her ass home so he

could focus all his attention on locating one very hard-to-find boy — and quit feeling responsible for the kid's mother.

5

At Columbia and East Eleventh, Lincoln Elementary School looked like so many others Amy had seen. Single-story. Brick. This one had a blue slide in the playground, instead of a silver one. The standard black leather swings. A bike rack. Maybe the paved playground set it apart a bit, but the art adorning the classroom windows wasn't extraordinary or even slightly different.

School after school. They were all the same to her. All part of the journey. Roads she had to travel to reach the end she had in mind. Charles, safe and warm, cuddled in her arms.

Happy.

Maybe her tears as she left the school were because her jeans were putting pressure on the ugly black bruise on her hip left by her collision with the steering wheel outside the A&W the day before. She was constantly aware of it. Aware of the pain.

She'd never been much good at tolerating physical pain.

She drove slowly past shops named Music Center, Picnics and Porches, Weepin' Willow. Weepin' Willow.

Weeping widow. "Yeah, that's me," she muttered.

On one corner downtown, a large statue caught her eye. Amy slowed, barely mindful of traffic that might pull up behind her as she craned her neck to study the sculpture.

The artist had depicted, in a very lifelike fashion, a group of boys and girls saluting the American flag. Their expressions, at once reverent and impish, pulled at her.

"Next time I'm home, I'm buying a statue," she announced to the empty car. Pewter, or maybe bronze. As she drove on, her gaze skimming the sidewalks, the street, the shop windows, a vision of her statue started to form, comforting her with the idea of strong, solid kids. Kids she could keep forever. It would be perfect out by the pond in the grounds behind the mansion. That way she'd see it every day from her bedroom window.

She wanted a log over a stream, with four or five kids crossing it. Some girls, some boys, maybe the smallest, a little boy, bringing up the rear. There'd be a pensive face. One frowning in concentration. Another looking fearful.

"I'll have to commission it," she said as the faces came to life in her mind's eye. And, with that decision made, she felt better. Renewed.

She had a plan.

Picking up the phone, she called Cara and asked her to find a sculptor.

Craig's Cruisers, a family-fun center, was her last stop in Holland. It had been a long, cold, mostly fruitless day. She hadn't been certain the place would be open in the middle of January, but she got lucky.

Amy hugged herself as she looked from the batting cages, past the go-cart track, over to the concession area and game room. Never sure what she was looking for, other than the longed-for sight of her small son, she tried to see everything. Catalog everything.

All the employees, she noticed, were teenagers. Young teenagers, who seemed barely old enough to work. Kids who were probably so caught up in who liked whom at their high school, they weren't likely to remember one small boy among the thousands of kids who surely frequented Craig's Cruisers.

Amy kept her distance from the children. After yesterday, she didn't completely trust herself. Once she'd calmed down and really thought about that boy at the A&W, she'd realized he couldn't possibly have been Charles. The boy had been the size Charles was five months before. The boy Amy remembered. But five months worked a lot of difference in a five-year-old. Her little boy would have grown by now.

She went up to the Rocky Mountain Mini Golf counter, mostly because the girl working there seemed to be a little older. And bored.

Not too many people interested in golf on a cold January day.

"Can I help you?"

"I'm looking for my son," Amy said, beginning her spiel. "He's with my next-door neighbor and I thought they were coming here." She pulled a less-used photo of Charles out of her wallet. "This is him. You wouldn't have seen him here today, would you?"

The friendly redhead gave the photo a serious perusal, then shook her head. "I haven't seen him, and I've been here all day," she said, her expression apologetic.

"Maybe they're at the bowling alley. Have you tried there?"

"Yeah," Amy said, frowning. Craig's Cruisers was her last stop and she didn't want to give up for another day. Didn't want to have to call Brad Dorchester and admit she'd made no progress, didn't want to hear those disapproving silences. Didn't want to hear him say — or imply — that she was wasting her time. Fooling herself into believing she might actually find her son. She didn't want his Goddamned pity.

She glanced up at the redhead. "I was sure they were coming here. You're positive you haven't seen him?"

The girl looked at the picture again. "Absolutely positive," she said. "He was in here a couple of months ago and there's no way I'd miss him if he came back."

Heart stumbling, Amy forced her face into a casual smile. "Oh, really? Why's that?"

"In the first place, he's so cute in those glasses."

Tears burned Amy's eyes as she nodded, not sure she'd be able to keep up the charade if she attempted speech.

"And he asked a million questions, wanting to know, for all eighteen holes, where to aim for a hole in one."

Yep, that was definitely Johnny's boy.

"But the reason I remember him is he insisted on holding the club upside down. Said he'd do better if he could pretend it was a bat. I think he played the whole course that way. And he did it again when he came in a day or two later. I haven't seen him since."

"And you say that was a couple of months ago?" Amy found her voice. The young woman gave no indication that she noticed any unusual thickness in it.

"Yeah, way before Christmas . . ."

"Huh," Amy said, frozen in the role she was playing while at the same time bursting with gratitude. With hope. "He never said anything to me about it. Did you see who he was with? My neighbor's a bit younger than me, dark-haired with bangs, slight shoulders, doesn't wear a lot of makeup. Do you think maybe it was her?"

"I'm sorry." The clerk frowned. "I was so taken with him I don't remember a thing about who brought him. Either time."

"Do you think it was the same person?"

The girl handed back the photo. "I really don't remember."

"Well, thanks, anyway," Amy replied,

taking her picture. She turned to go, anxious now to call Brad, to shake and grin, laugh out loud, whoop and holler and cry. This one was a positive ID of Charles. The redhead was certain.

"I'd still check the bowling alley," the girl called.

"I'll stop back by the house first." Amy tripped over her words. "Maybe they've gotten home by now."

She'd never thought herself capable of murder. She hadn't lived the easiest of lives. Hadn't grown up with privilege and class like that Wainscoat bitch. But she'd been raised with something that mattered more — a sense of right and wrong. Because she'd never had money to protect her, she'd had to rely on something that couldn't be taken away. Her values.

That didn't mean she wouldn't do everything she could to better herself, though. And hanging around this dingy place certainly wasn't an improvement. She sighed, looking at graying limp curtains that might once have been crisp, cheap carpet that, in patches, was worn down to the tweed matting, a sofa whose foam had long since deflated beneath the weight of too many heavy butts. As she stared at a chair with a cigarette burn on the arm that left the wood exposed beneath rusty-edged decaying foam, she had to face the fact that "better" wasn't going to be found here.

She'd really believed she was going to have it all this time. Love and money. Yeah, right. She groaned at her own self-delusion.

At that time in the morning, before the sun was up, she was alone. But she wouldn't be for long.

Sipping coffee grown cold, she grimaced and poured in another generous shot from the half-empty whiskey bottle she'd bought the night before. After a large, slow, appreciative sip, she decided that the booze warmed up the coffee nicely. She considered her problems again.

The whiskey hadn't changed them a bit.

She was trapped. With all the baggage she carried, the law would find her eventually.

She took another swig of the coffee-flavored whisky. There was only one option left.

Get rid of the kid.

The most memorable thing about Zeeland, Michigan, was the arched bridge.

The houses were redbrick, some with aluminum siding and porches. The grocery store was a D&W, the town was two blocks long and, on Chicago Drive, New Groningen Elementary School held classes without Charles.

It took her a week and a job bagging groceries to determine that.

Just outside Zeeland was a rest area where Amy spent several hours people-watching. And talking to truckers. She didn't call Brad that night.

A few miles farther up 196, Hudsonville had a Super 8 Motel where she spent ten nights. Hudsonville had a McDonald's. Amy got pretty good at taking orders — and making conversation. With other employees. With customers, especially the children. She carried Charles's picture in the pocket of her uniform — pulled it out so many times a day she'd lost count — and had to call Cara for more copies of the photo when successive ones became too greasy.

Groundhog Day came and went. Apparently the critter didn't see his shadow. And Amy found not a single trace of Charles. Nor was there any more word on her ex-nanny.

Jamestown. Grandville. Cold little towns

covered with slushy gray snow. They repre-sented six, long, jobless days filled with questions leading nowhere. And six equally interminable nights highlighted by frus-trating and much-dreaded conversations with Brad.

She was developing a dependency on the man she found unacceptable.

Grand Rapids was next. Brad's men were in the western part of the state, both in Grand Haven and Muskegon, still looking for leads on Kathy. Amy knew Brad had sent them there more for her sake than because he believed there'd be any answers at Kathy's door.

Still, there'd been a woman in Grand Haven who thought she recognized the picture they'd shown.

Tall trees lined 131 as Amy approached Grand Rapids. Leafless trees, which de-pressed her. As though the whole world was as devoid of life as she felt inside. But at seventy miles an hour, she passed those trees swiftly enough.

No matter that the next mile just brought more.

More time passed. More emptiness.

Grand Rapids was a big city. Amy took the first exit, fighting a familiar panic as she considered the immensity of the job ahead. Combing every inch of the city, seeing every school, talking to everyone who might have seen Charles. She usually skipped the big cities because they were harder to infiltrate, and because Brad and his men could move around more easily, using their authority to gain access and ask questions. But she had a feeling about *this* city.

As though Johnny were telling her to stop there.

Or maybe, exhausted as she was, she just couldn't figure out anywhere else to go.

"Big cities are really just a conglomeration of separate communities." Her own voice was a comfort as it bounced off the cold dash of the car. "When you're building a high-rise, you start at the beginning and take it one cinder block at a time."

She'd built some award-winning high-rises.

Cascade, Kentwood, Wyoming. All suburbs of Grand Rapids. She'd been to every one of them. By Valentine's Day, she still had nothing to report to Brad.

"Go home," he told her.

"No."

"You said yourself that I can cover the big cities far better than you can. You spent six days in the Grand Rapids area and you got nowhere."

"Go to hell."

He'd barely let her say hello before he'd started in on her. Apparently he had nothing to report, either.

She'd spent the day in Wyoming, Michigan, and now lay stretched out on the bed in a three-star motel there, still fully dressed in no-name jeans and a thick, though inexpensive off-white sweater. She was trying not to get sick looking at the intricate floral-and-diamond pattern in the red-and-gold carpet.

"I'm going to Lowell in the morning. I have a pretty strong feeling about the elementary school there."

Her tennis shoes were smudged. And might be leaving a mark on the red-and-gold floral bedspread.

"It's been more than a month since you took a break. You have obligations at home. If you don't put in an appearance soon, people are going to start getting suspicious."

"Everything's pretty quiet right now."

"But, if you're hoping to keep from alerting Charles's abductors to your presence on their trail, you need to be seen in Chicago."

"There's an industry conference in Jamaica at the beginning of April. Before all this started, I'd agreed to give the keynote speech. I can still do that."

"Will you know a lot of people there?"

"Undoubtedly." Something she'd hate. Being Amelia Wainscoat was becoming harder and harder.

"Can you get me a guest registration?"

"Why?"

"Wouldn't it be easier if you had a companion? Someone to eat with so you don't have to sit at a table full of people who'd tire you out?"

How did he do that? How did this man whom she'd only met a handful of times know her so well?

And why did it matter?

"Probably. Good idea. I can take Cara."

"I'd like to go, Amelia." The friendly tone was gone. "I want a chance to hang around and watch the people who compete with you for business."

"You really think someone in my professional life is behind all this?"

"Until we find your son, I'm not leaving any stone unturned."

"I'll have Cara make the reservation."

"Good. Now back to the original conversation. The conference is two months

139

away. You're going to kill yourself if you don't take a break before then."

She didn't have to listen to that. Not even when his words echoed the very plea she'd heard from Cara that afternoon. She appreciated that her absence made things tough for Cara, but her operations manager would just have to handle them, anyway.

And quit making up excuses to get Amy home.

"You're losing all perspective."

Amy studied the ceiling. And then, for a brief moment, the red-and-gold floral print on the wall behind her.

"That's rich, Dorchester," she said when she could trust herself to speak. "How do you suggest a mother *keep perspective* when her son's been missing for six months and the detective agency she's hired hasn't found so much as a hair from his head?"

The remark was followed by one of his trademark silences. God, she hated them. Hated him.

"Would I have enough perspective for you if I went home, waited until the walls closed in — which should take all of one day — and then cried until I had nothing left? No heart. No soul. No energy to drag myself up for yet another day?"

The silence continued.

"Or would the perspective be sufficient if I forgot the whole thing? Forgot I have a small son who knows where? With some person doing who knows what to him? Just pretend he doesn't need me, doesn't exist? Pretend my heart isn't crying out for him every second of every day? Would *that* work for you?"

Why the hell didn't he ever just hang up? It was what she deserved. The man was far too good to her, and she hated how much that made her need him sometimes.

If he wasn't going to say anything, there was no point in holding the phone to her face.

"It's Valentine's Day," she finally said.

"Yeah."

"I had a hard time avoiding the cards and hearts and advertisements for flowers today."

"Go home, Amy. Cara's there. She loves you."

The chill in the air made her hands feel numb. She didn't care enough to get up and adjust the room's heater.

"Don't start in on me again, Brad. Not now. Please."

Another silence. He was probably trying to translate that last word. She didn't know where it had come from herself.

"What kinds of things did you and your husband do to celebrate Valentine's Day?" The question was stilted. Awkward.

"We didn't."

"I don't mean last year," he said impatiently.

Of course not. As her private detective, he was fully aware that Johnny had been dead then. Hard to believe it'd been eighteen months since he was killed. Sometimes it seemed as if the police had come to her door just a week ago.

Amy shuddered, remembering that horrific night. The shock hadn't protected her from the sudden and overwhelming pain. She'd been in such agony she couldn't stand, had stumbled into her living room, fallen into a chair. Someone had touched her shoulder and she'd fallen apart.

Even now, these many months later, it seemed completely unreal that her husband was gone forever.

They'd never have a chance to mend the rift that had slowly dug its way between them since her father had died.

Sometimes it felt like only days had passed since that night and sometimes it felt like years. Occasionally she wondered if she'd just read about the whole thing in some melodramatic novel.

"Neither did I," she said finally, giving Brad a belated answer. "We didn't have time for Valentine's celebrations."

"You didn't spend any time alone with your husband?"

Now that sounded more like Brad. Accusatory.

"Of course I did," she snapped. "I just didn't have the luxury of doing so on a schedule dictated by minor holidays." And then, before he could pass some other judgmental comment, she said, "Those first years after my father died were hard. I'd expected Johnny to take over. He had no interest in it, no intention of being more than one of our construction bosses. He wouldn't even help me part-time in the office or accept a token seat on the board. And the board wasn't all that confident in my ability to take up where my father left off. I had to work harder than any man would have just to command the respect necessary to carry on. Whatever time I had at home was spent with Johnny and Charles together. There wasn't enough time for Charles as it was. I certainly couldn't exclude him from the few free hours I did have."

"Doesn't sound like much of a marriage to me."

She got up. Approached the heater. She should take advantage of having one. Many of the places she stayed in didn't have in-room controls.

"You ever been married, Dorchester?"

"Yeah."

That surprised her. As did the hint of something almost like jealousy that shot through her.

Though, considering that he had to be around forty, it shouldn't be such a surprise that he belonged to someone. Odd that the subject had never come up before. But then, their relationship was a professional one.

"You're married?" Her voice was impassive. No feeling attached one way or the other.

"No."

Oh. Well.

"Widowed?"

"Divorced."

There was absolutely no sane reason for her to be relieved. To feel anything personal about him.

Perhaps it *was* time to stop by Chicago for a day or two. Get in touch with another side of her life. Perhaps she *was* losing perspective.

But she was so sure that school in Lowell was calling to her . . .

"Twice," he added.

"You've been divorced twice?"

"Yep."

Well, she could understand that. Especially if he'd been anywhere near as bossy with his wives as he was with her.

Still . . .

"I'm sorry."

"Call me tomorrow. From Chicago."

Amy cursed as she abruptly ended the call.

6

The next day was Saturday. With a windchill of five below zero, it was a little cold to be spending the day in the park, but after arriving in Lowell mid-morning, that was exactly what Amy decided to do.

Monday was Presidents' Day, which meant it would be three days before she could gain entrance to the elementary school. A holiday weekend and a park spelled kids to her.

A curly-headed blond boy got there shortly after Amy. He rode in on a skateboard, hopped off as he reached the end of the sidewalk and landed, board in hand, on the frozen grass.

"Hi," he said, dropping the board as he hitched himself onto the swing beside hers.

"Hi."

"You waiting for someone?"

"No."

"Me, neither. Sucks not having someone to wait for, huh?"

Careful to keep her distance, Amy said, "Yeah."

He was a cute kid. She liked him.

"Yeah, my mom left us back before Christmas and my dad couldn't stand to stay in the old house, so we moved here. I don't really know anybody yet."

"How long have you been here?"

"Three weeks." He shrugged. "I know a couple guys from school, but not good enough to hang out with."

The matter-of-fact way he accepted the bad turns in his life touched Amy more than most things did these days. She wanted to tell him she'd hang out with him. That he didn't have to be alone.

He hadn't been in town long, but she showed him Charles's picture, anyway, simply introducing him as her son.

The boy didn't show the slightest sign of recognition.

Of course, he'd only been here a few weeks . . .

"How old are you?"

"Nine. I'll be ten next fall. Old enough to caddy for my dad during golf season."

"You have to be ten to caddy?"

"According to my dad . . ."

Half an hour later, the boy left, telling

her he hoped to see her around again. After that, a brother and sister pair roughhoused their way off the sidewalk and into the park. Bundled up in hooded parkas, jeans, mittens and scarves, they'd come from the church nearby, clearly filled with pent-up energy. Energy they spent the next twenty minutes expending on each other. They raced, chased, tackled, tumbled, yelled, punched a time or two and eventually left. All with only a surreptitious glance in Amy's direction.

She would have asked them about Charles, shown them his picture, but they'd seemed nervous of her and she wasn't going to risk scaring another child.

A young couple, both wearing hats that concealed much of their faces, circled the park a couple of times shortly after noon. The woman was very pregnant — and judging by the pinched look about her mouth, quite possibly in the early stages of labor. They smiled at Amy as she sat on a picnic table, rubbing her hands together, trying to convince herself that she wasn't as cold as she felt. She'd already jogged around the park a couple of times in an attempt to stimulate body heat.

She smiled back at the couple, her eyes drawn to the woman's extended belly. She wondered if the baby they were expecting was a boy. Hoped he was healthy.

And that they'd keep him safe forever.

"Hi."

Amy jumped, turned in the swing she'd returned to several minutes before. A pretty woman about her own age stood there in jeans, a cozy-looking light-blue jacket and thick white gloves. Her dark hair, cut in a nondescript bob, was uncovered.

In Chicago the woman's approach — a stranger walking up to Amelia Wainscoat from behind — would have prompted action from a Wainscoat bodyguard.

"Hi," Amy replied, slipping into the new role she'd created for herself. She identified with Amy a whole lot more than she did Amelia these days.

The woman took the swing next to Amy. "I live across the street," she said, pointing off to one side of the park. "I noticed you sitting here all alone . . . and thought I'd come over and say hello. You're welcome to tell me to mind my own business."

Amy grinned. "To be honest, I'd enjoy the company."

"I don't think I've seen you around here before."

"I'm new in town," Amy said. "I've been so busy getting on with the business of life, I haven't had time to get to know anyone yet."

"Well, I'm Ann. Ann Green." The woman grimaced, pushing lightly at the ground to set her swing in slow motion. "Could you find a more boring name?"

"I'm Amy. Amy Wayne."

Amy Wayne had a purpose. Hope. She couldn't bear to face Amelia Wainscoat's empty life.

"You married?"

Not missing the quick glance Ann gave her left hand, Amy felt with her thumb for the single, solid-gold band on her ring finger. She'd removed the diamonds Johnny had bought — with her money — but she still hadn't taken off the wedding band he'd bought her before they were married — with money he'd earned and saved.

"Widowed."

"I'm so sorry." Ann's remorse was as obvious as her friendliness. "See, you should've told me to mind my own business."

"It's okay." Amy smiled a little sadly. "It's been a year and a half."

The two women swung silently, their breath leaving wisps of steam in the air.

"How about you?" Amy asked, partially because she knew that if she cut to the chase too quickly she could raise suspicion. But also because, at that moment, she wished she really *was* Amy Wayne, new to town, free to open her heart to a new friend. She admired Ann's willingness to ignore social barriers just to ease the loneliness she thought she'd seen from her living-room window. "You married?"

"Yes," Ann said, though she frowned as she did so. "To my high-school sweetheart. We both grew up here. Graduated from Lowell High."

"He works here in town?"

"He did." Ann sounded somewhat despondent.

"He lost his job?" Amy immediately thought of possible jobs she could offer the couple. And gave herself a mental shake. As Amy Wayne, she wasn't in any position to dispense largesse. Apparently she wasn't as distanced from Amelia as she'd thought.

She was surprised when Ann shook her head. "He got a promotion. A nice one. To upper management. Which is especially impressive because he doesn't have a college degree."

"You don't want him working in upper management?"

"I don't want to leave Lowell," Ann said. "I've lived here my whole life. All of my family, all of his family, all our friends are here. I love this town. And corporate head-quarters are in Atlanta, Georgia."

Amy was beginning to understand. Far too clearly. "So which matters more — money and prestige or love and family?" she asked softly. It was a question she'd asked herself many times.

And she'd always come up with the wrong answer. She just hadn't known that until too late.

"He says it's not the money so much as the security. He wants to know that we'll be well provided for in our old age."

Yeah, she'd used that one, too. And then learned how easy it was for old age to be stolen away.

"So what are you going to do?"

"I don't know," Ann said, her feet scuffing the frozen dirt beneath their feet. She glanced in the direction she'd pointed to earlier. "He's over there packing his things. I'm staying here. At least for now. Until he finds a house for us. Or until I decide to tell him I'm not leaving here."

"You love him."

"Too much."

"Then if you stay, you'll be losing the one thing you're staying for, won't you?" Amy asked. "You'll be losing the love that means the most to you."

Wrapping her arms around the chains of the swing, Ann glanced again toward the home she so obviously didn't want to leave. "Maybe." Then she asked, "You have any kids?"

"One." Amy reached into her pocket.

She handed the photo to the woman next to her. "His name is Charles," she said.

Slowing her swing, Ann studied the image.

"We haven't been here long." Amy's words were said by rote. "Right now he's at his grandma's in Kalamazoo, but he loves baseball, would be in this park playing every second if he could get away with it. Maybe you've seen him?" She kept her voice casual, concentrating on instilling just the right amount of motherly exasperation.

"Actually —" Ann dragged the word out as she appeared to analyze the six-month-old likeness. "— if it weren't for the fact that you guys just moved here, I'd bet this was the little boy I used to see a few months ago."

Chest tight, Amy forced her foot to push the ground lightly. And then again. Maintaining the slow steady pace she'd been keeping since Ann had sat down with her.

"Charles has a twin in town?" she said. "I don't know if he'll think that's cool or the worst thing that could ever happen to him."

Ann, shaking her head, handed the photograph back. "The boy's not here anymore," she said. "I have a five-year-old son, too," she explained. "Who's also obsessive about baseball. For days all he could talk about was this little boy, Randy, who could catch and throw like a 'real' baseball player. I only ever saw Randy through my living-room window when the boys were in the park, but I'd swear that was him. Those glasses and chubby cheeks are hard to miss."

Amy could hardly breathe. The pounding of her heart reached an upsetting tempo. *Randy.* Her missing son had a name.

"What happened to him?" She prayed that her voice was even. That she wasn't revealing any of her inner turmoil. She was used to playing the part, asking the questions. Not to getting answers.

Ann shrugged one shoulder. "I guess his family moved. Sammy, my son, never said for sure, but you know how it is with five-year-olds. Sammy just came home crying one day because his kindergarten teacher had told the class Randy wasn't coming back."

"He was in school."

"Yeah." Ann gave her a questioning look.

Back off, Amy warned herself.

She was getting too intense.

"That's where Sammy met him," Ann continued after a brief pause. "Sammy just started school in September — and hated it until Randy moved here. Randy left after only a few weeks, but even with him gone, Sammy likes school now."

"And that was what, before Christmas?"

"I don't know," Ann said. "Yeah, it had to be cause Sammy got a new mitt for Christmas and spent a good part of the break complaining that Randy wasn't here to play with. . . ."

"I told you to call me from Chicago." At least a hundred times he'd told her. Most recently when she'd phoned him all excited about an ID made by some woman in a

155

park who'd only seen the boy across the street and through a window.

The caller ID on his cell had displayed the number from hers. She used that particular phone to call him when she was on the road.

It was late in Denver. Close to midnight. Which made it even later in Michigan.

"If you'd rather not talk while I'm in Michigan —"

"Amelia." He didn't even try to camouflage the harshness of his tone. "Don't hang up."

"Then don't give me a hard time. It's late and I'm tired."

"Where are you?"

"Lowell."

Still.

Lying shirtless on his king-size bed, Brad stared through the darkness at the shadow of a football. It was perched on the chest of drawers across the room.

He'd been a damn good noseguard in college.

"Did you find a job?"

"No."

Thank God. Not only were the positions she took far beneath her abilities, they only prolonged the cycle of false hope and failure.

Not that he could get the crazy woman to see that. How the hell she'd run a successful international company was beyond him.

"I had another positive ID today. That's two, Brad. The woman I met in the park and this one."

Brad had to listen. Just in case. But he sure hated to hear such an intelligent woman put herself through these continual episodes of denial and make-believe.

Sometimes he was glad she was far away so he wouldn't be able to act on the powerful temptation to shake some sense into her. Or kiss her just to shut her up.

"I was in a diner this afternoon. The waitress wasn't busy and she sat with me for a few minutes. She asked if I had any kids and I showed her Charles's picture. She said he'd been in the diner a couple of times."

Sitting up, Brad shoved a pillow behind his back. "Did she say when?"

"She wasn't sure."

"Was it before Christmas?"

"She wasn't sure." Her tone of voice signaled retreat.

Brad did the only thing he could. He moved in. "Amy, what did she say?"

"She said it was after Christmas, but she couldn't remember exactly when . . ."

"This is Friday. You've been there almost a week and you got only two IDs, neither of which corroborate the other, which doesn't make either one too reliable."

"Monday didn't count. It was Presidents' Day and everything was closed."

With difficulty he bit back a retort, although he would've felt a whole lot better if he'd gotten it out. She was in one of her unreasonable moods.

"It's not like you to stay in one place so long with so little evidence."

"I have to get into that elementary school. Charles was there, in Sammy Green's class. He *had* to have been registered and I'm not leaving until I know what those records say."

He frowned. "Don't do anything stupid. I'll get someone to check the records." He should have offered as soon as she mentioned the unknown Randy, but she came up with these useless IDs in more towns than not and there was never anything concrete he could ask the local cops to look for.

"All they're going to find is maybe an enrollment date. You know any address would've been false."

"Still, if they manage to get that, they'll

158

also get the date he was withdrawn from this school."

"How does that help?" she asked. "We already know from Ann that he left before Christmas."

"What about the waitress who saw him after Christmas?"

She didn't answer.

"It's the best we can do, Amy."

"It's not the best *I* can do."

"What are *you* going to find besides an enrollment date and a three-months'-old address?"

"I just think that if I have my hands on Charles's record, I'll recognize some detail. I'll have proof that this Randy was him and —"

"Don't do anything stupid, Amy," he said again, his entire body on edge. "I'll make some calls."

"Yeah. I know you will."

He didn't like the weariness overshadowing the acid in her voice. The acid gave her a fighting chance.

"I mean it, Amy."

"Yeah."

"Goddammit, woman, I —"

Brad stopped abruptly when he heard the sounds coming over the line.

Fuck.

She was crying.

"I . . . I have a feeling about that school," she said after a long moment. Her voice was stronger. "I *know* Charles was here and I'm not leaving this town until I see those records."

His jaw set, Brad didn't bother attempting to reason with her. "I'll see what I can do."

Jeans on, he flipped on a light, already compiling a mental list. The time had come to use that plane his employer had supplied.

He had to get her those records.

It was going to be a long night.

On Saturday, a full week after she'd met Ann, Amy awoke after a couple of restless hours with anxious energy singeing her veins. This day was not going to find her idly swinging in the park.

She'd spent a week in Lowell. First biding her time, drawing on patience she didn't have while she waited for Sunday to pass, and then, because it was Presidents' Day, Monday, as well. Tuesday, Wednesday and Thursday were consumed with trying every plan she had for getting into the local schools. There were no jobs. Not cafeteria, playground or even janitorial. She

160

was rejected as a teacher's aid because she didn't currently have a student enrolled.

The library didn't need any volunteers.

And if her son or his nanny had been in town, there was no sign of either of them now.

She'd knocked on Ann's door on Thursday, only to be told by a friendly neighbor that Ann had left on Tuesday for a house-hunting trip in Atlanta. The sixtyish woman said Ann's parents were keeping her three kids.

On Friday Amy was asked to leave the elementary-school premises unless she could state the specific business she had there. She would've offered to reupholster the chairs in the principal's office — and would've learned how to do it, as well — if school personnel weren't already starting to get suspicious of her repeated attempts to infiltrate their ranks.

She'd been tempted to pull out the picture of her son and beg for their help. If she hadn't been sympathetically escorted to the door in identical schools in too many identical little towns, she might actually have tried.

Her conversation with Brad last night had been the final straw.

After so many months on this quest,

Amy didn't need well-meaning people telling her that the police would take care of things, that the FBI was doing all it could.

She didn't need to be humored, advised or sympathized with. She needed to find her son.

Which was why, at six o'clock that morning, she was outside Lowell Elementary, dressed in black jeans, a thick black sweater beneath her navy parka, her black boots and her hair beneath a black wool cap. She'd checked out of the hotel. Had her week's worth of clothes, ones she'd taken to the Laundromat the evening before, packed in the duffel in the trunk of her car. She was ready to move. Just as soon as she had the information she needed.

Whatever it took, she was going to find her son. Get him back. Restore to him the safety and love that had been stolen from him.

They couldn't stop her. She *wouldn't* stop. Or it would all be over.

With her different interviews, she'd been in many of the administrative offices in the school. She'd walked up and down the hallways often enough to know which were the kindergarten rooms.

Hell, she knew which ones were first, second and third grade, as well. She just didn't plan to waste time in them.

And she knew that Bill, the old man who was in charge of maintenance, worked six days a week. And that when he was in the building alone, he usually left the alarm off and the side door unlocked so he could come in and out for his smokes. She also knew everyone seemed to have great affection for the rugged old man.

Judging by the quantity of butts she'd seen — and the number of times the custodian had gone outside during her week of reconnoitering the school grounds — Amy figured that Bill was damn lucky he was still breathing. She was fairly certain she'd never met anyone who smoked more than he did.

"Come on, old man." Teeth chattering, Amy was still waiting at six-twenty. She'd overheard a conversation between him and the vice principal one day that week while she was sitting in an office waiting to speak to the school's librarian. Bill was coming in early on Saturday to fix a leaky pipe in the boys' washroom before the Cub Scout derby descended that afternoon.

Amy was going to be in another town by derby time.

At ten minutes to seven, she heard the coughing of Bill's old Dodge pickup. Sliding behind the bushes she'd chosen the day before, she made herself as inconspicuous as possible, breathing as quietly as she could, and listened.

She was lucky it hadn't snowed or she'd be soaked.

As it was, the branches were frozen, jabbing into her shoulder, the small of her back, her right shin, with painful sharpness.

Less than five minutes into her vigil, Amy's entire body ached. She stopped noticing her discomfort the moment she heard the drag, tap, drag, tap of Bill's boots coming up the walk. She tried not to breathe at all when the custodian finally came into view.

7

He was in overalls again — as he'd been every previous day she'd seen him. And a gray jacket that looked as though it had once been stuffed with some kind of polyester fabric meant to insulate, but was now a bit of limp, dirty nylon with a big hole under one arm — presumably from which the stuffing had escaped. Amy didn't know if the jacket was unzipped because the old man hadn't bothered to protect himself from the cold or because the zipper was too toothless to use.

Just as predicted, he unlocked the side door. And then, pulling a crumpled pack from the bib pocket of his overalls, he lit up a cigarette. He took his time puffing, inhaling, and then slowly exhaling the tar and nicotine that seemed to carry him through his days. So much time that Amy had to start breathing again.

She breathed carefully. Slowly. Praying that his eyesight was either dimmed with age or he was distracted by his own thoughts. He'd have no reason to suspect that anyone was around; judging by the newspaper, Lowell didn't suffer from enough crime to warrant his concern.

Still, she'd spent much of the previous day and night running every element of this plan through her mind. She wasn't leaving a single thing to chance.

At seven-ten Bill entered the building.

At seven-thirteen, after a brief and very careful peek through the glass to make sure the custodian wasn't in the immediate vicinity, Amy slipped in behind him.

Each classroom door was inside an alcove. Amy tried the closest one — a fourth-grade room — and was relieved to find it unlocked. She didn't figure there was a single school in the city of Chicago that left classroom doors unlocked at night.

If that door was an indication of the others she had on her list, her plan had become almost simple.

With a covert peek at the empty hall, she moved quickly from alcove to alcove, door to door, until she'd reached the kindergarten room. She'd passed the boys' washroom, had heard pipes rattling inside and knew she was home free.

As long as she took into account those smoke breaks every fifteen minutes.

166

Breaking-and-entering was easy. Finding any record of a little boy named Randy was not. In the entire kindergarten room, in every desk, including the teacher's, there wasn't one single item bearing the name Randy. Not a crayon box. Not a picture hanging on the wall. Not a label by a hook on the wall or a class listing in a top drawer. The little boy who'd befriended Ann's son had disappeared from the classroom they'd shared as though he'd never been.

Which meant only that Amy was going to have to continue down the hallway to look for a way into the file cabinets fitted snugly along one wall in the administrative offices.

She would've preferred not to venture that far into the school's inner sanctum, but she wasn't afraid to do so.

It took her another ten minutes to make her way to the principal's office. The doors were securely locked.

"Damn."

Bill was outside. She'd have to wait for him to get safely back to the boys' washroom before implementing plan C — finding a way to squeeze through a small window she'd noticed in the back office. The hinge had been loose. Going in like this was less of a sure thing and it was much riskier, since she could be more easily seen, but she wasn't stopping now.

As she tried the door a second time, pain shot up from Amy's shoulder into her neck. A pain that used to accompany particularly important battles at the boardroom table. She'd always held her tension in her neck.

The outside door clicked shut. Bill's drag, tap, drag, tap sounded down the hall. Amy counted, waiting for the sound to stop when she figured he'd just about reached the boys' washroom. It didn't stop. Bill was getting closer.

She started to sweat. Wished she'd left her parka in the Thunderbird parked a couple of streets away.

Her alcove was still around the corner from his view. Was he coming this far down? Should she move?

The footsteps came slowly closer.

Glancing quickly around, Amy noticed another alcove toward the end of the little hallway in which she was trapped. Should she try to make it down there?

She'd have at least a chance of remaining undetected.

Bill was almost at the corner.

Amy half ran, half slid down the small

hallway, then slipped into the alcove. It was the door to a smaller washroom. And it was unlocked. She was inside before it dawned on her that Bill might be coming to do something with the pipes in there, as well. Maybe there was a main shut-off valve.

Plastered against the wall of one of the two stalls, her feet on the toilet, Amy looked frantically around. She didn't see any valves. But she wasn't altogether certain she'd recognize one if she saw it.

What she did see was a floor with cracks that weren't part of the design, dark stains here and there, and a couple of stray wads of brown paper towel that had somehow missed the metal waste can.

A sudden flash of herself in the private bathroom in her suite of offices at Wainscoat Construction, surrounded by marble and gold, plush carpet and soft, thick towels, brought a rush of hysterical laughter to her lips. Amy almost choked as she swallowed it back down.

The last time she'd seen Johnny, they'd stolen a couple of moments alone in that bathroom. She'd been sad that he hadn't kissed her and then he'd come back and given her a kiss that had left her wanting more. Their lovemaking had been so infrequent by then. . . .

Another couple of minutes, and Amy took a tentative step down from her stained ceramic perch. Bill had had plenty of time to come in if he was going to. Moving carefully along the dirty tile of one wall, she listened for any sound that would alert her to the old man's whereabouts.

Nothing.

She pulled lightly on the door, moving it only the inch necessary to let her look into the hall. No one was there.

Amy moved. As quickly and quietly as possible, she went back to the unlocked door leading to the outside, darting from alcove to alcove, listening, watching, prepared to duck into a classroom door at any second. It had to be close to eight o'clock. The derby wasn't until that afternoon, but surely there'd be people arriving early to set up.

She didn't know how much time she'd have.

Once outside, Amy ran so fast she slipped on the frozen ground, landing hard on her right knee. If there was pain, she didn't feel it, focused only on getting to the window she hoped she could enter.

She'd feared that with the cold, it might be hard to jiggle open. It wasn't.

It's meant to be. Amy hadn't felt this sure

about anything since she'd lost Kathy's trail more than a month earlier. She discarded her parka, hiding it in some bushes, and hoisted herself onto the sill. She squeezed through the window into the suite of administrative offices, leaving the window open to shorten her exit time.

And was inside the file drawer with student files seconds later. Her search slowed when she discovered there was no Wainscoat or Dunn. Of course, she'd already realized that whoever had changed Charles's name to Randy would have changed the last name, as well. And maybe Randy was only a nickname and he'd been registered under a different name altogether.

But a little thing like a name was not going to deter her. She was convinced that if she could just get her hands on Charles's record, she'd somehow know it was his. Of course, the job would be much quicker if she had access to computer records. She could at least sort by age.

She stared at the hundred or more files in the drawer she had open. And then at the eleven other drawers.

No matter. She'd sort by hand, and she'd started by making note of every five-year-old Randy in the school.

One of those files had to be her son's.

It took a little over five minutes to make it through the *A*'s. And by that time, Amy had a visual system for quick scanning, her eye immediately seeking the line that designated birth date on the first page of every file.

The *B*'s took a little longer as there were more of them. But no five-year-old Randys. If she got to the *Z*'s without finding any, she'd start again, checking six- and four-year-olds.

At the rate she was going, she could check all the boys in the entire —

"What are you doing?"

A *C* file in hand, Amy froze. And drew a total blank.

"Who are you?"

"I'm . . ." Slowly turning, she recognized Bill. How had the elderly custodian gotten in there without her hearing his boots?

And what the hell did she do now?

Bill was waiting for an answer.

The only thing she could manage was a surreptitious glance toward the next room and the window she'd left open. If she could get out, she could get back in later.

"Don't even think about it." Bill had a smoker's voice, gravelly and low. "I've already pushed the silent security alarm. The cops are on their way."

★ ★ ★

After a sleepless night, Brad should've been more tired. But he'd been able to catch almost an hour of sleep on the flight from Denver and got off the Wainscoat jet in Grand Rapids with more energy than he'd had in a while.

Probably because he was out doing things rather than holding court in his office.

As soon as he was on the ground, he tried Amelia's cell phone. There was no answer.

She'd told him she was staying at the Holiday Inn. Eight-thirty on a Saturday morning was probably too late to find her there, but Brad tried, anyway, keeping his eye out for her black Thunderbird as he drove a rental car through town.

He didn't have to rush. This was mostly a courtesy call. Just to make sure the school records would be checked. And to see what he could do to pacify her when she was told she couldn't have access to those records.

Still, the visit was overdue. It'd been a couple of months since he'd seen her. Mostly on purpose.

Amelia Wainscoat was the only client who'd made him consider another line of work. And the only one he thought about constantly, whether he was working or not. The woman wasn't good for him, not for his career success rate or for his peace of mind.

She was way out of his league.

Could he be blamed for keeping his distance?

There was no sign of the Thunderbird at the hotel. Nor at the park, the diner or anywhere else in town.

Brad had a bad feeling about that.

Hell, he had a bad feeling, period. He wouldn't have spent the night wrapping up enough business to allow him to leave town at five in the morning if he hadn't already summed up the situation. He didn't make courtesy calls.

There was only one reason he was in town — the desperation he'd heard in Amelia's voice the night before. Though he disagreed with her much of the time, he'd always been able to count on her to be rational in the end. Until now.

Back at the hotel, he stopped at the desk, intending to leave her a message to call his cell phone. He'd let her know he was in Lowell once he got her on the phone. Why give her a chance to skip town on him?

"I'm sorry, sir, she checked out this

morning." The uniformed young woman behind the desk gave him the bad news.

"Did she say where she was going?" He turned on the smile he used when he absolutely had to. It generally worked.

"I'm sorry, she didn't."

That didn't surprise Brad. It pissed him off, but it didn't surprise him.

Zipping up the bottom third of his black leather jacket, he strode back out into the midmorning sunshine that did little more than put a bright sparkle on the frozen landscape.

Pushing the six on his cell, he speed-dialed Amelia again. If she knew what was good for her, she'd pick up.

She didn't.

He sure as hell hoped she wasn't seeing his number come up on caller ID and choosing not to answer. He had too much work to do; he couldn't waste an entire day in some little town while she sped out of his reach.

Of course, if she left Lowell, maybe she'd have time to calm down. Come to her senses. Go home to Chicago where she had a staff to watch out for her. Be Amelia Wainscoat. So he didn't have to be bothered every hour of every day by Amy Wayne.

Back in the Explorer he'd rented, a newly purchased map spread out on his lap, Brad studied the lay of the land. Amy was methodical. Deliberate. And very organized.

She'd be going north out of the Grand Rapids area. Because his men were covering the western border of the state, she'd most likely go straight up. Which meant highway 37 or 131. There were no major towns for a while on either stretch. And many small, hidden-away, Amy kind of towns on 131.

Decision made, Brad threw the map on the seat beside him, went to a drive-through for a fast-food bagel sandwich and coffee, and settled back to see a bit of the Michigan countryside. He'd never been to this part of the state before and figured he might as well enjoy the view.

Until he caught up with the black Thunderbird and strangled its driver.

Munching on his snack, Brad drove by Lowell's two elementary schools. Amelia never left a place without becoming intimately acquainted with the schools. He was curious to see what captivated her.

He knew it couldn't be because she actually thought her son was going to come walking out of one of them.

She wasn't that stupid.

He had to cross town to get to the second school. With his coffee to his lips, Brad pulled around the corner. There were two police cars, lights flashing, outside the school.

It shouldn't mean anything to him. As an ex-agent, he knew he should just keep going and let the men on shift do their jobs without interruption or distraction. But he set his cup in the holder, dropped his half-eaten sandwich, wrapper and all, on top of the map and made a sharp turn to the left, into the school's parking lot.

"Shit."

Brad threw the vehicle into park so quickly it rocked back and forth. His insides churning with a protectiveness he could not acknowledge — and an anger he welcomed — he got out.

Although a quick perusal of the parking lot showed him that she'd stashed her car somewhere else, he knew he'd just found his client.

The food he'd just consumed sat heavy in his stomach as Brad watched Amelia Wainscoat, millionaire heiress and respected CEO of her family's Fortune 500 company, get pushed, handcuffed, into the back seat of a running patrol car.

Once again, he'd been too late.

★ ★ ★

Lowell hadn't been her proudest moment. Those hours in jail — another one of those places she'd only ever seen in the movies — until her lawyer and Brad Dorchester had come to her aid and she'd been respectfully released, hadn't been the worst of it, though.

"I can't believe I was that close to finding a name and address and messed it up," she lamented to Cara on her cell phone a couple of days later. She was driving on highway 10 toward Evart, Michigan, an hour and a half north and slightly east of Grand Rapids. Brad's men had had a tentative ID of someone matching Kathy's description in the area. Because Amy had nowhere else specific to go — and had been told to leave the Lowell vicinity well and truly behind — she'd turned her car toward the small town near Reed City.

"I can't believe you got arrested, Amelia. It breaks my heart to think of you sitting in that jail."

"It wasn't so bad," she said, one hand on the wheel as she drove the almost deserted highway. There were two lanes going west and, somewhere, on the other side of a tree-lined median, two lanes going back east. "I was the only one there."

"Were you in a cell with a cot?"

"No." Amy could hardly remember what the place had looked like. "It was just a room. With a table and chairs."

"Did it have a bathroom?"

"No. I was escorted to the ladies' room across the hall." Certainly one of the least-dignified moments of her life. And hardly worth a mention as far as Amy was concerned. What in hell did dignity matter?

Could it give her back her son? Her life?

"God, honey, I'm so sorry."

"It's really no big deal," Amy said, sorry, too. Sorry that she was upsetting Cara.

"They had no idea who you were or they'd have treated you with a lot more respect."

There was a barn off in the distance. All alone among the trees and the completely still countryside. Amy liked it. It looked deserted, but attested to life out there that couldn't be seen. Charles was that, too. He was somewhere out there — just couldn't be seen.

"Come home, Amelia."

"What?" She still held the phone to her ear and was a little surprised to hear the stern note in Cara's voice.

"You're not sounding like yourself at all."

"Or maybe I'm discovering how meaningless respect can be. Respect and dignity and —"

"You're scaring me!"

That made two of them. Sometimes Amy didn't even recognize the woman she lived with.

She'd been arrested. And although the charges had been dropped, she'd committed a criminal act.

Who was this woman who didn't stop at accepted boundaries?

"Don't worry, Cara," she soothed mostly out of habit. "I'm fine. Just tired."

"So what did Brad say?"

Amy sank a little lower in her seat, raising one booted foot up to rest against her thigh. "After he bailed me out, you mean?"

"I thought Frank took care of things."

Ah yes, Amelia's personal attorney. He'd been circumspect, had said a hell of a lot less than Brad Dorchester, but she'd still felt his — to put it gently — surprise when she'd used her one phone call to get him out of bed on Saturday morning.

"From what I understand, it was teamwork. Frank made the calls, Brad did the running around."

"I can't believe you called Brad."

"I didn't. He was here."

"You didn't tell me he was flying in," Cara said, her voice more excited than accusatory. "His men must have come up with a fairly substantial lead to call in the big guy."

She'd thought the same thing when she'd first caught a glimpse of him through the side window of the police car. Even handcuffed and on her way to jail, she'd been thrilled to see him. Not getting those records wasn't a matter of such importance if Brad had something else to go on.

Being arrested wasn't quite so frightening knowing that he was there to help her.

"He said it was a courtesy call. He likes an in-person meeting with his clients every few months or so."

"Seems like he'd have called and let you know he was coming."

"Yeah." It did seem that way. But Amy didn't want to look any more deeply into Dorchester's reason for showing up that morning. She'd wondered once or twice if his sudden appearance had anything to do with her state on the phone the night before.

If it did, she didn't want to know. Didn't

have the emotional wherewithal to delve into what that might mean. On any level. She was not going crazy. And it was nothing to him if she was.

"Did he stay long?"

"A few hours."

He'd bailed her out. Supervised a check of the elementary-school records only to come up with nothing. Waited around with her while Frank took care of getting the charges dropped, spent another hour having dinner with her — an hour during which he'd chastised her, reprimanded her and given her orders. And then he'd climbed back into her plane and left her alone.

She hadn't been sorry to see him go. The man exhausted her.

"Amelia, please come home."

"I can't."

"Yes, you can."

Amy pulled the elastic from her ponytail, shaking loose the unevenly grown strands. Maybe there was a salon in Evart where she could at least have the ends trimmed.

"Cara, you know I can't just come home and sit and wait."

"I know you *think* you can't," her friend replied, her tone lacking a bit of the supportive warmth Amy had come to rely on. "And I've been right there with you all these months. But you're going too far, Amelia. It's time to stop."

"You of all people know I can't do that until I find Charles."

"Looking for him because you can't stand to stay home is one thing. Losing your grasp on reality is another."

Losing her grasp on reality? That was harsh.

Her expression frozen, Amy moved only the muscles it took to drive.

"I love you, honey." Cara's voice had softened. "I'm worried sick about you."

"There's no reason to worry."

Cara paused, and Amy thought the conversation was over. "Yes, there is," her friend said suddenly. "You know I've always been honest with you."

"Of course. As I am with you."

"Right. Well, Amy, the truth is you're losing control."

"I'm in complete control of everything it's in my power to control," she said, immediately and fiercely defensive. Cara was pretty much the only person with whom she'd dared let down her guard.

"No, honey, you aren't."

"How would you know, Cara?" Her

question was fueled by intense disappointment. For Cara of all people to turn on her like that. She felt betrayed.

"What part of your life has given you the insight to judge how 'controlled' a mother should be when her young son has disappeared off the face of the earth?" she asked, her tone completely unlike any she'd ever used with Cara.

Amy took the next curve slowly. Deliberately. Aware of Cara's shocked silence. "For that matter," she continued, "what experience could you possibly draw on to know what it feels like to lose one's husband, let alone one's child?"

Amy knew how much it upset Cara that, at thirty-four, she'd never been in love. The blow was a low one.

"None."

"So don't tell me about control, okay?" Amy said, more scared by the tears welling up than by the uncharacteristic anger that was starting to fade as quickly as it had come. Anger kept her strong. Fighting.

Tears weakened her.

"Okay."

Amy felt so far away from Cara, much more distant than the miles between Chicago and Michigan. Amy Wayne and

Amelia Wainscoat were separating and she couldn't see how to stop them.

"Cara?"

"Yeah?"

"I'm sorry."

"I know. Me, too."

"Be safe."

"Yeah, you, too."

The lump in Amy's throat grew as she hung up the phone. Something had just changed, perhaps irrevocably, between her and Cara. Had she, on top of everything else, lost her best friend, too?

8

As small towns went, Evart was smaller. It didn't take Amy long to check the place out. There was no sign of Kathy, and no one recognized a small chubby boy who wore glasses and had a penchant for baseball. Amy hung around, anyway. Just the previous weekend, one of Brad's leg men had traced the ex-nanny to a bowling alley just outside town.

At least, he'd traced a woman fitting Kathy's description to the lounge inside the bowling alley. Kathy hadn't used her credit cards or bank account since leaving Chicago, which made tracing her that much harder.

Amy was surprised that Kathy — if it was Kathy — had been seen in a lounge. She hadn't been a drinker. But then, Amy had never been a woman who broke into elementary schools, either. Desperate times called for desperate measures.

Or maybe, as times became more desperate, people just changed.

Even though she hadn't yet seen a woman in that town who resembled Kathy, Amy continued to believe the sighting might have been legitimate. Which made her afraid to leave in case Kathy was still there.

There wasn't a lot to do in Evart, so Amy found herself gravitating more and more often to a makeshift ball field she'd happened upon her first day in town. Almost daily a group of boys, ranging in age from about six to twelve or thirteen, gathered to play a rousing game of baseball.

Sometimes when she watched, Amy could close her eyes and pretend she was back in Chicago, pretend that Charles was out on the side of the field, bouncing around near the dugout, begging for a chance to play. She pretended that Johnny was there, consoling the boy — who still needed a little more time to grow into himself — making promises, teaching his son the game.

Sometimes, she could even hear Johnny's voice.

And inevitably comfort would turn to bitter regret as she realized anew that she'd never have a chance to make things right with the man she'd loved so much when she'd married him — and had trouble loving as more than a father to her son as the years passed.

"I'm sorry to bother you, ma'am, but you got business here?"

Opening her eyes, Amy studied the police officer standing between her and the field. He was blocking her view.

"Here as in right here on this sidewalk? Or here in this town?"

Older than she was, he was a good bit heavier, too. Officer Peterson, his name tag said. Amy wasn't afraid; she just felt a little raw from the episode in Lowell.

"Both," he said, his bushy brows furrowed. He had bushy brown hair, too.

"I'm in town visiting a friend. And I'm here on the sidewalk enjoying the day."

"It's twenty degrees outside, not the kind of temperature anyone's gonna enjoy for long. And you've been on this sidewalk every day this week. Unless you can give me an explanation for watching those boys that I can give to their mothers, I'm gonna have to ask you to move along."

She wanted to challenge him about laws that forbade people from standing on public land, but was too shaken from her last run-in with the law. It was her goal to find her son, not become a convict in every town in the state.

"Please, tell the mothers I'm sorry for alarming them. I'll leave," she said, applying the style of Amelia Wainscoat, CEO and soother of frayed nerves, to the situation.

The uniformed officer was apparently not impressed with her attempt to placate. He frowned and walked slowly forward, forcing her to either let him bump into her or to back up.

She backed up. The Thunderbird was just around the corner. She wondered if he was going to back her all the way to the driver's door.

"What did you say your friend's name was?" he asked, still frowning.

"I didn't," she said. "But it's Kathy. Kathy Stead."

Maybe he'd know Kathy and where she lived, and then Amy could be finished with her business and get out of this man's town.

No such luck. "I don't know any Kathy Stead," he said.

"She's new here."

"It's pretty unusual for someone to move to a town this size unnoticed."

She could certainly attest to that. More than once, she'd felt prying eyes peeking out from between the lace-edged curtains on the windows of various houses in Evart.

"Well, I'll be on my way . . ."

"I'll walk you to your car."

The feeling of being unsavory was not something she could get used to. Amy picked up her pace.

"This is it," she said when they reached her car.

"So," Officer Peterson said almost conversationally, "you mind telling me why you told Sam at the bar that you didn't know anyone in Evart and were trying to find work? You've just told me you're here visiting a friend? So what's the real story?"

Damn. Word traveled faster in this town than most. Why in hell had she gotten greedy and hoped she could get the policeman to reveal something about Kathy? It had been a dumb move.

Dumb or desperate.

Neither of which was going to find Charles.

"I came here looking for an old high-school friend of mine," Amy said, all emotion aside as she slipped into the part she'd played so many times before. "I heard she'd moved to Evart after her divorce. When I spoke to Sam a couple of days ago, I hadn't found her yet. Now I have."

She delivered the lie smoothly. Another talent she'd picked up on the road. Another proud moment.

Kristen Miller had no idea who the woman with the haunted green eyes really was. She didn't know where she'd come from or why. She was just glad she had.

"So what made you choose Baldwin?" she asked her newest employee as they were closing the store on a Wednesday night in the middle of March. Amy had seemed particularly lost that day, doing her job impeccably, yet with an emotional distance that not one customer had managed to bridge.

"It was the next town on the map."

A grin accompanied Amy's answer, but Kristen believed the words held much truth.

Kristen counted the money in the cash register as Amy swept. She listened to the piped-in music as she made out a deposit ticket and slipped the day's earnings into a secured banking bag. Conveniently just off highway 10, Baldwin Convenience was doing a booming business.

Kristen had never had so much money in her life.

Buying the store was the smartest thing she'd ever done.

Amy finished her nightly chores, put everything away and came up front to wait. In the two weeks she'd been working for

Kristen, the women had made a habit of leaving the store together when they both worked the night shift.

"You're investing that, right?" Amy asked, watching as Kristen locked the bag.

"It goes into an interest-bearing account."

"No, I mean really investing it. Your money is your employee, every bit as much as I am," Amy said. "But it's only going to give what you ask of it. You have to *make* it work for you. There are hundreds of low-risk investments that, in the long run, stand to bring you a much higher return than a bank account will."

This wasn't the first time Amy had offered sound business advice. Because of it, Kristen had negotiated a much better contract with the beverage man when he'd been in earlier in the week. Amy had also come up with some dynamite remodeling ideas that would be relatively inexpensive yet would net Kristen a much larger yield per square foot.

"How would I find them?" she asked now, wishing she knew Amy's story. Not because she was merely curious. But because in the two weeks they'd worked together, she'd really grown to care about the other woman.

Kristen wished Amy would confide in her, let her help if she could.

"An investment broker."

Sitting on her stool behind the counter, bag still in hand, Kristen laughed. "In Baldwin?"

"No," Amy said, returning the grin. "In Chicago. Or New York. It can all be done by phone and e-mail."

"Would you walk me through it?"

Amy turned away to grab her purse from under the counter. "It would be the blind leading the blind," she said. "I had a job for a brief time as secretary to the CEO of a small construction company. I listened and learned a lot, but eavesdropping is a long way from hands-on experience. And he sure didn't pay me enough to have anything left over to invest."

Frowning, Kristen slung her own purse over her shoulder. It was times like these that she was certain Amy was lying. Initially she'd been indifferent, figuring the woman had a right to her secrets.

But as the only full-time workers at Baldwin Convenience, she and Amy had spent a lot of time together. Amy's intelligence was addictive, her kindness and conscientiousness compelling. And the dignity she wore so much more carefully than her jeans and cheap sweaters, drew Kristen. Kristen had been searching her whole life for a little dignity.

She hated the feeling that Amy was hurting and alone.

"You ever been married?" she asked, still sitting there.

Amy stopped on her way around the counter and glanced back at Kristen. In the dim light of the closed store, with no makeup and her hair in a ponytail, Amy looked about seventeen.

"Yeah." And then, "You?"

"Once." Kristen didn't want to think about that now. "So what happened?"

"He was killed."

Oh. God. She'd been thinking maybe she could help. Coming through a failed marriage was something she understood. But this . . .

"How?" she asked, instead, her heart open to Amy in a way it hadn't been open to anyone in a long, long time.

"A boating accident."

Horrified, Kristen stared. "Was he by himself?"

Amy nodded. "He was testing his new boat. They aren't sure whether the engine had a gas leak and exploded, or if Johnny hit a rock, which caused the explosion.

The first anyone saw was the remains of the boat burning on the water. Later his keys and part of his shirt . . . and other . . . debris . . . turned up."

Which would certainly explain the sorrow Kristen sometimes felt emanating from her new employee.

And she'd thought she could help. . . .

The night was dark and the little boy whimpered. The box of animal crackers she'd left him was clutched in his hand, but he didn't want them. He was alone again. And scared.

Something bad was going to happen to him. Worse than getting stolen or anything else.

Shaking as he lay on the cot that stank like someone wet his pants, he wondered what he'd done that was so horrible to make this happen to him.

He wished he could just say he was sorry and have Mommy back again.

Things weren't right without Mommy. He was afraid they would never be right without Mommy.

"You said you'd been married once, Kristen. Was it a long time ago?"

Stacking packs of cigarettes in their slots

195

over the cash register, Amy glanced down from her stool to the beautiful woman calculating stock and sales as she filled out a monthly order form for one of her suppliers.

"Yeah," Kristen said. And nothing else.

Staring for a moment at her slender neck, adorned only by the short strands of blond hair that was cut to look as though the wind had just blown through the store, Amy considered leaving well enough alone.

Lord knew she had enough trauma of her own without prying into other people's. She could certainly understand Kristen's need to keep her own secrets.

Marlboros. Marlboro Lights. Marlboro Light 100s. She was glad of the brief lull in business that allowed her to get stock out in preparation for the busy couple of days ahead. It was the Friday morning before St. Patrick's Day weekend and probably the last free minute she'd have until Sunday evening, when all the campers, hunters and fishermen went home and Baldwin settled back into the quiet, friendly town she'd grown to love. Or at least tolerate, with some degree of affection.

After the episode with the police officer in Evart, Amy had figured she might as well get out of there. With everyone suspicious of her, it wasn't likely that any confidences would be forthcoming. The chances of Amy learning anything about either her son or the vanished nanny were pretty slim.

She hadn't had the heart to go far — Evart being the last sighting of any kind at all — and had ended up in Baldwin, a stop on the highway between Reed City and Ludington. Located just off the middle branch of the Pere Marquette River, the town had a slow, steady pace and a tourist trade consisting mostly of hunters and fishermen and their families, dressed for the woods. There was one main street, a restaurant, a couple of bars, a bait-and-hardware store, a drugstore, a bank — and a shop that sold the best ice cream she'd ever had. Charles would love it.

A family-owned business, the Joneses had been making ice cream for close to a century.

They still gave the value of yesteryear, as well, half the price of ice cream in Chicago. And one scoop was large enough to fill her, even without a meal first.

"I grew up in Paw Paw." Kristen's words, coming out of the blue, broke through Amy's reverie. "You ever heard of it?"

Folding the stool, Amy slid it back into

place between the counter and the wall. Meeting Kristen's eyes, she shook her head.

"It's south of here — and smaller than Baldwin. Not much there except a few rich people who want to live out in the country and commute to Kalamazoo. And some white trash."

Pulling forward a box that sat on the counter, Amy started loading up the rack of mints and gum. Later in the summer, Kristen had told her, there'd be a rack of insect repellent, too. For now, it was all candy and gum.

She wondered which group Kristen had come from — rich or trash. Not that wealth had anything to do with a person's value in Amy's eyes. Not anymore.

A couple of guys drove up out front, pulling a boat. They bought some snacks, a case of cold beer and did their best to cajole Amy and Kristen into dates for the weekend.

The idea of dating was so foreign to Amy she didn't even think to respond. Kristen, on the other hand, turned down the offer in such a flirtatious manner it took Amy a few seconds to realize the other woman had said no.

"By the time I was fifteen, I was so sick

of my life I was willing to do anything to get out," Kristen said when they were alone again. She stood, her long legs in a pair of faded jeans something to envy. "Including sleeping with the guy who lived in the big beautiful house on the hill." She straightened the papers she'd spread on the counter, turned the key in the computerized cash register and ran the hourly report.

Kristen might have been talking to herself for all the attention she was paying Amy. But Amy was listening to what she was saying — and what she wasn't.

She'd finished setting up the gum. Had cans to stack on the one shelf that held real food — open-and-heat things like soup and stew. But she didn't want to do anything that might make Kristen stop talking.

She started to rearrange the turnstile of key chains.

And wondered what Kristen had had to endure, what had made her so desperate to escape by the age of fifteen. A time when Amy had been taking ballet, getting A's in her private school, going out any weekend night she wanted to, usually with whichever boy was her current crush, and anticipating the new Corvette her father was planning to buy her for her sixteenth birthday.

At fifteen, her only experience with the intimacies between a man and a woman had been what she'd read in the romance novels hidden under her bed.

"Of course, I *would* get pregnant," Kristen said. She ripped the report receipt off the register, glanced at it, pulled out the ledger under the register and logged that hour's earnings.

Amy would love to see her with a current computer program that would do all that work automatically and produce results in any number of areas and formats with a simple command.

"What happened?" she asked, re-alpha-betizing miniature license-plate name tags that were already in near-perfect order.

She'd had no idea Kristen was a mother. She must have had her baby at sixteen, which would put her son or daughter close to twenty.

"What happened is we got married," Kristen said. She shoved the logbook back into its slot and walked out in front of the counter, straightening cups at the soda machine. Checking the hot dogs spinning slowly on the rotisserie.

A family with a group of boisterous kids came in to use the rest rooms and load up on candy and chips, followed by a couple, another family and then a middle-aged man dressed in dirty jeans and a flannel shirt looking for a carton of cigarettes. One customer followed another until, as the day wore on, they were sometimes standing four and five deep at each of the two registers.

Amy and Kristen stood side by side for several hours, speaking almost nonstop, but never to each other.

"You still staying in the Three Sisters Hotel?"

It was Sunday night after a long but very successful weekend, and the two women, having said goodbye hours ago to the high-school student who came in part-time to help out, were finally closing up.

"Yeah," Amy answered her employer and friend. "They're letting me rent by the week."

"I don't live too far from there myself. How about we grab a bottle of wine out of the cooler and take it back to your room? Or my trailer?"

"That would be great. Let's go to your place."

Another time she would have refused, would've gone straight back to her room. Alone. Kept her mind focused on finding her son. But Brad was doing that. And he had her cell number if there was anything to report.

These days every single hope she had was wrapped up in that man. Not that she let herself think about it. Or him. They'd hardly spoken.

Baldwin — and Kristen — were perhaps easing Amy's way as reality finally caught up with her. As she finally saw the futility of what she'd been doing.

She could only run in place for so long without realizing that she was going nowhere. Being arrested and then chased out of town had a way of putting things in perspective.

She hadn't called Cara in two weeks. And she hadn't pulled Charles's picture out of her pocket once. Except when she was alone in her room at night.

When calling her cell garnered him nothing more than the damned recording again, Brad Dorchester tossed his phone onto the coffee table and stood.

Darkness had fallen while he'd been sitting there debating all the different angles with himself. He really should turn on a lamp. Heat up one of the gourmet dinners in his freezer. He walked to the bay window in his living room, instead, staring out into the night.

Sunday evening in Denver, and there were lights twinkling everywhere. Cars on the distant highways. People going about their business.

He gave her fifteen minutes and then tried again. Swore. And went for his brief-case. He'd had his secretary print out the number to the Three Sisters Hotel when Amy had called to say she'd stopped there almost three weeks before.

He dialed. Asked for her room. And listened to the ring. Again. And again. And again.

Brad didn't like it.

If something had happened to her . . .

He should be glad Amelia Wainscoat was staying put. Should be glad she wasn't wasting his time with a million phone calls leading nowhere, glad she wasn't chasing all over the countryside getting herself in trouble. Wearing herself out.

He should be glad.

Hanging up the phone, he went to get dinner out of the freezer. He was pretty sure that among the curries and masalas his housekeeper kept stocked, there was a man-sized Salisbury steak. He'd have it with a beer.

Brad stopped abruptly, the microwave dinner package half-opened. Leaving the box on the counter, he reached for a second phone sitting on the wet bar between the living and dining rooms.

He dialed with his thumb, waited impatiently for Sherry Down to pick up.

"How fast can you get started on a composite of the descriptions we've got?"

"Tomorrow morning," the retired agent and part-time portrait painter replied.

"I need a new one of the boy, too. Progressed eight months." They'd been staying true to Charles's age, but a life like he might be experiencing could easily age a person.

"No problem," Sherry said.

"What're you doing for dinner?"

"Leftovers."

"Want to meet me at Marley's?"

"Sure."

Brad appreciated a woman who didn't give him a hard time whenever he opened his mouth. Especially when he found himself missing the phone calls that had done nothing but frustrate and anger him.

The Salisbury steak was forgotten as he shrugged into his jacket and headed out into the night.

9

"I can't believe how big this place is," Amy said, looking around Kristen's living room. The light-colored spring theme in the floral upholstery was continued in the window treatments, the artwork on the walls, the handwoven tapestry area rug gracing the middle of the off-white carpeted floor.

"You've said that every time you've been here this week." Kristen handed her a glass of wine — still pouring from the bottle they'd brought home the previous Sunday — and took a seat on the opposite end of the sofa. They'd both changed into cotton pajama pants and tops.

Last time they'd had a late night of wine and conversation, Amy had had to borrow a pair from Kristen. Tonight she'd brought her own. And a toothbrush, too.

Easily ten percent of Amy Wayne's possessions.

"I always thought trailers were small and narrow, with everything in miniature. I had no idea they had rooms the size of standard homes."

"Some trailers are that way," Kristen said, sipping from her goblet. "The one I grew up in — on and off — was exactly as you describe. Our bathroom was so small you had to stand beside the toilet to shut the door."

Amy couldn't imagine living that way. Or worse, allowing a child to live that way. At times like these she felt completely overwhelmed by the number of things of which she'd been so ignorant. All the suffering. All the poverty and deprivation.

"What happened to the child you had?" she asked softly, starting to relax with the wine. The Friday traffic at the store had tired her. But settling into Kristen's home like this, late at night, made the tension disappear. They'd grown close, she and her new friend, over the past weeks.

"It died."

Amy sucked in a breath. She'd wondered, especially when she'd first visited the trailer and seen no pictures. She'd guessed something like this when Kristen never mentioned the baby again.

That didn't make hearing the truth any less painful.

"Before birth or afterward?"

"Before. I delivered prematurely — in my sixth month."

The night was quiet, comforting. Amy curled her legs up on the couch. "Oh, how sad. Was it a boy or a girl?"

"A boy."

Amy nodded. Studied the golden liquid in her glass. Tried not to feel too much.

"I named him Daniel, after the Bible story about Daniel and the lion. It was my favorite when I was a kid."

It didn't sound as if Kristen had been a kid very long.

"Mine was the fable 'Androcles and the Lion.' "

Kristen smiled, a surface smile, as her eyes met Amy's. "Kind of the same thing."

"Yeah."

"You'd think one of us would have gone for 'Goldilocks' or 'Little Red Riding Hood.' "

Amy shook her head. "I never got into 'The Three Little Pigs,' either." But Charles had. His favorite part had always been when Johnny would huff and puff to blow the house down. She flashed back to those memories, Charles sitting on his father's lap, Johnny giving a dramatic recitation of the story, complete with gestures and sound effects. . . .

"Where'd you go just then?" Kristen's voice startled her.

Amy had absolutely no idea what to say.

"You were here with me, and then gone," Kristen continued after a moment. "I've seen you do that before."

Amy shook her head. "Sorry," she said, sipping from her glass. "I didn't realize."

Even frowning, Kristen's features were perfect. Amy didn't think she'd ever seen a person so naturally beautiful.

"What happened after you lost the baby?" she asked.

Turning her head so Amy could no longer read her expression, Kirsten said, "I set out to be the best damn wife any man could ever have. Trouble was, Robbie Lawson didn't care to have *any* kind of wife, good or bad. He'd just married me to rebel against his parents.

"I put up with his cynicism, his cracks about me trapping him by getting pregnant, about how lucky we were that the baby died. I put up with the drinking and his taunts about how I was second-rate in bed, about his other women who were so much 'more woman' than I was. I kept telling myself I'd get better, if I kept working at it, I'd be the kind of wife who'd make him happy. That he'd learn to be happy about us."

Kristen's voice trailed off. For the first time since she'd known her, Amy saw tears well up in her eyes. Kristen bowed her head.

"I even put up with him hitting me. Twice. But when it happened a third time, I finally went to his parents. We were living in a cottage at the back of their property.

"You can imagine my surprise when instead of sympathizing, they looked at my bruises, my bleeding lip, and blamed the whole thing on me. Said I'd ruined Robbie's life."

"They should be shot."

Kristen gave her a brief, sad smile. "Yeah, well, I ended up okay in the end." She raised her head, took a sip of wine and sent Amy a sardonic grin. "I made out pretty well in the divorce."

"And you moved here and bought the store."

"Yeah," Kristen said, then shook her head. "Well, not quite. I was twenty-one, had a lifetime's worth of baggage and no high-school diploma. So I got my GED first, *then* moved here and eventually bought the store."

Amy had a feeling there was more heartache nestled in that "eventually" but she'd let Kristen talk about it in her own time.

"Can I tell you something?" Kristen asked.

"Of course."

"You have no idea how envious I am of you."

Amy grappled for a place to perch. Kristen couldn't possibly know about that other woman, the one who'd grown up with such privilege. The one who, even now, could own the city of Grand Rapids if her assets were combined. Amy didn't *want* her ever to know about that woman. Amelia Wainscoat and Kristen Miller had nothing in common.

"Why?" She was afraid to ask.

"Don't get me wrong, I know it had to be sheer hell to lose your husband . . ."

Amy nodded, hardly daring to breathe while she waited for her old world to crash into the tentative new world she was building.

"But at least you had it all once, you know?" Kristen's face creased in a grimace. "All I've ever wanted was to love and be loved. I think it would even be worth suffering the pain of a loss like that if I could at least have the memory of being loved."

Amy swallowed. Took a sip of wine. And choked.

"You okay?" Kristen asked a couple of seconds later. She was lightly rubbing Amy's back.

"Yeah," Amy said, trembling. The coughing fit had brought tears to her eyes.

And once started, they didn't want to stop.

She looked over at Kristen. Her employer. A woman who felt like the only friend she had in this new and often frightening world.

She hadn't called Cara in two weeks. She'd only spoken to Brad twice. His men were hitting the northern part of the lower peninsula pretty heavily with a new round of photos, but they'd had no conclusive results. They'd unearthed some serial numbers on cash Kathy had withdrawn before leaving town. The money had been resurfacing in various parts of Michigan.

She was glad, in a distant sort of way, that Brad was finally taking her seriously about Kathy.

In the same distant way, she was glad he was handling the search and making the ex-nanny the focus of his inquiries.

She just had to keep him out of her new life. The only way she could survive at the moment was to concentrate on the here and now. To defer hope until Brad came up with something definite.

"I wasn't in love with my husband at the end."

She owed her friend as much of the truth as she could give.

Kristen's mouth fell open.

She sipped slowly from the wineglass she'd been holding, peering up at Amy as she did so.

"I loved him," Amy finally said. Thinking back to that time in her life was like remembering a novel she'd once read. Some scenes were clear and vivid, others hard to recall. "I was . . . just no longer in love with him."

"Did he love you?"

Now there was the billion-dollar question.

"I was completely sure of that when I married him."

"But by the time he died?"

Amy remembered that last day in her office. Johnny had wanted her home for dinner.

"I think so," she said slowly. He'd kissed her so tenderly. Or had he merely responded to the tenderness in her kiss? "Maybe."

Rising, Kristen filled both their glasses, then sat down again, facing Amy.

"We were great friends," Amy said. Even now, after more than eighteen months, she didn't have any true perspective on the relationship with Johnny.

"I loved spending time with him. I loved his way of looking at life. And the way he genuinely cared about other people. But we didn't have the same values. At least not when it came to working and providing for a family. He had pretty traditional views on the matter. I guess I didn't realize that immediately. . . ."

She'd figured that if being the main financial support of the family didn't bother *her*, it wouldn't bother him, either. She'd figured wrong.

"I have a strong work ethic, taught to me by my father. After . . . we were married for a couple of years, Johnny started to resent that about me, which interfered with everything else in the relationship."

"Did you ever think about leaving him?"

"No." Amy shook her head. She would never have left Johnny. Never have broken up their family. Not while Charles was young. Probably not ever. Johnny had needed her. She'd taken him from a lifestyle he'd never have been able to go back to, from an anonymity he'd never have re-captured. Even though he'd worked, he'd needed her support, financially and emo-tionally. And in her own way, she'd needed him, too. "I was certain we'd grow old to-gether."

She looked up, a half-smile on her lips. Kristen's blue eyes were warm, filled with understanding as they met and held Amy's. "I always hoped that one day, the breach between Johnny and me would mend."

Amy awoke sometime around dawn, the coffee table holding an empty wine bottle and two empty glasses in her line of vision. Her head was propped up against one end of the couch. Kristen was in the same half lying, half sitting position on the other end. They must have fallen asleep at about the same time.

This wasn't the best night's sleep she'd ever had, but it was heaven to wake up and not be alone.

Glancing at the clock on the wall, Amy realized they'd only been asleep a couple of hours at most. There were still another couple of hours to go before they had to open the store. As she drifted back to sleep, thankful that the aching loneliness inside her had eased, Amy wondered if maybe this was what her life would be like now. The loneliness broken by the occasional moment of peace.

That was probably the best her life could be without Charles.

Six days later, Brad Dorchester called Amy at work.

"I'm in Reed City," he said when she answered.

That was less than an hour east of her. Not quite halfway between Baldwin and Evart.

Her legs suddenly weak, she slumped onto the stool behind the counter. She was vaguely aware of Kristen giving her an odd look, but couldn't face her friend right then. Brad only traveled if there was some development in the case.

"Tell me," she said as soon as she could speak. Her throat was so dry she felt as though she might choke.

If he had bad news, he should tell her in person, not over the phone. But this was Brad Dorchester. He'd tell her in a voice mail.

But only if he was completely sure . . .

"I have a positive ID on Charles."

"What?"

Kristen turned from the register in a

flash. And the customer whose purchase she'd been ringing up stared at Amy. She hadn't realized she'd been so loud.

"It's not fresh," he said. "But it's conclusive."

"Where? When? Who?"

"A manager at the McDonald's off highway 10 in Reed City."

Oh my God. I drove right by there. Amy pressed a hand to her forehead, as though she could keep the dizziness at bay.

"She recognized the age-progressed photo. Because she was so certain, Fleming called me and I flew in. I just finished meeting with the manager, a Ms. King."

Fleming was the FBI agent in charge of Charles's case.

"What did she say?" Amy got the words out through gritted teeth.

She couldn't look at Kristen. Couldn't face the questions — and concern — she'd seen in her friend's eyes.

"That the woman he was with called him Randy, but earlier, the manager had seen the boy looking at the display of Happy Meal toys while he was waiting for his mother to come out of the ladies' room. When Ms. King went over to say hello, he said his name was Charles."

"Oh, my God." The world was spinning

216

in earnest now. She was going to be sick.

In Lowell, Ann — the woman Amy had met in the park — had said the boy in the photograph had called himself Randy.

Amy jumped up. Sat back down. She was trembling so hard she could hardly hold the phone.

Her mind flew over a series of plans. Of ideas and guesses and probable next steps. Landing nowhere.

She was going to be sick.

Somewhere in the midst of her confusion, Kristen's hand gripped her shoulder, squeezing softly. Offering the reassurance that she wasn't alone.

Brad gave her a few more facts, which barely registered, and then hung up.

While the FBI and some local officials, as well as Diane Smith and Doug Blyth, were continuing to follow up, he was flying back to Denver with Ms. King to have his own artist create a composite of the woman Charles had been with. He said it didn't sound like Kathy, but Brad wouldn't put any stock in that until he had a computer-generated drawing.

By the time Amy was back from the bathroom, her face splashed with cold water and a compress on her forehead,

Kristen had called in someone to watch the store. Thursday afternoons were usually busy, and even though it was the end of March and unseasonably warm, this Thursday didn't seem any different.

Amy couldn't stand still while Kristen gave the young man instructions. She paced the aisles of the store and then the parking lot outside. Her car was there. She could leave.

But she didn't have anywhere to go.

And a very strong reason to stay. The news, the resultant questions, the screaming for answers, the thought-numbing relief, the inability to *do* anything with the information, were sending her out of her mind.

She was afraid to be alone.

"Let's go."

She hadn't heard Kristen come out, but followed blindly, silently, when her friend grabbed her by the arm and led her to the passenger door of her little pickup truck. They didn't go to Kristen's trailer, as Amy had assumed they would.

Instead, after a drive that could have been five minutes or twenty-five, Kristen stopped the truck on the side of a dirt road.

"Come on," she said, climbing out and heading toward an old wire-and-post fence that was partially down.

"This is private property." What an inane thing to care about.

"It's okay. I know the people who own it. They don't get up this way as often as they'd like and they're happy to have people on the property now and then."

Kristen led her through some brush and into a forest of pine trees. They walked for several minutes before they came to a clearing.

There was a freshly mown yard, at least an acre in size, and in the middle of it a picturesque cabin with a stone chimney, shingled roof and wooden shutters.

The front door had a full-length wood-framed screen with a metal handle.

Amy wondered why she was cataloging such meaningless details, then decided that only by noticing ordinary objects in an ordinary world could she maintain any kind of grip on reality.

After following Kristen around to the back, Amy walked down the cement steps behind the cabin, then down a slight hill to more steps, three of them, that ended at a bridge.

Halfway across, Kristen sat on the bridge, her legs dangling over the side.

Amy did likewise. She stared at the water rushing by several feet beneath them. Even though the weather was warm for the end of March, nearly seventy, she figured the water had to be freezing because of the snow coming down from the hills. It was only about a foot deep and crystal clear. Amy studied the variously hued rocks that swayed a bit with the force of the current. Oranges. Dull browns and beiges. An occasional yellow, shimmering like gold. And black.

She wondered if the rocks had been there long. Maybe for years. Maybe since before she was born. They'd probably be there long after she was dead. They —

"Who was that on the phone?" Kristen was swinging her feet, staring upstream. Her short blond hair glinted in the sun, lifting almost imperceptibly with the light breeze.

She wasn't frowning, but there was definite concern in her eyes.

"Brad Dorchester."

"Who's he?"

"The detective who's looking for my son."

Kristen's feet stopped swinging.

Amy had been trying to find a way to tell Kristen about Charles, but she'd never considered blurting it right out.

The stream gurgled over the rocks beneath them. It seemed serene, yet full of energy. Amy looked up at the shuttered cottage. A narrow porch, empty except for an old white rocking chair, ran almost the whole length of the building. She tried to imagine being inside the cottage, knowing she was there to stay. With time enough to allow the peace of this place to settle over her. Around her. Inside her.

She wondered if the owners would be willing to sell.

"I'm sorry I lied to you."

"You didn't lie." Kristen didn't move. Her hands clutching the edge of the bridge on either side, shoulders hunched to her ears, she just sat there and stared at Amy.

"Not technically, maybe, but by omission."

She needed more time to absorb the peace and tranquility that the stream, the land, had to give her. Her heartbeat was returning to normal. Her thoughts, too, were starting to focus.

"Honesty was one of the things I always prided myself on," she said. She could have been talking to a client. Explaining a time-line for constructing an office building. "In recent months, I've found that lying is something I can do without a blink."

Kristen sat there silently.

"I hate that about myself."

Farther upstream, beaver-constructed dams lined the banks. Amy wondered if there were any fish.

She wondered, too, if there'd ever been little feet crunching along the pebbles at the bottom of the stream on a hot summer's day.

"But you know, maybe I've been lying my whole life." Aware that she was babbling, Amy continued to talk, anyway. "Before, I was lying to myself. About life, about who I was and what I wanted, about the things I did and didn't see in the world. Now I tell lies to others."

"Amy." Kristen leaned over, pressing Amy's shoulder with her own. "Tell me what's going on."

10

Amy considered what she should say. Kristen hated rich people, and she couldn't lose Kristen: It would mean losing the chance to be a friend to a woman who could use one. It would also mean losing the chance to be a normal person in a little town far away from everything.

"A little over a year after Johnny was killed, our son was abducted." Amy's mind backed away from the images, the memories. She couldn't do this. She had to move forward, stay focused on finding Charles, not on his loss.

Except that, in the past weeks, the clarity of that vision had disappeared. After the situation in Lowell and then in Evart, when she'd scared herself with a desperation that had gotten her arrested and then run out of town, she'd tried to concentrate on ordinary life, on the mundane tasks that kept her sane.

"How old was he?" Kristen's voice was

low, filled with caring.

"Five. Just."

Kristen's fingers slid beneath Amy's, holding on. Amy was watching for fish. Because there might be fish if she watched.

"Where was he?"

"An amusement park. On a kiddy ride. I was there with him."

A mental flash to that sun-filled afternoon, the glint off the metal of the ride, Charles's face as he rode past.

"The ride stopped . . ." *She could see it slowing, slowing. Where was Charles?*

"He was on the far side, where I couldn't see him."

There were happy faces everywhere. Running kids. Excitement.

"I didn't even wait for him to come around the ride. I went after him. . . ."

All the kids were gone. Others were starting to get on.

". . . but he wasn't there."

He wasn't there. She'd thought it was a mistake. That she just had to wait for a few more minutes and everything would right itself.

"I've been on the road ever since, looking for him," she said, wiping at her tears.

"I'm so sorry."

Somehow Amy wasn't surprised to see tears in Kristen's eyes, as well. In a very short time, Kristen had become a dear friend.

"I'm going to find him," Amy reassured her.

Kristen looked at her a long time. And then out at the stream again.

"Do you have any idea who might have him? Does the detective?"

Amy told Kristen about Brad. And about Kathy Stead. Charles's baby-sitter. She told her that in spite of Kathy's alibi, she was convinced the ex-sitter had her son. She told her about the months in Wisconsin. Her sighting of Kathy in Lawrence two and a half months before. About the woman's abandoned car the very next day. And about meeting Ann Green in Lowell. They were still on the bridge, she and Kristen, although they'd turned, feet out in front of them, to face each other.

"How could you afford all this? The detective, the time you've spent searching . . ."

Amy glanced downstream. Thinking about the lies. Thinking about Amelia Wainscoat.

"There was insurance money from Johnny's death." It was the truth.

Birds twittered back and forth in the

225

trees flanking the stream. Amy wished she could lie down on the bridge, beneath the comforting heat of the sun, with the breeze on her skin, and go to sleep.

Kristen tapped her tennis shoe against Amy's calf. "So what happened today?"

"They have a positive ID on Charles."

"Alive?" The word lost none of its intensity despite the whisper in which it was uttered.

Amy just nodded. And swallowed the lump in her throat. She told Kristen about the manager in McDonald's, the boy with two names.

"Randy was the name that woman in Lowell called him," Kristen said.

"Mm-hmm." Amy looked across at her friend. "It's the first absolutely positive assurance I have that he hasn't been dead all this time," she said, her vision blurred with fresh tears.

She couldn't hold back any longer. As hard as she tried, she couldn't restrain the anguish — or the relief. Her shoulders shook as sobs convulsed her body.

"Ah, honey, come here," Kristen said, reaching over to pull Amy into her arms. Curled up like a baby, Amy leaned against her friend, vaguely aware of Kristen's fingers running softly through her hair as the torment she'd carried for so long broke free.

"Seven months," she sobbed. "He could be with some maniac who likes little boys!"

It was the first time she'd spoken that thought aloud. And it almost killed her.

"Oh, God, Kristen, what will I do if my baby boy's been molested?"

"Shh," Kristen said. "Don't do this to yourself, Amy."

"It's possible." And it was only one of the indescribable horrors that had been haunting her.

"Yes, it's possible. It happens. But it sounds far more likely that the baby-sitter has him." Kristen's shirt was soft against her face. Amy tried to concentrate on the softness. And to Kristen's words.

"She was unhinged," Kristen continued in the same soothing voice. "She'd convinced herself that Charles belonged to her. When you tried to deny her the right she felt was hers — to raise him — she'd do whatever she had to in order to preserve that right."

It did make sense. Amy sniffled. And quieted for a moment while rational thought once more took hold.

"And if she's got him, you're pretty much assured that he's being well cared for."

"You think he's happy?" Sometimes, when the darkness consumed her and she wasn't sure she could go on, Amy dreamed about Charles in a house somewhere, warm and cozy. Forgetting her. Happy.

"Probably not," Kristen said, reminding Amy of Brad with that blunt honesty. But then, that was a trait Amy valued. "If nothing else, he's got to be missing you terribly."

"Do you think she'd turn on him if he couldn't forget me? If he cried for me? Wouldn't that seem like he was rejecting her?"

Kristen's fingers started stroking her hair again. "It's possible."

A shard of fear shot through Amy.

"The McDonald's manager didn't recognize Kathy from the picture."

"How long ago was he there?"

"A couple of months. Sometime in January. She was sure about that because of the kids'-meal promo they were running at the time. Charles was looking at the display."

"Kathy could have any number of disguises for herself."

Which was exactly what Amy had told Brad. More than once.

Head down, Amy gazed out over the side of the bridge. "The manager said Charles was rubbing his ear, said it hurt. He was prone to ear infections during the winter months. He usually had at least two between November and March."

And if they weren't treated, her son could eventually lose part of his hearing. But that wasn't anything she could worry about at the moment. The possibility of a deaf Charles wasn't nearly as terrifying as a dead Charles.

"Sounds like the woman had quite a talk with him," Kristen mused.

Things Brad had said slowly filtered back as the shock and numbness began to subside.

"He told her he was going to be starting Little League soon," Amy said now, smiling. She sat up, hugged her knees to her chest as she once again faced Kristen. "Starting T-ball this spring was all Charles talked about. He had to be five to join, but on his third birthday, Johnny bought him his first real ball and glove." Her smile grew as she remembered warm fall evenings out on the back grounds of the estate. She'd sit on the patio with her laptop and a coffee as Johnny pitched balls to their son, his patience unending. "Johnny spent hours teaching Charles the ins and outs of the game."

They'd had season tickets to the Chicago White Sox, too, and hadn't missed a game in four years.

"Sounds like Johnny was a great father."

"The best." Amy had loved him for that.

"It also sounds like whoever has your son is trying to keep him happy. Going places like McDonald's, taking him to baseball . . ."

Her chin resting on her knees, Amy peered up at Kristen. "Sounds like Kathy, doesn't it?"

"Yeah."

"The manager also said he talked about going fishing. He didn't say where, but Brad's men are going to check all the fisheries in the area that allow kids to drop in a line, and check all the lakes and streams, as well."

"That'll be one hell of a job." There was a mural painted on the outside of the brick building that housed Jones' Ice Cream Shop. It was a picture of a lake and a deer, and said that there were ten thousand lakes in Michigan.

"Johnny was teaching him how to fish, too."

"And I'll bet Kathy knew that."

"Yep."

Silence fell between them. Calmer now, Amy listened to the stream. And the birds. And hoped that the God who'd made them would keep her boy safe. That He'd help him forget Amy, help him accept Kathy as his mother, if it would keep him safe and cared for.

"So if your entire life is consumed with looking for Charles what've these weeks in Baldwin been?" Kristen asked, her voice oddly tentative.

"After Lowell and Evart, I think I was afraid to keep looking," Amy said. "Everything was starting to backfire on me. I'd lost my touch."

"So you've given up?"

"I might've been thinking I had."

"And now?"

"Now I think this time was about me finding you." Only because they'd shared such intimate sorrows could Amy admit that. "Emotionally I was running on empty and I needed to get filled back up." She grimaced at the trite image and gave a short laugh, but Kristen didn't join in.

Amy risked a quick glance at her; Kristen was once again staring upstream.

"I think, when I was at my lowest, fate

sent me to you," she said. "A rare, once-in-a-lifetime kind of friend . . ." This was so hard. And yet, life was too precarious, too frightening, not to take the chance. "I hope I'm not the only one who found that friend here."

Withstanding Kristen's studied glance was hard, but Amy persisted. It mattered that much.

"You aren't," Kristen said simply.

Amy smiled — inside, as well as out.

Thursday, March 27. It had been a good day.

Jamaica was a lot warmer than Denver during the first weekend in April. Warmer than Michigan, too, not that he expected Amelia Wainscoat to notice. She hadn't been outside the hotel since they'd arrived separately that afternoon.

He'd been busy following her, alert, every sense tuned to the people around her. Anyone acting nervous, refusing to meet her eyes, avoiding her. Anyone who was acting too friendly, or watching her. He was the best in the business when it came to surveillance.

So far, his skills had been completely wasted.

From the very beginning, Amy hadn't

given much weight to his theory that someone from her professional life was involved with Charles's disappearance. He suspected she might well be right.

Sipping from a very weak bourbon, he looked at his employer.

Impeccably dressed in a designer silk gown that moved seductively with every step she took in her very expensive leather shoes, she worked the crowd of dignitaries as smoothly as though she'd never left their realm for a day.

Hard to believe this was the same woman he'd bailed out of jail just six weeks before.

"You said you'd sit down with me and show me every detail of the search if I came here," she said softly as she passed him in the crowded ballroom during the evening's cocktail party.

"I have charts, graphs and more reports than you want to read upstairs in my suite. As soon as you give your speech and we're finished down here, I'm ready to go to work."

After Ms. King's confirmation that Charles had been alive — and in Michigan — Amelia had tried, repeatedly, to get out of this conference. In the end, it had only been his promise to use their spare time to update her on every single detail — and his reminder that if she truly wanted to find her son, they had to check every possible angle — that had gotten her on the plane.

He stood, drink in hand, in his favorite tuxedo, not in the least intimidated by his million-dollar client.

A slight relaxing of her shoulders was all the response he got. At that moment, the president of a national electric company greeted Amelia by name and escorted her over to the CEO of one of the nation's leading developers.

He was glad she'd come. With the progress they'd made this past week, he was starting to believe they actually might find her son. And if they did, the little guy was going to need his mother strong and healthy.

Assuming they didn't find him dead.

Not that it was any of his business either way. He wasn't a baby-sitter — of small boys or their mothers. He merely located them.

"How did I get so lucky as to find a great-looking guy like you all alone at this shindig?"

Brad hadn't noticed the woman walk up. An oddity, considering the fact that with her shoulder-length blond hair, generous cleavage and long legs, she was exactly the type Brad went for.

Judging by her skimpy dress and the amount of makeup she wore, he assumed she was there working the party — a classy and expensive call girl for very rich and not-so-classy men.

Brad's league on both counts.

"Your lucky day, I guess," he said, offering to buy the woman a drink. And wondering if he should think about taking her upstairs. Strangely, he felt no desire to do so.

Even as he shared the drink with this gorgeous and fully accommodating woman, his attention was on the one across the room. As much as she drove him insane, Amelia Wainscoat compelled probably the strongest admiration he'd ever felt for anyone.

She'd been through hell. Twice. And was still standing.

Standing nicely, he noticed as he extricated himself from the voluptuous woman at his side, not wanting to take up her time when he knew there'd be no payoff for her.

Keeping to the fringes of the crowd, Brad watched Amelia during the next hour, impressed anew. Her thick dark hair, with its stylish cut done specifically for this little jaunt, skimmed her bare shoulders.

He'd never realized she had such small, fragile-looking shoulders.

Her conversation, intelligent and informed from the snippets he heard, flowed easily, naturally.

Not that Brad had any interest in being on the receiving end of the socially polite chitchat. He much preferred her straightforward honesty.

Her keynote speech, delivered confidently, commanded the attention of the crowd. She spoke about ethics in business and about loyalty. About companies that deliver, to their clients and their employees. And she talked about the responsibilities of success.

If he was the type of man to be intimidated by a woman, it might have happened right about then.

Thank God he wasn't that type of man.

Amy was relieved when at last she made it up to her suite. She'd planned to slip away immediately after her speech, but it had taken almost two hours to even reach the door of the ballroom.

In another life, the time would have melted away without notice. Now every word took effort.

Before she called Brad, she took a moment to dial the trailer in Baldwin. Hearing about the store, the day's sales, the weather in Michigan, a date Kristen went on, all bolstered her in a way Amelia Wainscoat would never have been able to understand. Kristen grounded her when she couldn't ground herself.

And then she changed out of the gown and shoes Cara had bought for her, thinking fondly of the good friend she'd grown up with. The friend who knew Amelia and didn't understand Amy at all.

Hair in a ponytail, dressed in jeans and a red T-shirt from Jones' Ice Cream Shop, Amy opened her door to Brad ten minutes later. She was glad he'd traded in his tux for a pair of jeans, too. That tux had made her uncomfortable.

Two hours later Amy was exhausted — yet energized, too. Her suite was completely covered with charts, graphs, maps, pages of statistics and bound reports from each field representative working the Wainscoat case.

She pushed away from the table, sliding down until her head rested on the back of the upholstered chair. "We're really making progress."

Methodically checking out fishing lakes and streams, his men had unearthed several more sightings of a young boy who loved baseball and fishing, traveling with a woman.

On a couple of occasions, the woman had been with a man.

Unfortunately none of the sightings were recent.

"Yeah," Brad grunted.

"Enough progress that you can go home to Chicago."

"Forget it, Dorchester," Amy said automatically. "Do you think Kathy's got a boyfriend?"

"That's one possibility."

"You have another?"

"The woman might not be Kathy."

"It makes sense that she is," Amy argued.

"The composites don't all match up."

"But enough of them do."

"To make it a *possible* yes. But not conclusive."

Amy looked away from hazel eyes that saw too much and showed too little.

"What's your gut feeling?" she murmured.

"That it's probably Kathy."

His craggy, lived-in face gave away as little as his eyes, but she knew he wouldn't tell her something just because she needed to hear it.

"The lack of a ransom demand makes total sense if Kathy's the kidnapper," she said.

"It also makes total sense if Charles's kidnapping was random. Either someone who wanted a child and saw the chance or —"

"Yes, well, it's Kathy." She couldn't let him say it, couldn't let him finish that last sentence.

Coming from him, the keeper of her hopes, that would be more than she could handle.

"At the moment, I agree."

"Thank you."

Amy was struck by the odd look in his eyes. When he didn't glance away, she did.

They were finished. They both had an early flight in the morning. She expected him to go. And wasn't sure what to do when he just sat there, twirling a half-empty glass of warm whiskey.

"We know what we're doing, Amy. You can have complete faith that we'll find your son."

That theme again, although the tone was different. Almost human. But then, it was the middle of the night and they'd done some good work piecing a couple of things

239

together. Like the fact that there were no sightings of Charles anywhere during the week Kathy had been in the Lawrence area. They'd also added miniature golf courses to their list of sites to check.

And somewhere along the way, they'd become friends.

Sort of.

"I'm not the type of person to sit back and let others do all the work," she said quietly. "I'm honestly trying to play by your rules, Brad. I know you're the best and I'm not stupid enough as to ignore your experience, but I have to play."

Running his thumb around the edge of his glass, he glanced up at her. "How long are you going to be able to survive like this, running from town to town? Uprooting yourself at a moment's notice, your only possessions what you can pack in one duffel?"

"As long as it takes." She shivered, although it wasn't cold in the luxuriously appointed suite.

"We're still a good eight weeks behind her," he said. "It could take months."

"I know."

He shook his head. "Do you think you can keep your claws sheathed for a second while I tell you something?"

Because she needed to know what he had to say, Amy said, "Yes."

"I've been working on missing-persons cases for almost twenty years, Amy. I've seen what this kind of thing does to families. Mothers are always hit the worst."

She started to speak and he held up a hand to stop her.

"In every case, the ones who come through it best are those who keep up a semblance of life during the search. You have to have normalcy, some everyday living, to sustain you through the emotionally debilitating ups and downs."

"I've already lost my husband, Brad," Amy said softly, allowing some honest feeling to accompany the words. "And now, with hope dwindling, I'm losing my son. There *is* no normalcy. There *is* no life to go back to — no life at all without Charles."

In a low voice, almost so low she couldn't hear, Brad said, "What if we find a dead boy?"

Amy's heart dropped inside her. Brad hadn't said those words lightly.

"Then I focus on getting through the rest of my life," she said. "And wait for it to be over."

11

Charles thought about going outside. He thought about throwing the ball up in the air and seeing how often he could catch it.

But he lay on his blanket on the floor and hugged the wall, instead. He didn't feel very good.

He understood that bad men had Mommy. He worried about her. He missed her a lot. *She* wasn't like his mommy at all. She said they were playing a game, pretending to be different people all the time.

He was tired of playing the game. And he was real tired of the chocolate milk and Rice Krispies she gave him, even if they were things his mommy wouldn't let him have.

The door across the room slammed and Charles jumped. He closed his eyes real fast, hoping if he was asleep, she wouldn't bother with him.

He tried to think about school. He guessed it was good that he still got to go to school. It was just that his school at home was different. People there knew you. And he didn't always have to be the new kid.

He heard her footsteps coming closer. He felt like he was going to throw up.

"You awake?"

Her voice had changed a lot from when she'd first started playing the game with him. She used to like him.

"I know you're awake."

He kept his eyes shut so tight they hurt. He hated that every time he made a new friend, he had to move.

"Caleb, you answer me right now."

He hated his name, too. What if when they moved, it changed again and he forgot it?

She'd hit him for sure.

"Caleb, tell me I'm your mommy now," she said in that squeaky voice he hated most of all.

He missed his real mommy. And got scared sometimes, even though he didn't want to be a sissy.

Her toe caught the middle of his back and Charles began to cry. But he didn't make a sound. His tears just trickled out in secret.

She'd never kicked him before.

He tried his hardest not to, but when her foot jabbed his back a second time, he started to shake.

After the conference Amy went back to Baldwin. She'd told Kristen she was flying out to meet Brad for an in-depth update, a reason Kristen unhesitatingly accepted. It was certainly true enough, Amy figured. Though she was no longer working at the store, she'd left her things at the trailer. On her return, Kristen offered her one of the extra bedrooms, and Amy gladly accepted.

She spent the next couple of days traveling to nearby lakes and campgrounds. She'd come up with a story about wanting to surprise her husband and son with a fishing trip for her son's birthday but couldn't remember which lake they'd gone to the summer before. She showed Charles's picture everywhere, hoping someone would say that was the lake. Or the campground. Or the shop where they'd bought their bait.

She didn't have one nibble.

And every afternoon was spent at ball parks, watching boys of all ages dressed in official-looking uniforms arrive for their Little League games. Hoping. Always hoping.

The Friday following her trip to Jamaica, Amy got a call from Brad.

"Where are you?" he asked without preamble. Curt, even for him.

Heart pounding, she replied, "Paris." Sitting in a ball park about an hour southwest of Baldwin. "Why?"

"I have a lead on Kathy. I just landed in Grand Rapids and there was a message on my cell."

"What've you got?"

She and Brad had developed a respectful truce after their night in Jamaica. He didn't exactly welcome her involvement, but he tolerated her presence on his case.

"An address. She rented an apartment in Big Rapids last week. I just got off the phone with the rental agent who said she'd seen Kathy go inside an hour ago."

His men were all over the western part of the state and heading toward the Upper Peninsula, still combing lakes, streams and miniature golf courses looking for Charles. That left him — and Amy.

"I'm less than an hour from Big Rapids," she said, already moving toward her car.

"Amy, she's living alone."

"As far as the agent knows, but —"

"I don't want you to do *anything*. Just

stay in your car and watch her door until I get there." It was the Brad of old.

"Fine. What's the address?"

She wrote it down in the little notebook in her wallet while she walked.

"It's kind of odd that after all this time she'd do something so easy to trace, isn't it?" she asked, her mind only half on what she was saying as she climbed into her car and started the engine.

"Yes." Brad's succinct reply grabbed her complete attention. "Which is why you're not to do anything until I get there."

A knot in her stomach, Amy drove to the highway, trying to be prepared for whatever lay ahead. Brad wasn't expecting it to be good.

But even Brad Dorchester wasn't right all the time.

The apartment complex was relatively new. Nice. Part of a growing neighborhood in a Big Rapids suburb, it sprawled among beautifully manicured lawns with a well tended private park at its center. The park had swings, a slide, a sandbox and shaded benches for mothers to sit on while they supervised their kids. And plenty of room for small boys to play an impromptu ball game.

She was surprised to read on the sign that the apartments weren't furnished. Kathy was on the run. As far as Amy knew, she didn't have a bed or any other furniture. Let alone all the boxes of little things, like dishes and silverware and towels.

The white-brick, two-story buildings were well marked. Amy found Kathy's second-floor front door without any trouble at all. Each unit appeared to have one covered parking slot, but there was plenty of guest parking, as well. Amy drove into one of these spaces.

On the short trip from Paris, Amy had maintained her calm by rehearsing what she'd do upon arrival. If she could, she'd park so that her windshield faced Kathy's door. And then she wouldn't blink until Brad got there and they could go up.

The nanny was not getting away again.

Simple though Amy's plan might be, she went over and over it in her mind. The second she stopped thinking about it, her mind was going to race out of control. She'd obsess about the possibility that she was finally going to see Charles. That her son was very likely on the other side of that door.

Right now. That door right there. It was after three. He'd be home from school.

Watching television maybe. Having an afternoon snack. Or a really early dinner if he had Little League practice.

Did they even have a television? And what in hell was Charles sleeping on? With the money Kathy had to be paying here, she could've afforded a smaller apartment in a complex that was a little older but fully furnished.

She could hardly bear to sit still knowing that Charles might be inside that very apartment. So close after so long. She could feel his chubby arms around her neck, hugging her so tightly it hurt. Tears sprang to her eyes, blurring her view of the door, and she hurriedly blinked them away. She could feel her chin trembling, her heart pounding.

Charles. Just feet away . . .

She climbed out of the Thunderbird and almost forgetting to shut the car door, took the steps three at a time. Kathy had lived with her, in her home, as part of her family, for more than four years. Why had she let Brad convince her that she needed to wait for him? Amy *knew* Kathy. She could probably handle this better than Brad could.

Funny how, after all the months of frantic searching, she was about to knock on a door and — she prayed — be reunited with Charles. Amy paused at the top of the cement steps, one hand on the black wrought-iron railing. She yanked the light-blue, going-out-of-business-sale sweater down over her no-name jeans suddenly feeling decidedly less powerful. Would Charles even recognize her like this? Dragging the elastic from her ponytail, she shook her head. Thank goodness she'd had her hair cut and shaped for the conference the weekend before.

Taking a deep breath, she lifted her hand to knock. And then stopped. What if her son *wasn't* there? What if Kathy still refused to tell her what she'd done with him?

What if Brad's earlier suspicions were right and Kathy *hadn't* been the one to take him?

No. Straightening, she rapped sharply on the door. She wasn't going to do this to herself. Brad had admitted just the weekend before that a lot of the evidence and all of the motive pointed to Kathy.

No one answered. Amy knocked again. There was no window by the front door. No peephole. No way for Kathy to know that it was her standing out here.

Of course, the woman was on the run. She might not answer her door.

Looking around, Amy noticed a young man climbing the stairs to an apartment across the drive. A sedan went by with a woman driving and a car seat in the back. Inside, Amy could see little arms and legs thrashing about in the haphazard way of young babies.

She knocked a third time. Harder.

Kathy might be tough, but Amy was tougher. She wasn't going to leave. She was going to win this one.

She wondered now if Kathy had looked through a window and seen her in the parking lot. If she knew who it was knocking on her door. If she knew this was the end of the line.

And that scared Amy. What was Kathy doing in there? Panicking? Would she hurt Charles in her desperation?

The rental office was just across the way and, keeping a watch on Kathy's stubbornly closed door, she ran over. The agent was young. A brunette who was tall, slender and beautiful enough to be a model. She smiled, her navy suit and pumps giving her a very professional appearance.

"Can I help you?" The woman's name tag read Jenny.

"I was supposed to meet my friend fifteen minutes ago," Amy said. "She just moved in to 6402 and she's not answering her door."

"Kathy Stead. Yes, she just rented from us last week. She seems to be quite popular. You're the second person who's asked about her today."

Amy was having a hard time maintaining any semblance of calm. "She's expecting me, but not answering my knock. I was wondering if we could give her a call."

"Sure," Jenny said. "I know she's home. I saw her come in and that's her car out there." She pointed to a blue compact. She pushed a couple of keys on her computer, then picked up the phone.

"No answer," she said a minute or two later. "Maybe she's in the shower."

Amy prayed that Brad would get there soon.

"Kind of odd that she'd take a shower when she's expecting company, though, huh?" the friendly agent asked.

"Yeah."

"Let's go try the door again."

The young woman put a Be Right Back sign on the front window ledge, grabbed some keys and locked the door of the rental office. High heels clicking on the blacktop, she accompanied Amy to Kathy's door. It was nearly impossible for Amy to maintain the slow pace. She needed to run up those stairs, pound on that door, get her son free.

Of course she couldn't tell Jenny that. She couldn't go around accusing one of the tenants of kidnapping and expect the agent just to open the door without calling the police. But if she could convince the woman that there might be an emergency, that Kathy might need help . . .

Kathy still didn't answer the door. Jenny frowned. "I hope she's okay."

"Did she tell you she was diabetic?" Amy had no idea where the lie came from. "I know once before she had a problem with her insulin level and passed out. . . ."

"You stay here and keep trying," the agent said, a new note of urgency in her voice. "I'll go get the master key."

The Explorer Brad had rented pulled into the drive just as the agent was heading across the street. Amy, shifting her weight from one foot to the other, was starting to feel sick to her stomach. She was trying not to think about what might be happening in that apartment while she stood helplessly outside.

"I told you to wait." Brad came up the stairs ahead of Jenny.

Amy was surprised at how much comfort she took simply from having him there. "She's not answering."

"I've got the key," Jenny said, sliding between the two of them to put the key in the door.

She went in first, followed by Brad.

"Oh my God!"

Amy was barely in the front door when the agent screamed.

"Don't touch anything. I'll call the police." That was Brad.

Amy faltered. Afraid to move forward and find out what the others already knew.

Another two steps and she saw what they'd seen.

Kathy Stead, lying in the middle of the empty living-room floor, dead in a pool of her own blood.

Still lying in one hand was a knife. In the other was a picture of Charles and Johnny, taken on the grounds of the estate in Chicago. Not far away from the dead woman lay an empty pill bottle and a half-empty paper cup of water.

Brad was already on his cell phone, calling the authorities.

"It's like she wanted to make absolutely certain she didn't fail," Jenny said slowly, shock slurring her voice as she nudged the pill bottle with her foot. "God, I was just joking with her yesterday about the fact that she still didn't have any furniture. I told her I'd love to go shopping with her. And all along, she knew she wasn't going to be needing any. . . ."

The young woman's voice trailed off. Her face a ghostly white, she looked as sick as Amy felt.

Amy knew she should be doing something. Finding a sheet to cover the body, crying, feeling anything at all. There should be something to say to the young agent, who'd just had the shock of her life. Jenny had probably never seen a suicide before.

But then, neither had Amy.

And she was terrified that this wasn't the only body she was going to see. Phone to his ear, Brad was searching the rest of the apartment. Amy was afraid to breathe. Her gaze flew to his when he came back to the living room.

One quick shake of his head and Amy wilted. Her shoulders slumped. Her knees lost their strength. Down on the floor, head in her hands, she tried to assimilate the horrors washing through her. Charles wasn't here. But Kathy was.

The woman who'd been family to her,

who'd raised her baby for more than four years.

Her hands still covering her face, Amy raised her head enough to take another look at her ex-nanny. Kathy had apparently dressed for the occasion — she wore a black sheath, hose and black pumps. Her hair seemed freshly washed, her bangs curled. She'd paid far more attention to her makeup than she ever had while living in Amy's house.

Climbing to her feet, Amy stumbled into the bathroom and retched.

"She slit her own throat." As usual Brad didn't mince words.

It was late that night, and he and Amy were sitting at the butcher-block table in Kristen's kitchen. An hour before, he'd driven Amy back to Kristen's trailer, Diane Smith and Doug Blyth following with his rental. They'd already returned to Big Rapids. Now he was waiting for Kristen to get home before leaving.

"And took pills," Amy said. Her face drawn, she looked worse than he'd ever seen her. He hadn't met Amy until the day after Charles's abduction, but wondered if this was how she'd looked the night her son had been taken.

As though she'd rather be dead than have lived through that day.

He didn't like to think about how she was going to cope if they didn't find her son soon. And alive.

"I can't believe Kathy's dead," she said. "She used to be almost a sister to me." The shock in her eyes, the loneliness, tugged at him.

But soothing her wasn't his job. Wasn't something he'd be good at.

He could sure use a drink. First bar between here and Grand Rapids, he'd go in, have a belt or two. Amy had expected him to stick around for a few days, but he needed to get back to Denver. To coordinate all the information that would pour in over the next week.

Fingerprints. Autopsy. Death report. And once the article ran in newspapers across the state with a sidebar about Charles's disappearance, he hoped there'd be more information about her whereabouts and doings these past months.

Amy, he knew, hoped for a miracle.

For someone with so damn much pigheaded, stubborn strength, she had some unexpected vulnerabilities.

"Not only was there no sign of Charles in her apartment, no little-boy clothes, no toys, there wasn't even a second pillow to go with the blanket she'd spread on the floor in the bedroom," Amy said, her voice expressing quiet disbelief.

"And there was nothing in her car," Brad felt compelled to remind her. "Not a French fry or animal cookie dropped on the floor. She didn't have him, Amy."

"I can't believe there was no sign of Charles," Amy murmured, as though she hadn't heard him. "And no suicide note. Just that picture in her hand."

"Odd that it was of Johnny and Charles. Did she have a thing for your husband?"

Amy shook her head. "That was always her favorite picture of Charles. . . ."

"You're just going to have to face it, Amy. She didn't have him. All the schools in the surrounding area have been checked and rechecked tonight," Brad told her. "Not a single new five-year-old has registered lately. No one recognized Charles. Even the agent had never seen him."

"She was off work for a few days right after Kathy moved in," Amy was quick to point out.

Before he could do more to help her see the hopelessness of hanging on to Kathy as a suspect, Amy's friend Kristen arrived at the trailer. Brad thought it was best to keep things simple, so they told her only that they'd had a promising lead on Amy's babysitter, but it had turned out to be disappointing.

Eyes clouding in sympathy, Kristen took Amy's hand, squeezing it. He wasn't sure what a multimillionaire CEO and the owner of a small-town convenience store could possibly have in common, but he was damn glad Amelia Wainscoat had found a friend.

12

It was raining as she took highway 10. West of Baldwin, 10 was mostly woods, pine trees, a turnoff now and then. Little produce markets. Isolated bars. Random homes, an occasional trailer. Amy passed them slowly; she just didn't know what she was looking for. She felt lost now that Kathy was gone.

But while the nanny's death left her without a theory, it also saddled her with fears that would destroy her unless she kept moving. Kept looking. *If Kathy didn't have Charles, who did?*

And what did she tell herself, late at night, if she couldn't pretend that Kathy loved Charles as much as she did, that her son was cared for and safe?

What would Johnny make of all this? "Where are you?" She glanced up at the dark sky as she spoke. "Tell me what to do."

Another couple of houses, seen through the steady back and forth motion of the

Thunderbird's windshield wipers, and then the Lazy Days Motel. White with red trim, the place was old but well maintained. If there was a town nearby, it would've been her kind of place.

She could hardly remember what it felt like to be in that luxury suite in Jamaica the week before.

Slowing, she scanned Fox Lake as she drove past. There were no boats on the water, no fishermen on the banks. Odd for a Saturday, except that it was raining. And cold.

She'd said goodbye to Kristen that morning. Her friend had hugged her tightly and there'd been tears glistening in her eyes as she'd told Amy to keep in touch.

Kristen didn't have to worry; Amy planned to call her every night. Those times in Lowell and Evart had taught her a very important lesson — she wasn't invincible.

Walhalla, Michigan. A post office. A few buildings. Open grassy fields. A farm. The town came and went to the pattering beat of rain on the roof and the slush of tires against wet road.

Amy heard a crack of thunder in the distance and wondered how long the stormy weather would prevail. And whether or not Charles had a Little League game that was getting rained out.

Custer showed a little more life. She passed a market. A post office and a bank. Johnny's Restaurant.

Simply because of its name, Amy pulled in. Ordered a cup of coffee. Listened to the locals talk about the upcoming holiday weekend and the Easter pageant a customer's kid was in. And then she left.

She passed Crossroads Church. She wondered if that was where the pageant would be — and whether Charles would get an Easter basket this year. If not, would he think the Easter bunny had forgotten him?

Or had he figured out, sometime these past months, that all the best things in life were make-believe?

Rather than just scattered houses, Custer had actual neighborhoods. Aluminum-sided homes, some quite nice.

And a ball field. It was wet. Muddy. And deserted. Amy stopped there, anyway. She thought about calling Kristen and asking if she thought Amy was losing her sanity. Except that the answer wasn't going to change anything. Amy would continue to do what she was doing.

She wished Cara could accept that. She'd called her earlier that morning to tell her about Kathy. Cara had been shocked, of course. And scared.

She kept begging Amy to come home where she belonged; she couldn't understand that Amy didn't belong there anymore. And Amy was afraid to pursue things too far, in case she found out that Cara's place in her life was gone, too. Cara was the closest thing to family Amy had left.

She wasn't going to lose her.

At least Wainscoat Construction was doing well. Brad had pretty much given up on his theory that a business motivation lay behind Charles's disappearance. She owed Cara more than she'd ever be able to repay for these months of carrying the load.

She couldn't believe Kathy was dead. No one had any solid theories as to why the woman took her life. No one except Amy. She suspected it had been because of *her*. Because she'd taken charge of her own son — and in doing so, she'd taken away Kathy's purpose in life.

The rain hadn't let up at all by the time Amy approached Scottville. The first thing she noticed was a veterinarian's office. It was a good sign, she decided. Charles had always wanted a dog.

An Amoco food shop was next. Then some kind of factory building. Scottville High School was on her left, amid two-story homes with aluminum siding. Pale blue. Yellow. Welcoming.

Mason County District Library on Scottville's main street had a story time. And that was when Amy knew this was the town where she'd stop. Charles loved to be read to, and Amy couldn't leave until she'd talked to the librarians.

She passed Scottville City Hall, Nichol's Pharmacy, a law office. She missed what was next because the UPS truck blocked her view but caught the window of an antiques store. The Shell station and convenience store was busy, but not as busy as Kristen's, although Wesco Gas across the street, which claimed to be "your neighborhood store," seemed to be doing quite well.

She drove until she found the elementary school. Always, she had to know where the elementary school was. At first she thought it was in the Old School House, but the big redbrick building was permanently closed. It didn't take her long to find the newer structure that served as

263

Scottville Elementary. An attractive woman with stylishly cut long blond hair and a pinstripe suit had just left the school and was walking toward some very nice homes across the street. Amy hadn't seen so many trampolines and aboveground swimming pools since leaving Chicago.

And best of all, the playground was behind the school.

This was a town she might choose for Charles. He could be happy here.

When she saw Hungry Howie's Pizza, Amy stopped. She needed a newspaper. And a place to sit. It was time to get a job.

"Amy? Your cell phone rang so I answered it." Amy glanced up from the eager faces around her as the young day-care worker approached with Amy's cell. There were only three people who had her number, and none of them would call in the middle of the day unless it was important.

Leaving the half-dozen four-year-olds with a promise to be right back and what she hoped was a warm smile, Amy took the phone and stepped outside the Little People Day Care on Main Street in Scottville. She'd been volunteering there for five days already — having used her fake credentials to get the position — and had learned absolutely nothing about her son.

A couple of older ladies, obviously sisters, were coming out of Frick's Old Country Store, both carrying bags and chattering. Amy envied them.

The call was from Cara. An envelope bearing a Paris, Michigan, postmark, with Amy's name and address pasted in cut-out newspaper type, had arrived in the mail at the Wainscoat estate that morning. The police wanted Amy home immediately.

Brad arrived in Chicago a few minutes ahead of Amy. Cara, picking them both up, was relieved to get Brad first, as though the detective would be some kind of buffer between her and Amy. Guilt-ridden, feeling disloyal for the way she felt, Cara hardly spoke to him as they drove from Midway Airport to O'Hare to meet Amy's flight.

"I hate it that she won't use the company plane," Cara ventured only that one comment as they pulled up to the passenger pickup area where Amy was to meet them.

"It would be a little hard for her to travel incognito if she arrived in a Wainscoat jet."

Nonsensically, Cara felt a bit betrayed by his response. She'd thought Brad was on her side, knowing that Amy was on a crash course to self-destruction. But then, Brad Dorchester didn't have a lifetime of loving invested. And anyone else who would care was completely ignorant of Amy's double life.

The burden was a heavy one and she was carrying it alone.

Cara didn't say anything else during the remaining few minutes of their wait.

The local police, Agent Fleming and a couple of Brad's men met them at Amelia's home. Entering through the gates, Cara turned up the drive with hope in her weary heart. These months without Charles and Amelia had been lonely beyond description.

"It's so good to have you home," she said, glancing at Amelia in the front seat beside her.

In the back seat, Brad was on the phone.

There was none of the peace she'd hoped to see on her friend's face. No sense of pleasure or comfort at being home. Amelia's expression was tight as she looked straight ahead, as though she couldn't even bear to see the beautiful grounds Cara had overseen with such care.

"I've missed you," Cara whispered.

Amelia's eyes softened, although they revealed no less pain as her gaze met Cara's.

"I've missed you, too," she said. "A lot."

The ache in Cara's heart eased just a bit.

"Don't worry about touching the envelope, since it's been through the United States mail and has likely been handled by so many people we won't be able to lift any clear prints." The detective handed Amelia the letter-size envelope Cara had left on the massive mahogany table in Amelia's formal dining room. Seven of the twenty chairs were currently occupied, all by various law-enforcement officials in suits and ties. Amelia studied the envelope and passed it on for each of the room's occupants to have a look.

Cara didn't need to look. The sick feeling that had consumed her when she'd first seen the letter that morning was still with her.

Was no one else petrified that the letter spelled danger for Amelia? Cara couldn't even fathom a life without her mentor, boss and best friend.

"We can run a check on the newsprint," one of the agents said.

"It was sent from that town where the nanny died," another said.

"We've still got a man there," Brad pointed out. "I doubt whoever sent it hung around afterward. . . ."

Cara kept a close watch on Amelia as the conversation jumped around the table. Remembering Amelia's collapse the night Charles disappeared, Cara didn't know how much more of this Amelia could take.

Ruling a boardroom Amelia could do with one ear pressed to the phone and her eyes on a computer screen. But emotionally Cara's friend had been shielded for most of her life. Too shielded, Cara had always thought.

"Let's open it and see what we've got." It was the first thing Brad had said since they all shook hands and sat down. He was the only man there not in a suit and tie. And maybe the most commanding of them all, in spite of his Dockers and rolled-up cuffs, as he moved to stand behind Amelia's chair.

Fleming started to shove his hands into a pair of surgical gloves.

Cara held her breath. She'd been fretting all day over what was in that envelope.

"I'll open it."

Cara stared at Amelia, her stomach tensing when she saw the determined look on her friend's face.

"Do you really think you should?" Cara couldn't understand why Amelia didn't spare herself some of this. "We don't have any idea what's in there." And anyone who'd paid the least attention knew there had to be more than just a letter. Through the envelope, the contents felt uneven and slightly slippery — as though someone had sent Amelia threads of silk.

"It was tested for anthrax," Amelia said, accepting gloves from the detective. She'd been told this earlier.

"Be careful not to touch anything more than absolutely necessary," Agent Fleming said. "I'm sure whoever we're dealing with wore gloves, but just in case there are any prints, we don't want to smear 'em."

Cara was choking on fear as she watched Amelia carefully tug at the flap of the envelope, then pull out a folded piece of white bond paper.

Three of the detectives joined Brad behind Amelia's chair. Cara kept her seat directly opposite her friend. She cared more about the expressions crossing Amelia's face, the signs that would help Cara know what she needed, than what the hateful letter might contain.

She'd never seen color drain from a person's skin so fast. Her cheeks white, the sickly paleness made more prominent by two splotches of a feverish red, Amelia slowly unfolded the letter.

Several clumps of dark hair slid to the table, getting lost against the deep mahogany.

"Honey?" Cara said softly. Amelia didn't move. Didn't speak.

Cara leaned over until she could see the paper. The tension in her stomach became a burning line of pain when she saw what was obviously a child's drawing of orange and yellow box figures representing a woman and a small child, covered in the middle by pasted newsprint letters. The note demanded $250,000, the drop time and place to be divulged at a later date — and only if the search for Charles was called off.

According to the note, if Amelia wanted her son to stay alive, she had to give up any hope of seeing him again. If the search didn't end, he'd be killed. Either way, she wasn't ever going to see Charles again.

Cara's arms were open and ready to catch her friend, strong enough to hold her up through this newest onslaught.

"I'm to assume the hair is Charles's," Amelia said, her voice empty, unlike anything Cara had ever heard.

"We'll send it to the lab, but it's obvious that's what they want us to believe," Brad said. He turned to Agent Fleming. "How soon do you expect answers on the newsprint?"

"Within the hour."

"And the rest?" He indicated the contents of the envelope on the table in front of Amelia.

"Before nightfall."

Amelia nodded and, with one last look at the drawing, turned and left the room.

Cara didn't know whether to follow or not.

She shouldn't have come here. Amy knew that. Yet here she was, sitting in the little chair at the miniature table in Charles's nursery, seeking whatever comfort there might be in getting close to his things. Things he'd loved. Things he might be missing.

There was no torture worse than helpless waiting. Being beaten, even killed, would be easier.

When she could tolerate sitting still no longer, she moved about the room, scooping up a tiny teddy bear, holding it almost unconsciously in one hand as she reacquainted herself with Charles's various attempts at art that were hanging on the walls.

She remembered the picture he'd drawn to put on Johnny's grave last August. Remembered Kathy in this very room.

Was it only eight months ago?

It seemed like thirty years.

Dammit, Kathy, why?

She should really go and do something productive. Quit torturing herself. Except that Charles's rooms were the only place she could find any sense of self, any sense of the things that mattered to her.

She'd lived at the mansion her entire life and couldn't find anyplace within its protected and luxurious walls where she could still be comfortable in her own skin.

Except here.

A white T-shirt Charles had worn to do fingerpainting the day before he'd disappeared was thrown over the top of the easel, on which the half-finished masterpiece still hung. She hadn't allowed anything to be moved, half-believing that if she could preserve Charles's room the way he'd left it, he'd be able to walk right back into his life.

Amy picked up the blue-and-red-spattered T-shirt. Held it out in front of her. And knew that Charles was never going to be able to walk back into the life he'd left. He would have outgrown that shirt. And other things . . .

Wadding the shirt in her hands, Amy buried her mouth and nose in the soft folds, muffling sobs that erupted out of depths she'd thought completely plumbed and drained. Her fingers closed around the tiny teddy bear she still held, squeezing hard enough to bring pain to her fingers and the palm of her hand, not caring how badly it hurt.

Other than Cara, every person she'd lived with in that house, every person she'd loved and depended on, was gone. Her father, Johnny, Kathy.

And Charles.

When would the grief ever end?

"Amy."

She heard the voice, but couldn't respond, lost as she was in a confusing haze of pain.

"Amy." It came again. She wanted it to go away . . .

There was a hand on her back. Rubbing, moving up to her neck to lightly massage cords that were tense enough to snap. Amy went with that hand, focusing on the unexpected comfort. And as she did, the sobs tearing through her lost some of their intensity.

She took a shuddering breath. And then another.

"It's good news," Brad said.

She was afraid the hand was going to stop. "Mind . . . telling . . . me . . . how?" She struggled to get the question out, her voice muffled by the shirt she couldn't let go of. It still smelled a little like Charles, like the baby shampoo they'd used to wash his hair.

The strong hand at her neck led her slowly over to a Winnie the Pooh-upholstered love seat. Urged her down. Followed her. Continued to rub lightly. Neck, back and up again.

"I think we just got a response to the newspaper article."

"Yeah?"

"Something tangible to investigate."

She was very thankful for that.

"It's possible we've scared them. Which means we're getting closer." The voice sounded different than she'd ever heard it before. More human.

Wholly reassuring where it was usually succinct.

She lowered the shirt, but only to her chin, her eyes studying the grain pattern in the hardwood floor.

"Doesn't it also mean they'll be getting more desperate?"

"Yes. Which can work in our favor. Desperate people make mistakes."

"So you think Kathy was involved."

"No. The article about her death — with the sidebar about Charles and his abduction — got published in all the papers. We were hoping for a response to the item about Charles. We got one — the ransom note."

"I thought we were looking for anyone who could shed some light on her life to come forward."

"That would've been nice." The soothing motion continued. "Takes weeks sometimes for someone to find the courage to speak up."

"But the ransom note — does that mean Kathy *wasn't* involved?"

"I don't know. If she was, then someone else is involved now."

Yeah. And knowing that had been one of the hardest things for Amy to deal with this past week.

"She might have passed him off as her son and made arrangements for someone to take care of him if anything happened to her. If so, that person might only have realized now that Kathy lied. He or she could be trying to figure out how to come forward."

"Wouldn't make much sense to send a ransom note, then, would it?" she asked dryly.

"Maybe. The amount of ransom was far too small, considering how much you're worth." He brought up something that had seemed odd to her, too. But then, she didn't know anything about typical ransom demands. She just knew what she'd be willing to pay to get her son back. And it was a hell of a lot more than a quarter of a million dollars.

"Kathy was traveling in small towns, living among simple people. To someone who makes ten thousand a year, a quarter of a million would be a fortune." She really liked this theory. "If it was professionals who had him, someone who took him just for the money, they'd have asked for a lot more and they'd have asked months ago." She continued to work out the idea. "The low amount suggests the ransom's an afterthought."

"Or from someone who doesn't have any idea of the high stakes they're dealing with."

"That would explain the amount, but why, if they were in it for money, did they wait until now to ask?"

"My guess is they don't want money now and never did."

"You think they did this just to scare us off?"

"Yes."

She thought about that.

"And they know they need to scare us off because of the article about Kathy. They know we're getting close."

"It's a theory," he said. "But not the only one. That note could have come from anyone who read the stuff about Charles in that article. Someone who's never had him could be trying to make a little cash."

"But the picture today —"

"Any kid could've drawn it."

"But Charles always drew his people with box torsos."

"So do a million other kids his age."

She shuddered again. Shook her head.

"There's something you have to consider, Amy."

She didn't want to hear it. Amy knew instinctively that she couldn't handle what he was about to say.

He rubbed a little harder, moving up to her neck. "There's a chance that Kathy killed Charles before she killed herself. Agent Fleming and his men are looking for a grave. It would be remiss of me not to tell you that."

Oh. God. Remiss of him? Would being remiss have been so bad?

"Suicidal people often get into the 'If I can't have you, no one can' mode. And then once the victim's no longer around, they no longer have a reason to live, either."

Her entire body focused on that hand at her neck.

"Is that what you think?" She couldn't allow herself to think. She'd have to rely on him.

"No."

Amy almost started to sob again.

"I'm working under the assumption that this is still a living-person search. I'm not yet convinced there's any reason to change the direction of the investigation."

Was there no end to the torment?

"It kills me not having any idea who might have him. Or why. When I believed it was Kathy, at least I knew he was loved. At least I understood. . . ."

"You've got to train your mind to stay away from thoughts like those. Be aware of possibilities, but don't dwell on them."

That was more like him, commanding her to do the inconceivable.

"Look at this place," she said, her voice stronger now but still thick with tears. "It's a mansion and I support it single-handedly. Look at the malls I've built, the thousands of people I employ. The offices I own and run. I can do all that . . ." She stopped, swallowed and then, in a smaller voice finished, "And I can't do one single, solitary thing about anything that really matters."

"You've been a thorn in my ass for months. Don't disappoint me now, woman. Don't you *dare* give up."

His hand massaged the muscles on either side of her spine. Down low, up higher.

Giving up. Was that what she was doing?

"I'm not."

"Good."

Amy nodded. "So we have two impossible choices. Which one do we take?"

"Depends on what you see as the choices."

"Either we call off the search and never find Charles and we just hope they're good to him, or you and your men keep looking and we risk Charles getting —"

She couldn't make herself say the word.

"I see a third option."

Amy's heart leaped, her head whipping around. "What?"

"We make it *look* like we're calling off the search."

"How?"

"I can't speak for the FBI, but I can pull my men out of Michigan."

"And . . ."

"You stay."

He moved his hand from her back as she straightened and stared at him.

"I can't believe I'm even suggesting this. It's highly unusual and completely crazy, but you've done a good job with your metamorphosis," he explained. "I don't think they know you're out there. If they did, they'd have mentioned it in the letter."

She still didn't speak.

"I think you've become our most valuable tool."

Amy hadn't thought there was anything that could possibly ease the horrible, helpless desperation eating her from the inside out.

"Okay," she said.

Hazel eyes that revealed nothing studied her unrelentingly. "You have to go into this knowing that he might be killed, anyway. And that, regardless of what happens, you are not to blame."

Amy nodded.

"I mean it, Amy." Those damned eyes saw too much.

Contemplating that cynical, lived-in face, Amy decided to be honest. "I have to believe that wherever he is, whoever he's with, he's playing ball. Fishing. Learning to read. And that, in the end, he'll come home again. If I don't, I won't make it through this."

13

The newsprint on the ransom note came from a Michigan paper with state-wide distribution. Which gave Amy a reason for heading straight back to Michigan on a commercial flight first thing in the morning. Brad, using a Wainscoat jet, had already left for Denver.

Amy wasn't even surprised at how sorry she was to see him go.

"I wish you'd take a little more time to think about this," Cara said late that Thursday night. "At least stay through the weekend. It's Easter. We could go to church together."

In her suite, packing a small case with some of her underthings and a couple of pairs of lighter pajamas — ones she was prepared to leave behind in a hotel room if need be — Amy sent her friend a warm look. "I wish I could, Car. I'd love to have the time, just you and me. But Charles might not be able to wait."

"I heard Brad tell you it wasn't Charles's hair."

Amy didn't need the reminder. "That's right." She shrugged. "The lab report was definite on that."

"So you could be risking everything chasing nothing at all."

"That's always been true."

Cara picked up a pair of blue cotton pajamas. Rolled them to fit more easily into the limited space. "It's not that I don't want Charles back as badly as you do," she said.

Amy stopped. Sat down on the bed beside her childhood friend. "I know that."

"I miss him so much."

She took Cara's hand. "I know."

"He's the closest thing I've ever had to a child of my own."

"He loves you very much, too."

Cara's eyes, so close to her own, were earnest, yearning and filled with pain. "There are professionals to see to Charles. But no one to see to you," she said softly. "I feel like I'm not only losing him, but you, too."

Amy lifted a strand of hair that had fallen over Cara's forehead, hooked it behind her friend's ear. "I'm right here, Cara. Always."

"You're changing, Amelia. Sometimes it's like I don't even know you."

Amy tried to maintain eye contact, knowing how badly Cara needed reassurance. But she was looking for answers Amy didn't think she could give *herself*, let alone anyone else.

"What about the company?" Cara said. "You used to care about what we did, about the people there, the deals. Wainscoat Construction really mattered to you. Now I can hardly get you to remember a client's name."

"You think a company should matter more than people?"

"Supporting Charles used to be as important to you as spending time with him."

"And you don't think that was wrong?"

Cara frowned. "How can supporting your son be wrong?"

"He doesn't need a suite of rooms to himself, Cara. Or private grounds, an Olympic-size pool or a Jacuzzi in his bathtub."

"Surely you don't expect me to believe that you'd prefer some dirty motel room to *this* place," Cara made a sweeping gesture with her arm.

Amy didn't know what to say, how to explain what she herself didn't quite understand — the guilt, the self-loathing she carried with her to every bathroom stall she cleaned, every customer she waited on, every child she helped.

She didn't want Cara to think she looked down on her for the life they'd always lived. She just knew she couldn't live that life ever again.

At least not with the blissful ignorance she'd clung to before.

"You're under more stress than most people could deal with," Cara said. "And you've been away too long. You're forgetting who you are inside. And maybe outside, too. You need to come home. I know you, Amelia. This is me, Cara, remember? I *know* how much this place means to you. How much living here means to you. And I know it's important to you to be treated with respect. You get all that because of who you are. You'll never be happy without everything that comes with being a Wainscoat."

A year ago Amy would have agreed with that.

"Cara, listen to me. In a way, you're right. I'm changing. Or maybe I am. I'm not sure." Cara turned away, but not before Amy saw the stricken look in her eyes. She didn't let that deter her. "But the things that matter aren't changing — like my love for you. Your place in my life, in my heart, isn't changing."

That was all she could say with absolute certainty.

Still looking out toward the darkened grounds visible through the bay window, Cara didn't respond.

"*You* might be certain that being a Wainscoat is a vital part of who I am, but *I'm* not," she went on, hoping Cara would love her enough to stand by her no matter who she turned out to be. "I'm thirty-four years old and I'm just starting to find out what really matters to me."

Cara stood and resumed Amy's packing. "You're overwrought."

With a firm but gentle hand, Amy stopped Cara, pulling her back down. "No, Cara." She looked around the room, at the opulence, and compared it to the room she'd had in Kristen's trailer.

"Don't you ever think about all the people in this city who go hungry? Who scrape and struggle just to be able to afford a shabby room somewhere?"

Cara's expression was perplexed. "You give generously to charities. Why, last Christmas you —"

Amy shook her head. "I'm not talking

about donations, Cara. I'm talking about a way of life. About awareness. And compassion."

"You think you have to give up your birthright to have compassion?"

"No!" Head bowed, Amy wondered when she and Cara had lost their ability to instinctively understand what the other was thinking.

"If . . ." Cara stopped, sent Amy a guilty look. "When you find Charles, are you planning to sell all this? Or give it away?"

"No!" Amy said again, frustrated. Not just with Cara, but with herself. "The thought never crossed my mind. Not once. I don't know what I'm trying to say, Car."

Cara's eyes softened. She nodded, and Amy was afraid she'd just given her friend false hope. But hope of what? She really wasn't sure.

"Stay home, Amelia. We can get through this together."

"I can't."

"You can't do it all alone, either. Let me help you."

She supposed Cara was right. Yet Amy didn't like the way Cara's words made her feel. As though she wasn't strong enough, capable enough, to do what she had to do.

There was something else she was sure

she'd never be able to explain to her friend. She didn't have the emotional energy to even try.

"Just stick with me, okay?" she begged.

"Always."

That single word eased some of Amy's tension. She knew now that *always* meant no more than the moment, that *always* could change in the space of a second — in the second it took for a heart attack or a car accident, in the second it took a boat to explode. And yet it comforted Amy to hear Cara promise her an eternity of friendship and faith.

At six the next morning, after only an hour or so of restless sleep, Amy dressed in cheap jeans and a plaid blouse. Her hair in a ponytail and her face devoid of makeup. She left the house and walked the short distance to the cemetery just down the road.

She'd made the trip many times. By herself. With Charles. With Cara. She knew every step of the way, every ditch and rise, every tree.

And she knew exactly how many headstones to the left of the drive she had to go to see the mother she'd hardly known. And the father she'd adored and lost far sooner than she'd expected.

She stopped to pull weeds, rearrange the flowers in the urn, and then moved on. To the man she'd once loved with every passionate bone in her body.

"It wasn't supposed to be like this, Johnny," she said, kneeling in the dewy grass in front of his stone. "We were supposed to prove all the critics wrong, beat the odds, live happily ever after. We were special."

They'd had it all. Not just love, but anything money could buy.

"Why didn't I know that money couldn't buy me one damn thing I really wanted?"

She listened to the silence of early morning, which only seemed amplified by the sounds of birdsong and a few distant cars. There were no answers in that silence.

"Did *you* know?" she whispered, tears filling her eyes.

Money had never meant as much to Johnny as it had to her. But then, he'd lived his whole life without it.

What had mattered to Johnny was his son. *He had known.*

Irrational as it might be, she felt as if she had an answer, after all.

"I'll find him for you," she whispered as she stood to go. "I promise, Johnny, I won't let you down this time."

She brushed a leaf off the five-foot-high family marker and didn't look back.

By eleven-forty-five the next morning, after cramming weeks' worth of business discussion into a few short hours, she hugged Cara goodbye outside the terminal at O'Hare. And was the first to say, "I love you."

"I love you, too."

"Thank you for everything, Car, I —"

"It's okay." Cara hugged her again. "It's okay."

"Be safe."

"You, too."

Amy could hardly make herself leave. Yet when she finally did, she was almost light-headed with the relief of being free.

Brad had a female artist on his team, but he'd never had a female field agent. He didn't like it one bit. Didn't like how it changed things. He could send a man any-where and move on to the next assignment without a second thought. But wherever Amy Wainscoat was, part of Brad's mind went with her.

And yet, impossible as it seemed, his ad-miration for her had grown during the ten days since she'd returned to Michigan. Sitting in her private jet for the flight from Denver to Baldwin, wearing his usual Dockers and a tan polo shirt, Brad sipped from a glass of iced juice and contemplated what he'd gotten himself into. He was far too uncomfortable with the current situation — flying to Baldwin to accompany his client, who was now working for him without pay, while she followed up on an anonymous tip he'd received.

Yet what choice did he have? Walk away from the job? Never. Risk the boy's life by going in with his team when there was another viable option, a *better* option?

He'd never had an agent with more indomitable determination. Nor, unfortunately, one who dared talk back to him so much.

Hell, he didn't have an agent on staff who dared talk back to him at all. Any employee of his dumb enough to try it once wasn't on staff to try it a second time.

When word had come that there were no identifiable prints on the letter, giving them no place to start looking, she'd returned the very next day to Little People Day Care and the room she'd had at the Ramada Inn six miles or so down the road. She wasn't finished with Scottville.

She'd said the town "spoke" to her of

Charles. When he'd asked why, she'd hesitated, then said because the water tower proclaimed Scottville as home to the Clown Band. And there was a Clown Town Café.

Brad had had to remind her that she wasn't looking for a town Charles would like, but one where his abductors could easily hide. And then he'd had to shut up. What he needed from her was exactly what he was getting.

He finished off the juice, wishing it was a little later in the day this last Sunday in April. He would have preferred dipping into the bottle of well-aged whiskey under the bar. He chewed his ice, instead.

Working mostly under her own direction until he had some direction to give her, Amy was doing what she'd been doing so well for so long. This time, she was getting to know the mothers and children of Scottville.

She'd been paying special attention to miniature golf courses since her hit in Holland, as well. Just the day before, her friend, Kristen, had made the half-hour drive from Baldwin and the two of them had spent the afternoon at Adventure Island Family Fun Park. If Charles had ever been there, no one had noticed him.

And in ten days' time, there'd been no follow-up to the ransom note — leading both him and the FBI to believe the note had nothing to do with money at all and everything to do with warning them away.

Which was a good thing.

If it was a warning rather than an extortion, the note probably meant the boy was still alive.

Unless it had been sent by some sicko as a joke.

He hadn't yet approached Amy with that particular theory — though he suspected she'd probably come up with it on her own.

Brad spoke to Amy every night now, sometimes only for the few seconds it took to report no news. Which was how he knew that she was spending today at AJ's Family Fun Center, not far from downtown Scottville.

Kristen was waiting for him, looking slim and lovely in jeans and a white blouse, at the private airstrip just outside Baldwin.

There was none of the awkwardness there could have been at a meeting between two people who hardly knew each other. She greeted him easily, asked about his flight, joked about the color of her

bright-yellow Ranger truck as she unlocked the door for him.

It was a far cry from his reception at the
airport in Chicago ten days before when
Cara Carson had hardly said a word.

"Where are we meeting her?" Kristen
asked as soon as Brad had thrown his
duffel in the bed of the truck and climbed
in beside her, his knees doing a tango with
the dash. A thing this small shouldn't be
allowed to bear the name *truck*.

"In the parking lot of AJ's. You know it?"

"Yeah." She nodded, short blond hair
bobbing. It was cute, windblown. He liked
it. "What time?" She glanced at the black
band of the man's wristwatch she wore.

"Whenever we get there," Brad said, ap-
preciating the classic beauty of his chauffeur.

Pulling out into a lane of traffic, Kristen
took a moment to frown at him. "You've
got her just sitting there waiting?"

"She doesn't know we're coming."

Amy's friend had a foot as heavy as his
own. Brad liked that, too. As a matter of
fact, from the little he'd seen, he liked a lot
about Kristen Miller. He was going to be
in town for a day or two; perhaps he
could . . .

He didn't complete the thought.

There was far too much ground to cover on this trip to get sidetracked by a woman.

Or so he told himself.

It was easier than admitting that since he spent so much time with Amelia Wainscoat on his mind, he'd lost interest in other women.

Signaling, Kristen pulled out into the oncoming lane of traffic to pass an elderly couple in a twenty-year-old sedan. "So why the secrecy?" she asked.

"Did Amy tell you about her little side trip in Lowell?"

"The jail?"

"Yeah. Or about being run out of town in . . ."

"Evart. Yeah."

"There was another time she went knocking on a door, alone, when I specifically told her to wait for me."

"So what're you saying? You don't trust her?"

"I'm saying I don't want to find her dead in Ludington next."

He'd told Kristen, when he'd called before leaving Denver, that he had a lead. Nothing more.

"So this lead you're chasing, it's dangerous?"

"Not necessarily, but it could be. Any

anonymous tip has the potential to be a setup. I'm not willing to take that chance."

She nodded, leaning forward to turn the radio on to a light-rock station, then adjusted the volume and started to sing along. Brad had a feeling both the radio and her accompaniment would have been a lot louder had she been driving alone.

"She's busting her ass for this kid," she burst out in the middle of crooning one of the sappy love ballads he considered a waste of radio waves. "I think you can trust her."

"The woman's done some damn crazy things." More than he could recount. Pretty much every step of the way.

"She's a mother defending her child."

"Somehow I think she'll be much better equipped to do that if she's alive."

"She's been alone on the road for all these months and she's still standing. Amy is one of the most intelligent women I know."

"I don't doubt her IQ," Brad said, hoping this AJ's was going to be right around the next corner. He didn't need another defensive female. "My problem is with the way her common sense flies out the window every time her adrenaline gets going."

He tried to shift in the seat, make his legs more comfortable, but there wasn't much room.

"You're wrong, you know," Kristen said so quietly he barely heard her over the radio. She pulled out to pass another Sunday driver. "Amy never acts senselessly. Every time she takes a chance, she's made a very conscious decision to do so. She's thought about it and determined the risks involved."

"She's been on the road a long time," he replied, taking in the sunshine, the rolling green fields, occasionally punctuated by pine trees.

Country without the trappings of civility. A place where a man could just kick back and be a man. Territory made for male pleasures — hunting, fishing, forgetting to shower or shave.

"The chances are getting slimmer and the risks more foolish," he added for emphasis.

A series of ads came on and Kristen turned the volume down to almost nothing. "I don't think so," she said. "The chances might be getting slimmer, which makes the risks greater, but they're no less calculated."

It spoke highly of Amelia Wainscoat that she had such loyal champions in her friends. You generally had to *be* a great friend to have friends like that.

Or you needed enough money to buy them.

Brad suddenly remembered what Amy had told him on the way to Kristen's trailer from Kathy's apartment that day: Kristen didn't know her real identity. Which meant there was no way Kristen was in this relationship for the money.

"It's easier to take risks when you don't think you have anything to lose," he said.

"Or maybe you take risks when you know that what you have to gain is worth any risk it takes."

"But is it?" he asked. Not one to involve himself in introspective conversations, at least not with anyone but himself and then only over his second or third glass of whiskey, Brad wondered again which bend up ahead signaled this journey's end. "Amy is young, healthy, beautiful . . ." and richer than hell. "Is it worth losing another promising life on the off chance that she'll find a piece of information that might or might not lead to her son?"

"I don't think Amy sees any promise in her life without her son."

He didn't, either. And that bothered him a lot.

"Then it's time she found it."

"Obviously you've never had a kid."

"Obviously you don't know the statistics on missing kids," he retorted, the cords of his neck tight again. "When they've been gone this long, they usually don't make it back."

That shut her up.

Brad wished he could have found satisfaction in that.

Busy watching a little guy playing a video game, Amy almost missed the ringing of her cell phone. She caught it just before her voice mail did, her heart hammering as she recognized Brad's number flashing on the screen.

Two seconds later, she was running out the door, only vaguely aware of the curious eyes following her.

"Where are we going?"

Amy was already on highway 10 heading west. Kristen had had to get back to the store and Amy had given her a quick hug, the promise of a phone call and then, following Brad's pointing finger, turned the Thunderbird onto the highway.

"Ludington."

She'd heard it was a pretty town on the

shore of Lake Michigan. Knew it was where folks took the ferry across the lake to Wisconsin.

Knew, too, that Brad wouldn't be here unless he had something significant.

She was afraid to ask what it was.

But she was glad to see him.

"I got an anonymous call," he said, stretching his long legs out in front of him. "Someone who saw the picture in the paper said that Charles was playing T-ball in Ludington."

The first thing she saw as they left town was a cemetery.

And then a bowling alley. She assured herself that the place meant for fun was a good omen that would cancel out the bad.

" 'Was' as in a while ago or as in still is?" she asked, trying to keep calm. She couldn't get so worked up every time they had a lead. Now that she was the only one on the road, she had to make damn sure she had the stamina to do the job.

"I don't know," Brad said. And that insidious thread of hope wound itself around her heart again. Her son might be only ten minutes away. Playing T-ball at that very moment. Would she pull up to a ball park and see him there?

"There was a message on the machine.

The call was made from a pay phone." Brad's voice brought her out of her son's arms and back to her driving. "It was a man's voice. He said that Charles was going by the name of Caleb, but that once, when another boy on the team was being called, Caleb responded automatically. The other boy's name was Charles."

"Caleb," Amy said, her voice uneven in spite of her self-control. "Caleb what?"

"Didn't say." He paused, glancing at her and then quickly away, almost as though debating whether or not he should say more.

If he *knew* more, he'd darn well better spill it.

Another time she would've told him so, but now, strangely enough, she just waited. She really was glad he'd come. Hadn't realized how much she hated forging into these situations without him.

And she was well aware that if she waited, he'd tell her whatever he knew. He always did.

"The man recognized Kathy's picture, too." He spoke nonchalantly, as though he'd just told her he'd had French fries for lunch.

"He said she'd been at one of the games, cheering for Charles. Since we have no idea who the guy was, we'll do what you always do and canvas the town."

Amy hadn't had lunch. And that was probably a good thing as her stomach cramped with the shocks coursing through her.

Charles was close; she could feel it.

This time it was really going to happen.

It just had to.

14

Memorial Medical Center welcomed them to Ludington. A sprawling complex, it seemed to Amy to go on and on.

"Look." Brad pointed to a billboard advertising a radio station on the other side of the street.

"WMOM — 102.7. Always Listen to Your Mom," it read.

Another good omen to cancel out a bad.

Amy discovered that Brad had very definite ideas about where she should slow down, turn, stop, whereas she had perfected her own way of doing things. Get the lay of the land. See the neighborhoods, the businesses, find the elementary school. And stop when she got a strong feeling that she should.

He leaned an arm on the console between them. "Let me make something perfectly clear," he said in such a congenial tone her hackles rose. "I am the boss here. We do this *my* way. Period."

"Funny, I've always thought the person signing the paycheck was the boss."

Was Charles in one of those big Victorian homes? Had he ever played on the grass at the courthouse? Or visited the public library across the street?

"If it's going to keep you alive, you can keep the damn paycheck," Brad's words were surprising enough to freeze the retort on her lips.

"We don't do this unless you agree to follow my orders," he said.

There was no doubt he meant every word.

"Okay," she said, but she didn't like it.

Brad sat back. "Nice town."

At another time, Amy would have appreciated the sprawling yards, the all-wood Victorian homes — complete with turrets — that sometimes took up an entire block. At another time. Maybe.

At the moment she was practically crawling out of her skin with the need to find her son.

She slowed down as she drove by the Family Barbershop. "I wonder if he got his hair cut there," she said out loud — just as she would have if she'd been alone.

"Don't do this, Amy," Brad said. "Don't

start torturing yourself with scenarios that probably never happened."

He was way too late there. "It's a comfort, Mr. Dorchester, not a torture."

He let it go, but Amy knew he wasn't satisfied. The car was suddenly far too small for the two of them.

Brad tried to be patient. To let Amy do things her way. Until she started seeing her son in every building they passed. She wasn't saying anything, but he read the expressions as they crossed her face. Hope. Anticipation. Longing. He had a sick feeling that she'd been doing this to herself the entire time she'd been on the road.

And wondered how on earth the woman was still standing.

When he couldn't sit there any longer watching her agonize, he suggested they find some ball fields. Hang out. Talk to some people. On Sunday afternoon, the parks would be pretty populated.

The third ball field they visited turned up a young boy and his dad practicing T-ball.

Brad moved in.

It took only a couple of minutes to get the name of the man who ran the local T-ball league. Henry Vallen and his wife, Lorraine, had no children of their own but were actively involved in volunteer work for the youth of Ludington. In addition to T-ball and numerous other activities, they hosted a summer acting camp that put on a play at the Kiwanis Bandstand every August. They lived in a large, light-blue Victorian home on the lake.

Back through a lovely, old-fashioned downtown, past A Bride's Time bridal shop, which she figured Brad wouldn't even see, by Captain John's Party Port, which she pegged as much more his style, toward the harbor and Lake Michigan.

She silently chanted, *This is it,* over and over in her mind, in rhythm with the tires humming on the road. Had she been alone, it wouldn't have been silent.

"How do you want to play this?" she asked Brad, conscious of his solid presence at her side. It had been a long time since she'd shared a car with a man.

"Let's go with what you normally do," he said. "Sounds like you've got your patter down to the point of sounding natural."

"Okay," she nodded, adrenaline pumping as the harbor came into view. The certainty that she was getting closer to Charles was overwhelming. "We're new in town and have a friend who's arriving soon. Our friend has a young son who'd like to play T-ball, and we were told about the Vallens by my sister, whose son played ball here for a little while. That should garner questions about my nephew, at which time we show them Charles's picture."

"Got it."

Amy glanced over at him as she pulled to a stop just before turning onto First Street. Brad wasn't such a bad guy when he wasn't telling her what to do. If only he'd agree with her more often . . .

After all the buildup, the Vallens weren't home.

"Let's find a place to stay for the night, get something to eat and come back in a couple of hours," Brad suggested when he saw the crestfallen look on Amy's face. What he really wanted to do was sit down and have a beer.

He supposed he still could. He considered how nice it would feel sliding down his throat.

But he couldn't leave Amy alone; she spent far too much time alone as it was.

And she was paying him a hell of a lot of money. The least he could do was see that she ate a decent meal.

★ ★ ★

Snyder's Shoreline Inn, a charming, two-story motel, was just across the street from a half mile of beach, complete with picnic areas, a playground with swings and, in season, water activities. Amy could see boats sailing in and out of the harbor from her second-floor balcony.

Much nicer than most of the rooms she briefly called home. Amy appreciated the antique furniture and handcrafted decorations — all of which, she felt certain, were lost on Brad in his room next door.

The big bed, covered in a quilt with a matching canopy, was inviting. After staying up late talking with Kristen the night before, she wanted a nap much more than the meal Brad was insisting they get.

With the butterflies swarming around in her stomach, how could she possibly eat?

Of course, there was no way she'd be able to sleep, either, so she might as well go.

Besides, she didn't want to be alone.

Henry Vallen was much younger than Brad had expected, midthirties at the most. His wife, with perfectly dyed auburn hair, was a good five to ten years older. They were dressed as though they'd just come from church, Henry in slacks and tie, Lorraine in a calf-length silk dress. She was still wearing hose and heels.

Obviously a couple who stood on ceremony, even in their own home. He'd go crazy living like that. Before they'd even spoken, Brad had mentally raised the validity of their information a notch. They'd both looked him in the eye, confidently held out a hand.

The couple was kind, gracious and obviously fond of each other. One way or another, they were always in physical contact. A shoulder against a shoulder as they stood at the door. A hand resting against an arm while they were in the foyer talking to their guests. And now, on the Queen Anne love seat in the formal living room, they were sitting close enough for their thighs to touch.

And they completely fell for Amy's well-practiced line. She and Brad hadn't been there five minutes before she was taking out the picture of Charles they'd asked to see.

Brad watched intently as Henry and his wife studied the picture.

"Yes, I know him!" Henry said. "Never met a kid more excited to get signed up."

"Wasn't he the little guy who caught that

fly ball?" Lorraine asked before he'd even finished.

Henry nodded, looking from the picture to Amy and Brad. "You have to understand, the bat's bigger than most of these kids. If we have one hit all season, it's remembered all year. And along comes Caleb. He's five going on twenty-five. Probably knew as much about the game as his coach." Henry moved to the edge of the seat.

And Amy, sitting next to Brad on the couch, was holding herself so tensely it was a wonder she didn't snap.

He wasn't so sure it might not happen yet.

She was damn good, though. If he didn't know her better, he'd think all her smiling and nodding was that of an aunt hearing about a beloved nephew.

"It was only the second game of the season," Henry was saying, "and we got our one hit of the year. Timmy Randall. He's a year older than most of the boys and big for his age. And here comes little Caleb, running so fast he was practically tripping on his own feet."

"He was so cute!" Lorraine said, her lips spreading in a warm smile. "We're all waiting to cheer him, anyway, when the ball zoomed in ten yards behind him. You can imagine our shock when —"

"He caught it!" Henry finished. "And it wasn't any old 'look what I got' catch! The kid ran it in like a pro and made a double out."

"We've never had one of those before," Lorraine offered, leaning against Henry's shoulder as her husband settled back into his seat.

"How long ago was that?" Amy asked, her voice a bit higher than normal.

"I know his parents told me about it," she rambled on in an un-Amy-like fashion, "but I've been so frazzled, getting ready to leave the town I grew up in . . ."

"Season starts mid-March, weather permitting, so we can get enough games in before all the boys start to leave on family vacations."

Six weeks ago. Brad was disappointed.

"Did he get to play a lot of games?" Amy was one hell of a doting aunt.

Henry shook his head. "I only saw him once more after that. . . ."

So emotionally charged she could've swum to Wisconsin, Amy had a hard time sitting still on the short drive back to the inn. She turned on the radio. Wanted to sing along. Felt as if she was going to cry. Turned it off.

"Okay, let's have it," Brad said. He was slouched in the passenger seat, watching the buildings go by.

"What?"

"Whatever it is that's going to come exploding out of you — most likely in some inappropriate fashion — if we don't urge it along."

A retort came automatically to her lips, but she couldn't get it out. She sighed, instead. "I'm just frustrated that once again, I'm too late. Why is it that we can't ever be in the same town at the same time?"

"Luck of the draw." Brad's laconic reply was no surprise. And no help, either. "But we're making progress."

She stopped, signaled the turn into Snyder's. "How can you say that?"

"Because the IDs we're getting now aren't merely possible likenesses, vague remembrances. They're completely positive."

"I had some of those before."

"But they're starting to gel with each other. He was Randy twice."

Amy nodded, sliding expertly into a parking slot by the stairs. "And he's been Caleb twice, too."

"That's significant progress."

Perhaps, if she'd doubted those earlier accounts as much as he had, these *would* seem vastly different. But he was right. The name repetition was good.

Brad didn't get out of the car immediately. "You want to walk?"

"Sure." Especially if her other choice was sitting in a motel room all by herself. It was only eight-thirty.

They went down to the beach. Amy couldn't see much in the darkness — the blink of a lighthouse in the distance, the shadow of swings — but she loved the sound of the waves rushing at the shore. And the cool breeze that cooled her heated skin.

"You going to be warm enough in that sweater?"

"Yeah." The weather was quite balmy. Besides, she wore jeans and tennis shoes.

She thought about the woman Lorraine had described, the one she'd assumed was Caleb's mother, given the enthusiastic nature of her cheering. She'd only seen her at one game, but then, Lorraine didn't attend them all.

"The woman at the game was Kathy," she said to Brad now.

"Sounds that way."

"So she did take him."

He didn't say anything, just walked slowly beside her, their feet sinking into the sand. His loafers were going to be filled.

The lake sounded as turbulent as she felt. "So who has him now?" she asked, a catch in her voice. Her words were barely loud enough to be heard over the waves.

"Right after we figure that out, it'll probably be us."

The words, spoken as succinctly as everything else Brad said, quieted the fear threatening to overwhelm her.

Brad was planning to find Charles.

She'd just have to hang on to her faith. Trust him. Trust herself.

"Randy, Caleb and who knows what other names." She broke the silence that had fallen between them. "He's got to be pretty confused. . . ."

"Kids have amazing resilience."

Yeah. "I remember when Johnny was teaching Charles to ride his bike. Up and down the drive, over and over. Johnny would let go, Charles would fall. They'd patch up a skinned knee or elbow and be right out there again."

"Johnny pushed him that hard?"

"No." Amy smiled sadly, kicking up sand with the toe of her tennis shoe. "Charles was that determined to learn. He'd beg Johnny relentlessly."

"What about you? Didn't you have a turn out there on the drive with him?"

Lips pursed, she shook her head. "Johnny and Kathy did most of the teaching." The pain of that admission tore into her. "I was working."

Once again Brad fell silent, leaving Amy to wonder what he was thinking. It was odd having this kind of conversation with him, since there was nothing personal between her and Brad.

At least, she didn't think there was.

Still, she wanted to know if he'd judged her and found her wanting. If so, it wouldn't be anything she hadn't already done herself.

As they walked along the dark moonlit beach, she thought back over the months of conversations they'd shared. And couldn't place exactly what their relationship was. Far more than employer and employee, anyway.

Or was it just the nature of the job that made it seem that way?

When all this was over, would he take his money and disappear, never to be heard from again?

She supposed he'd have to. He certainly

couldn't maintain relationships with the families of all the children he'd found.

From the sound of things, he didn't maintain relationships, period.

"How old are you?" she asked.

"Does it matter?" His voice wasn't as gruff as it could have been.

"No, just curious." And then, "You know my age." Pretty much every fact or statistic concerning her was in one of his reports.

"I'm forty."

"You live alone?"

"Yeah."

"Have you been alone long?"

"Ten years."

Ten years — when eight months seemed like a lifetime to her.

"Do you ever get lonely?" She'd probably cringe in the morning when she remembered this conversation. But the night made it so easy. And she was trying desperately to escape the thoughts that spun around and around her head until she grew dizzy and unsure.

"I don't think about it much."

"But when you do think about it . . ."

She felt more than saw his big shoulders shrug, could picture the grimace on his craggy face. "I don't know. I guess. Maybe on holidays."

Holidays. She'd made it through Christmas Day with the help of tranquilizers. Kristen and a bottle of wine had seen her through Easter the week before. Charles's birthday wasn't until August. She had to have him back by then.

Several feet from the water, the beach was no longer smooth. Amy and Brad stepped over the mounds of scattered brush growing in the sand.

"It gets easier," he murmured.

"What does?"

"Being alone."

"Maybe." She didn't think so. "For some people." Amy wondered if that was really true. Or if some people were just better at convincing themselves than others.

They turned silently, followed the beach back to the motel, walking closer to the water. Amy had never before found companionship in the simple presence of another person. Had never found companionship in silence. She'd always thought companionship meant conversation.

"Can I tell you how sad it makes me that I didn't see that catch?" she asked.

"You don't need to tell me. I saw the look on your face when the Vallens described it."

Amy suddenly stopped. Stamped her foot. "Dammit, Brad! It's not right. It's just not right." Her voice broke. She looked up at him, furious, frustrated and so lonely the thought of walking into that lake and letting it close over her head was tempting. "How do parents survive this?"

Hands in his pockets, Brad stared out at the lake. "I don't know," he said, his voice filled with a compassion she hadn't heard before . . . "It's a question I don't ask."

She nodded, stood beside him gazing out over the water, shivering although she wasn't really cold.

"So where do we go from here?"

"I'll be flying back to Denver in the morning."

She'd figured as much.

"You need to stay right here."

She'd already decided that, too. "Since Charles lived here," she said, "people are going to have known him." She assumed this was what he was thinking. "One of them might have some idea where he went from here."

"And with whom."

She'd come full circle. Back to the fiery pain lining her stomach.

And back to the ever-increasing fear that someone evil had possession of her son.

15

She got a tan out on the swings at the beach. There were several sets from which to choose, and over the next several days, Amy chose them all.

One day, she hung out at the harbor with the seagulls, watching the ferry leave at eight-thirty in the morning, and was there when it returned from Manitowoc, Wisconsin, at seven o'clock that night. She wanted a feel for who was coming and going.

One night, about five days after Brad left, a small boy on the deck of the boat caught her eye. At first glance he could've been Charles. He had the same pudgy build with the promise of muscles to come, the same dark hair, cut a little long. His face was turned away. Amy stopped, standing there in the middle of the dirty cement parking lot, facing the white, black-trimmed door of the ticket office — a door that looked more like the front door of someone's home — surrounded by old shipyard fencing, and stared.

The boy's dad was standing directly behind him, hands on the rail of the ferry, arms on either side of his son, enclosing him in safety. In love.

The ferry made its way slowly into the harbor to dock. The closer it came, the more her spirit yearned for her young boy.

And when the ferry docked and the little boy turned and Amy saw that he didn't even resemble Charles, she turned and walked away.

All four movies at the Ludington cinema were new to her. She bought tickets to all of them that first week so she could sit through the fifteen or twenty minutes before the show started, watch the families come in, listen to people talk. Chocolate from the chocolate shop adorned the top of her dresser at Snyder's. And she knew that the shift changes for the officers at the downtown police department were eight in the morning and four in the afternoon.

In six days' time, after striking up conversations with mothers and kids on the beach, in line at McDonald's, bowling, with the innkeepers and everywhere else she happened to be, Amy had found a total of two people, besides the T-ball players, who'd known her "nephew" Caleb. Neither of them knew he'd left town.

One man had seen him at the Jaycees' miniature golf course and later seen him getting into a car with a woman driver whose appearance was hard to discern. The other saw him tossing a ball by himself on the beach.

With the first man, Amy joked about the way "Caleb" held his putter. And was rewarded with an answering laugh and affirmation that she was right, confirming her suspicion that the little boy at the fun park last fall had definitely been Charles.

She wanted so badly to ask if Charles had been wearing his seat belt in the car with the woman. But she didn't.

Kristen drove over from Baldwin that Saturday to play at a miniature golf course with Amy. They played more than ten games of golf before Kristen headed back to the easier job of managing and owning the busiest convenience store west of Reed City.

As she lay in her bed that night at the inn, trying to lie still enough to drift off, Amy reviewed the day, the games, the conversation, and she felt *loved*. A feeling she used to take for granted — like every other good thing in her life.

Her mind returned to that morning when she and Kristen had just arrived at the miniature golf course. They'd paid for their first game, chosen putters and walked toward the course.

A man and a little boy were playing as they approached. The man stood right behind the boy, with his arms around the small body, his hands guiding the little boy as he held the club.

It was the two from the ferry. Father and son. She wondered where the mother was. If she was dead. Or divorced. Or maybe just at work.

She wondered if the little boy had a nanny who loved him.

There were tears on her pillow when she finally drifted off to sleep.

Josh Dillon had a thing for ice cream. Or rather, for the new employee at the House of Flavors in his hometown of Ludington.

"Can I have chocolate this time, Dad?" Danny asked, his five-year-old legs walking twice as fast as his father's to keep up. Josh's son insisted on dressing just like his dad, which made things easier for a single guy trying to do it all. Jeans, T-shirts, tennis shoes, and they were done.

"Sure, sport," Josh said, smiling down at the little guy. Danny always had chocolate. But he always asked permission, as though there might be some doubt. Some other choice that might be made for him if he didn't make sure.

"You're hoping Amy's working today, huh?" Danny guessed, skipping a couple of steps.

Josh shoved the tips of his fingers in the front pockets of his jeans. A few seconds later Danny did the same.

"So what if I am?"

Danny grinned. "I'm kind of hoping so, too."

Looking up as the door to House of Flavors opened, Amy missed a beat, dropping a scoop of ice cream back into its bucket.

It was them. Again.

First at the harbor.

Then at miniature golf.

And three times this week at House of Flavors. Three of the four days she'd worked since being hired here, they'd come in for ice cream. She'd waited on them two of those times.

Quickly finishing up with the double-dip,

mint-chocolate-chip cone she'd been scooping, Amy handed it over to the pimply-faced young man across the counter.

"Can I help you?" she asked, wiping her hands on her apron as she immediately moved down the bar to the father and son before someone else got to them.

Though it was only the second week in May and not all that hot, House of Flavors was busy that Friday afternoon. Still, they'd managed to grab two free stools.

"He'll have —"

"I know," Amy interrupted with a smile. "A single scoop of chocolate on a cake cone."

She wasn't quite sure how to interpret the over-the-top meaningful look the boy gave his father.

"Right," the dad said, obviously trying to ignore his son's message.

"And for you?" Amy asked one of the best-looking men she'd seen since Johnny.

She could hear the little boy's tennis shoes kicking back and forth against the counter.

"I'll try black cherry this time."

"A double on a waffle cone?"

His grin was a great reward for her good memory. "Yeah," he said.

With the overly-generous scoops she'd

given them, the treats took about ten minutes to eat. Amy served other customers, but she was always aware of the father and son. Pulling at her.

Haunting her with a past come to life. *Her* past. Her husband and son . . .

"Ask her, Dad," she heard the little boy say once in a loud and insistent whisper.

She turned on the blender then to make a shake and didn't hear the father's response. Focused, instead, on the wallpaper and the Norman Rockwell prints, some of which she recognized.

Father and son finished their cones. But didn't leave.

"Can I get you anything else?" she asked when there was finally a lull and she could get back to them.

"We want you to have dinner with us," the little boy said. He had both arms on the counter and was pointedly ignoring his father.

Captivated by big brown eyes beneath unruly dark curls, Amy smiled in spite of the painful catch at her heart. "What are you having?"

"Macaroni and cheese."

"What else?"

The little boy frowned. "Do you need more than that?"

"What about vegetables?"

"Oh." His face brightened. "Don't worry, we don't eat those."

The little boy's father, who'd been silent throughout the exchange, coughed.

"Yes, Danny, we do," he corrected, but the words lost a bit of their firmness due to his obvious need to laugh. "Sorry about that," he said, looking up at Amy with brown eyes identical to his son's. "I'm Josh Dillon, landscaper and Ludington native. This is my son, Danny."

"Pleased to meet you, Josh and Danny," Amy grinned again. Something she hadn't done much of these past months.

Before they left, she'd accepted their invitation to dinner, too.

"There was this really cool kid there," Danny was saying, his mouth full of hamburger. He was talking about the one and only game of T-ball he'd ever played. "He could catch and throw as good as the older guys."

Her stomach tensing, Amy tried to smile with interest. She had to fight off a sudden and severe longing to see Charles.

She'd been fighting the excruciating ache all day. Mother's Day.

"His name was Caleb . . ."

Danny knew Charles. Even if only briefly. This little boy had seen her son sometime within the past two months.

Amy felt closer to her son and more hideously alone at the same time. She wanted to hug Danny and never let him go.

"That wouldn't happen to be Caleb Brown, would it?" she asked, always prepared to do her job. That was the name the Vallens couple had confirmed. She put her burger back on the paper plate, unable to eat.

"You know him?" Josh asked. He'd just finished grilling the second lot of burgers down at the beach. It was Sunday afternoon, and Amy had been with the pair almost every waking moment of that weekend.

At first because they'd asked and she'd felt drawn to them. Or at least to what they represented, the memories they evoked. And then because she'd felt drawn to *them,* to the people they really were.

They'd bowled, played miniature golf, walked the beach, built a sand castle, taken a drive to see some of the beautiful gardens Josh had created, using shrubs, trees, rocks, waterfalls and flowers.

All things she'd never done with her own husband and son.

She'd accepted that her time with them was meant to be. A gift to see her through Mother's Day — maybe even to start the healing that had completely eluded her so far.

"He's my nephew," she finally said. "That boy lives and breathes baseball. His father had him watching a game the day he came home from the hospital. He was just a day old and already cheering for the White Sox."

"Small world," Josh said, his eyes warm as they met and held hers. They'd been doing that more and more, finding each other and hanging on.

"Small town," Amy replied. It wasn't much, but it was the best she could do.

Once she'd made the decision to stay in town, Amy had rented a room in an old Victorian not far from the harbor. It had its own entrance and bathroom, so unless she wanted to use laundry or kitchen facilities, she never saw her landlady, an unmarried accountant who'd inherited the home from her parents.

She was glad of the privacy as she returned home Sunday evening, not certain she could've managed another moment of congeniality. Living two lives was getting harder, wearing her down until she wasn't sure who she should be anymore.

Being without her son, without anyone who remembered that day almost six years before when she'd become a mother, had left her limp and exhausted. Inside as much as out.

"Hey," she said. She was lying on her stomach, on top of the quilted blue-and-green bedspread, her head and one elbow hanging over the side while she held her phone to her ear.

"Hey, yourself! How are you?" Cara's familiar warmth washed over her tired body, soothing her. Amy grimaced. "Bushed."

"You sound it. So how are things going?"

Amy loved her friend for not really asking.

"The day's almost over and I'm still alive."

"Did you spend it alone?"

"No."

She wasn't ready to tell Cara about Josh and Danny yet. Wasn't ready to have her friend asking questions she couldn't really answer.

Cara didn't know much about Kristen, either. Other than as a name. One of her bosses.

Again, Amy just wasn't prepared to define or explain what she didn't fully understand herself.

"Another one down, honey. I'm proud of you."

That meant a lot to Amy. Still.

Cara spent the next couple of minutes chatting, her way of easing hurts, getting beyond the pain. She talked about the weather. About the grounds at the estate. Her idea for painting the suite of rooms she'd moved into after Kathy moved out. Then she asked, "Anything new since we talked on Thursday?"

"Not really." Another couple of people had seen Caleb, but they hadn't had anything to add, nothing that told her any more than she already knew: that Charles had been there.

"You don't sound good. What's up?"

She guessed she needed Cara's concern. Or maybe it was her friend's perspective she was seeking. Cara was the only person left in the world who knew her entire history. The person she'd been at ten. And fifteen. The woman who'd lost her husband.

Cara had been there the day she'd lost Charles.

She'd known Kathy. And Amy's dad.

"Nothing, really," she said. "I'm just feeling lost."

"Because you're missing Charles?"

"Partly, yeah. Will the pain ever let up?"

"We've been told again and again that time heals."

"Do you think there are some hurts that are bigger than time?"

It was the kind of conversation she and Cara had had during their teenage years, when they'd been discovering the world outside of childhood. And again in college, when the boundaries and rules changed all over again.

"Maybe," Cara said slowly. "And maybe this is one of them. But that doesn't mean time can't help."

"How much time?"

"I think that all depends on the person and the circumstances."

"It's taking too long, Car."

"That's because you aren't letting time do its work."

Lying there staring at the hardwood floor, her chin resting on the edge of the bed, Amy thought about that.

"Because I'm not getting on with my life?" she asked.

"Yeah. And because you keep opening the wound. Over and over. Every lead you chase gets your hopes up. Which keeps the pain alive."

"So you think I *shouldn't* have hope? I should just give up?" But that meant accepting that her son was lost to her forever and she just couldn't do that.

Could she?

Was there going to come a time when she'd have to? Was that time now?

"I think you should stay home and let the professionals you've hired do their jobs. There's been no further word from whoever sent that note."

Amy pushed herself up, to sit cross-legged in the middle of the bed. "Do you think I should give up hope?" she asked again.

Cara was silent a long time and Amy waited, not sure whether she even wanted to hear Cara's answer.

"No," she finally said, far too softly. "But I do think you've worked beyond your emotional capacity. If you don't stop torturing yourself every single day, if you don't come home and . . . and replenish yourself, we're going to lose you, as well as Charles and Johnny."

Amy pulled at a loose thread on the hem of her jeans. She'd always been able to trust Cara's advice. Her friend had a better understanding of people and motivations than almost anyone.

"It's just living a double life that's hard," she said, although she didn't know if she was honestly trying to help Cara understand or if she was trying to convince herself. "I've met some great people on the road, some I'd like to keep in contact with, but they don't really know me. To them I'm Amy Wayne."

She thought of Kristen. She'd grown to love her. Without Kristen, life would never be as happy as it could be.

Danny's grinning face floated before her mind's eye. Followed immediately by his father's.

"The only difference between Amy Wayne and Amelia Wainscoat is some money," Cara said. "The woman inside is the same."

If that was so, then why was it so hard to imagine going home? Every time she thought about her old life, about Wainscoat Construction, she no longer seemed to fit into that picture.

Kristen had left a message on her cell phone earlier. Amy wanted to call her back. She wished Kristen was there, sharing a bottle of wine with her, letting Amy talk. . . .

Brad had called, too, but she figured he wouldn't even know it was Mother's Day.

And he certainly wouldn't think to offer condolences if he did know. The thought made her sad.

"You know me better than anyone, Car. Do you honestly think I've lost perspective? That I'm fooling myself by thinking I'm doing some good?"

"You've done some good, Amelia, but so have Brad and his men." Cara paused and then went on. "You need to ask yourself something. Are you doing this because you're determined to find your son? Because you believe your involvement is necessary to the cause? Or are you doing it out of desperation? Because you can't bear to come home and face a life without Charles?"

Amy considered the question, but she didn't know the answer.

The house was clean — or as clean as Josh and Danny ever managed. The dishes were done, everything was in a closet, a drawer or under a bed. And there was nothing sticky on any of the larger surfaces.

A minor miracle for a Monday evening.

He'd been a little late picking Danny up from his after-school day care, but the macaroni casserole was in the oven and the fresh precut veggies he'd bought were on a tray in the refrigerator. He had a pitcher full of lemonade, a six-pack of beer and some chardonnay.

He and Danny were entertaining.

"She's here!"

Josh's heart pounded when his son came charging into the kitchen with the news.

Damn! He'd forgotten to set the table.

"Are you going to ask her to marry us tonight, Dad?" Danny asked, jumping up and down on one foot. "I think you should."

"We only met her last week, sport. It takes a little longer than that."

"Oh." Danny's face sobered, and then he grinned again. "Can we keep asking her to come over until it's long enough that we *can* ask her?"

Danny needed a commitment. And while his son ran off to answer the door, Josh wondered what in hell he was doing. It was one thing for a man to pursue a woman. But quite another for a man and his son. A man understood going in that no matter how well a relationship might start out, nothing lasted forever.

And a little boy? A little boy didn't understand that at all.

16

"What happened to Danny's mother?" Amy had been wanting to ask the question since she'd first seen Josh and Danny on the ferry ten days earlier.

"She left a couple of years ago. After Danny was born, she wanted to go back to school, and so she started taking classes at West Shore Community College. One day she came home and told me she was going to New York to be a fashion designer."

"Just like that?" She was sitting with Josh at his kitchen table, antique wood with mismatched wooden chairs, everything but the dessert plates in the dishwasher behind them. Danny had gone to bed, with much protest, almost an hour earlier.

Josh fiddled with the tines of his fork. "Not quite. One of her classmates, a man, went with her. In fact, he not only drove her there, he had family in the city that they moved in with."

"Oh."

"Yeah."

"I can't believe she'd just up and leave Danny like that. He's her *son*."

After tucking Danny into bed that night, Amy wasn't sure how she herself was ever going to leave this house.

"I've never been able to figure it out."

"Does she ever see him?"

"If you call once in two years seeing him."

"Did she marry the guy?"

"Not that one, but she is remarried."

"Is she a fashion designer?"

"Nope. A housewife. Last I heard she was pregnant. I'm guessing that'll put an end to the few phone calls she deigns to bestow on our son."

Josh appeared to be more upset on Danny's behalf than his own.

She got caught up in those brown eyes of his again. "You seem to have recovered."

He shrugged. The sight of his grin made her stomach flip-flop. "Time does that. And maybe I didn't love her as much as I thought."

"Funny how you can be so sure and then, when you least expect it, that can change on you."

"You sound like you're speaking from experience."

Amy gave herself a mental kick. "Yeah," she said. "Though not anywhere near as serious as yours."

"Have you ever been married?"

"No." She hated the lie, but it was easier that way. She pulled the elastic out of her hair, swinging her head as the dark tresses fell around her shoulders.

"You're so good with Danny," he said. "I can't believe you haven't had kids of your own."

She didn't normally eat as much as she had for dinner that night, and now wished she hadn't. "I've just never met the man I wanted to spend the rest of my life with."

"So where were you before coming to Ludington?"

That was the problem with getting to know people. They had this irritating habit of wanting to know her, too.

Making a mental note to remember the stories she was making up so she could fill Kristen in, just in case she and Josh should ever meet, Amy said, "Chicago. That's where my brother and his family live."

"What did you do there?"

"Office work."

She'd been much better at this in the beginning, when she'd believed so much in

338

her goal that the means didn't matter. These days the lies were getting to her.

Because they were accumulating, one on top of another, until their weight was too much to bear? Because she was lying to people she knew and was starting to care about? Or because she was losing belief in the likelihood of accomplishing her goal?

How would all the lies be justified if she didn't find Charles?

Josh was gazing at her. With that look in his eye.

She was looking at him, too. And couldn't stop. Fingers of desire unfolded from deep in her stomach, spreading lower. She'd been so long without the sensation, it shocked her. She'd thought herself immune, dead to anything except the pain of losing Charles and the desperation to find him again.

And maybe the very tentative, needy love for her friends.

None of those had abated. And yet, something else had emerged.

Josh took her hand. Deliberately threaded his fingers through hers. "I have a comfortable bed upstairs," he said. "Would you like to join me there?"

Amy just kept gazing intently ahead.

She'd known this was coming, but she had no idea what to do about it. Even before those erotic sensations had begun to tempt her, she hadn't known.

"I —" She broke off. Begged him with her eyes, begged for time to decide.

Josh was still holding her hand, his thumb rubbing slowly. Seductively.

Patiently.

Even if Cara was right and Amy *had* lost perspective, even if Kristen and Brad were wrong to support her in her quest, she couldn't go home. She no longer understood who she was, where this journey might lead her. She didn't know if Amy Wayne and Amelia Wainscoat would ever be able to coexist as one woman. Or what she'd do if they couldn't.

But she knew Cara was right about one thing. Amy had reached the limit of her capacity. She'd tortured herself enough with false hopes.

She stood up.

"Is that a yes?" Josh asked, rising, too. "Or are you leaving?"

His jeans fit him to perfection, hugging long muscular thighs, shaping a bulge she wanted to explore.

"I . . ." She licked her lips.

What kind of fool was she? Right here

for the taking was a ready-made family. So much like the one she'd spent the past eight months trying frantically to recover.

She was pretty sure she loved little Danny already.

And his father?

Amy tugged at the hand holding hers.

He turned her on. Was smart and kind and gorgeous. A great father.

And he was offering her something she needed almost more than breath. Something not even Brad Dorchester could give her. He was offering her a chance to recapture what she'd lost. "Let's go," she said.

Leading him toward the stairs, she didn't look back.

For the next several days, Josh was in paradise. Amy settled into his little family as easily as if she'd done it all before. She encouraged him and Danny to continue their "guy time" as she called it. And other than putting in her shift at the House of Flavors, she was home with them. He'd always wondered if he'd ever find a woman capable of loving Danny as much as he did, and he was beginning to think his prayers had been answered.

Amy doted on the little boy. She traded

shifts with one of the women at work so she could get off in time to pick Danny up after kindergarten. That way, he didn't have to go to day care.

She oohed and aahed over his artwork until you'd think the kid was Picasso.

And in bed . . . he'd never had better.

He was actually considering throwing caution to the wind and following his five-year-old son's advice. So what if it had only been a couple of weeks? It was obvious Amy needed to marry them.

There was just one small wrench in the plan. It was those times Amy didn't think anyone was looking, the times he'd walk quietly into a room and catch glimpses of extreme pain on her face. The time he'd woken up and found her sobbing in her sleep.

Saturday morning, a hand slid over his back, up his side to his nipple.

Instantly aroused, Josh lay there, pretending sleep. It was early, they had lots of time.

The tip of one slender finger teased his nipple, while the weight of her wrist tickled his ribs. He had to physically restrain himself from reaching up, grabbing that hand and sending it straight down to the results of her devilish torment.

He was achingly hard.

Still, he didn't move.

Slowly, tantalizingly, she ran her finger across his other nipple and then down the line of hair that started at his chest, crossed his stomach and disappeared into the hair covering his groin.

Where this woman had learned to love, Josh had no idea, but he was grateful from the bottom of his heart — and other places — that she had.

Amy's touch was seductive without being sleazy. Bold without losing any of the gentleness that made her so special.

Her hand moved lower. Josh sucked in a breath before he realized the sound had probably given him away. Her tongue darted out to lick his shoulder blade and he convulsed.

"I'm guessing you woke up." The teasing voice was his complete undoing.

"I'm guessing you're right," he growled, quietly reaching for the condom they never did without. He rolled over, taking her beneath him and thrusting inside her. She was hot and moist, as ready as he was.

And while he enjoyed her firm breasts, while he touched every inch of her body, bringing them both to mind-splitting

343

climax again and again, Josh wondered just what it was that Amy was trying so desperately to escape.

Brad had hardly spoken with Amy in more than a week. She was talking to people, collecting frustratingly little information and scooping ice cream. He needed to get her out of that town.

At his office on the Saturday after Mother's Day, he went over the notes he'd taken during the meeting with the Wainscoat-case staff. While his men were no longer in the field, all were actively searching for Charles. They were back to using tools like the telephone and the Internet, reading and rereading reports, gauging mileage, putting different pieces of the puzzle together on the off chance they'd make more sense.

His team had unanimously accepted the theory that Kathy Stead had taken Charles in the beginning. But unlike Amy, none of them believed the boy's ex-nanny had kept him. The FBI, the cops, his team had all been too thorough during the weeks immediately following Charles's disappearance. She'd been exonerated because she was clean.

So the questions remained. If she'd kidnapped him, where had the boy been during those first few weeks? Had she taken him back? When and where? Who had him now? And why?

The last, more likely and less palatable question was, had she killed the boy before taking her own life?

It was the only explanation that fit cleanly into every theory.

Rubbing the back of his neck as he stood staring out at the sunny Denver afternoon, Brad seriously wondered if he should take himself off this case. The answers were beginning to matter too much.

They mattered so much that he insisted on looking beyond the answers because he didn't like them, didn't like what he was seeing.

He was losing perspective.

When his cell rang, Brad grabbed it off the desk eagerly. He'd been waiting for a call from Amy; he hadn't heard from her in several days except by quick voice-mail messages. That made him uneasy, too.

"Brad? It's Kristen."

Brad braced himself. This couldn't be good. "What's she done now?"

"I was hoping you could tell me. I talked to her about an hour ago and she sounded depressed. I was afraid you guys had found out something bad and wondered if I should get someone to watch the store so I can go to Ludington to be with her."

"If she's found out anything at all, good or bad, she hasn't told me."

"I guess she's okay, then."

"She's a big girl." So why in hell had Kristen's words put such lead in his gut?

"Yeah, but it's been one hell of a long haul, and she's there all alone."

He didn't like it, either. Not one damn bit.

It was just as he'd thought. He was losing perspective.

"I'll call her," Brad said.

"I'll be at the store. Let me know if I need to drive over."

Amy was on the beach with Josh and Danny when her phone rang. Confused, with a headache that was making her dizzy, she wanted to ignore the call. But it could be about Charles. And Charles came first.

A glance at the screen told her the call was from Brad. All week, by leaving voice-mail messages or calling on her way to work, she'd been able to avoid this — speaking with Brad while she was with Josh. Partially because Josh knew nothing about Charles. But also, although she had

346

no logical explanation at all, because she felt guilty about Josh. As if she had something to be ashamed of.

She didn't want Brad to know she was sleeping with him.

Josh had stopped midway through a Frisbee throw when her phone rang. He watched now as she said hello.

Amy turned around. She couldn't handle both men at once.

"It's time you moved on." As usual Brad dove right into the reason for his call.

"Okay." Amy didn't have the stamina to argue with him. Wasn't even sure she wanted to.

"I've had a couple of men checking the records we've subpoenaed from the hotels, motels and campgrounds in all the towns we think Charles has been." Heart hammering until she could feel the pulse of blood rushing through her temples, Amy silently listened. While she'd been playing house, he'd been working.

Thank God he'd been working.

"They've come up with a list of names that have appeared more than once. One couple, Ray and Julie Court, has come up four times. They always pay in cash. It's a long shot. No one's ever seen a child with them, though."

"If no one's seen a boy, then . . ." She went for disappointment rather than hope this time. It seemed healthier. Safer.

"They could be hiding him, keeping him in the car, sneaking him into the room after dark. If you had a stolen child, would you parade him into a motel lobby?"

"No, but then why parade him around a miniature golf course or a T-ball field?"

"I admit it's a long shot."

"Okay. Sorry." And she was — for more than he knew. She heard Josh tell Danny not to get too close to the water. And then heard him come up beside the picnic table a few feet away, where she'd left her purse.

In capri pants and a blouse, she should be cool on the beach, especially with the breeze coming in off the lake. Instead, she was sweating.

She didn't turn around.

"They were in Manistee last month. At a small motel close to Douglas Park. There's a House of Flavors there, as well. Try to get a job transfer to the Manistee store. Let's see if we can place Charles in another town with the Courts."

"Okay."

"You'll call me from there tonight?"

She frowned. Didn't like the way Brad was pushing her.

"Yes," she said, and clicked off her phone.

And then she turned to face the questions in Josh's eyes.

Danny was building a sand castle several yards from where Amy sat with Josh. They were on the sand, leaning against a tree, their shoulders touching.

Waves were steadily chasing the lake-shore, breaking and receding.

"You ready to tell me what's going on?" Josh asked after Amy made several unsuccessful attempts to speak.

She should've been honest with Josh from the beginning. She knew that now. Maybe she'd known it all along. The lies, the role she played, had become confused with reality. She'd wanted a new role for herself and had invented this fantasy — using Josh and Danny to do it. Fashioning her new world out of theirs.

Was that what came from living dishonestly day in and day out? A change in values? Did the end not justify the means, after all?

She didn't know.

Head in her hands, Amy shuddered. It was time to be strong again.

To get back to doing what was right. She only wished she hadn't messed up two very special lives before she'd made that discovery.

Lifting her head for a moment, still holding it with both hands, she watched Danny build his sand castle. The look of concentration on his face brought tears to her eyes.

She hoped he was strong enough to withstand the defection of a woman who'd let him think she'd be staying around. A woman who'd pretended to herself that he could fill the hole in her heart.

She wanted to wrap him in her arms, to ease every pain he'd ever had. To make life a place where innocent children could grow up happily.

The sand had seeped over the tops of her tennis shoes.

In this world, heartbreak wasn't reserved only for those who'd lived long enough or who were strong enough to survive the onslaught. Agony came to little boys who lost their mothers to selfish acts. Little boys who lost their fathers in senseless accidents. And it didn't always stop with one blow. Charles had been forced to suffer much more. He'd been snatched away from the arms of love, taken from everything dear and familiar, from his own mother, hidden away like a criminal, denied the use of his own name.

She couldn't even think about what else he might have suffered.

"My name isn't Amy Wayne."

17

Josh was silent as she told him everything. Starting with her family's wealth, through her marriage to Johnny and on to everything that had followed.

"You're the only person I've met in the past seven months who knows who I really am."

She didn't blame him if he didn't preserve her secret, but she knew he would. In another time, she could have fallen for Josh. If her life had been as guileless, as simple, as she'd pretended. If she'd been Amy Wayne, not Amelia Wainscoat.

If she hadn't met a man with a craggy face and a softness buried so deep inside him he didn't seem to know it was there.

Danny had found a friend at the beach. It looked as if they were building an entire village in the sand.

Josh still hadn't said a word. Just sat there, knees pulled up, arms wrapped around them, staring out at the lake — and his son.

"I'm sorry, Josh. I know that doesn't make one single thing right or easier, but I am so sorry."

"Why us?" His voice was dry, cracked. "Why now?"

"People have been telling me for months to get on with my life. Telling me I'm losing perspective. I didn't listen. Until I ended up in jail. And then was practically escorted out of another town by the police. It scared me. Made me think my . . . friends were right. That I was losing it."

She picked up a handful of sand, let it sift slowly through her fingers.

"And we come in where?" He was obviously trying to be fair. And she could hear what the effort was costing him. "Danny and me . . ."

"I guess I was trying to get on with my life."

"I'd think the millions of bucks in Chicago might've been a more likely place to start."

She shook her head. "I can't go back there. At least not to the life I had there. Money meant too much to me. And in the end, it stole from me everything that was truly important. I'm pretty sure now that I lost Johnny because of it long before he was killed. And I suspect I lost my son for the same reason. My money made him a target."

"I thought you said his nanny took him."

"But if I hadn't left my son for her to raise during the first four years of his life — while I made more money than we ever needed — that wouldn't have happened, either."

"So you decided an affair was the way to start a new life and I just happened along."

Amy shook her head, wishing she was back in bed with him. Just long enough to make him feel good again.

"It's all mixed up, Josh." She wished they could leave it at that. "In some ways you're a lot like Johnny." That was the best explanation she could give.

"I think I'll take that as a compliment." There was an edge of bitterness to his voice, but understanding, too.

"It was meant to be one. Johnny was the best father I've ever seen. He probably made a mistake or two, but I sure never witnessed them. He taught Charles. He disciplined him, but he never lost patience. Never raised his voice. And he never got tired of playing with him. That first time I saw you and Danny on the ferry, you had your arms on either side of him, keeping him safe. It reminded me so much of

Johnny with Charles. And everything I've seen since does, too."

"I'm beginning to understand," Josh said. "You weren't really starting a new life so much as trying to capture the one you'd lost."

"Minus the mistakes," she added. "Minus the money. I think this was my twisted attempt to get it right."

"Which is why you didn't tell me who you were."

She supposed it was. At least in part.

"For nine months now, people have been looking at me and seeing a broken woman. They look at me and see a mother who lost her son. They see suffering. You and Danny looked at me and saw a woman."

"One we wanted to keep around," he said quietly.

"You guys rescued me from the loneliness that was beginning to destroy me."

He was silent for a long time. Amy understood; it was a lot for anyone to digest.

"I'm not going to pretend it doesn't hurt," he finally said.

She wished she could change that. She wished she could take back the damage she'd inadvertently done.

"But I find that I can't really blame you, either," he went on. "In fact, of the two of us, I think you're the one who needs sympathy most. I might have lost a girlfriend, but I've got Danny. I can't imagine going through what you've been through."

"Yeah," she whispered. "Me, neither."

"You mean her little boy might be dead?"

It was late that night, and Josh had Danny in the big bed with him. Josh had changed the sheets to get rid of any traces of Amelia Wainscoat — her scent, a stray hair, a sock she'd left behind. Then he and Danny had watched a movie together, eating popcorn and doing a pretty good job of wiping away all reminders of the woman who'd shared his life, his bed, his heart for such a short time.

Sometime during the evening, Josh had decided he wasn't sorry to have known her.

He was more like Amelia's Johnny than she knew. He would've had a problem with her money, too. Would've hated having a wife who could buy him a thousand times over. Hated having a wife support him. But he'd sure loved the time Amy Wayne had given him.

"Is he, Daddy?" Danny asked again, moving his face right up to Josh's in an attempt to get his attention. "Is her little boy dead?"

Josh hadn't told Danny that Amy's son was the great little baseball player Danny had known as Caleb.

"It seems pretty likely, sport," Josh said. He didn't want to believe it. But chances were good that before the nanny had killed herself, she'd killed the boy.

He hurt for Amy. Ached inside when he thought about her looking for a little boy playing T-ball when, in reality, the child she was seeking was probably going to turn up lifeless.

If he turned up at all.

Pulling Danny close, Josh held on uncharacteristically tight. Danny seemed to understand, since he leaned into Josh and clung. It cut at Josh's heart to think of a young boy Danny's age suffering who-knew-what kind of atrocities. What if it had been Danny? He didn't think he could have survived it with his sanity intact.

He was never going to forget Amy Wayne. Or the lesson she'd taught him. He would never again resent his wife's leaving him to raise a child alone. He would never let one day pass without giving thanks for his son. Amy had shown him what an incredibly lucky man he was.

And when, later that night, he lay awake

in bed, his son sleeping soundly against his chest, he did something he hardly ever did. He prayed. And after thanking God for keeping Danny safe, he asked that by some miracle little Charles would still be alive.

And that Amy would find him.

Amy had only been in Manistee for a couple of days when she got a very strange phone call from Cara.

"Amy?" Her friend didn't sound like herself at all. "Are you okay?"

"Fine." She was in her car waiting at the bridge; it opened occasionally to let larger boats travel up the river from the marina to Lake Michigan.

"I came home for lunch and in the yard by the front door, someone had spelled out the word *stop* with rocks."

The bridge lowered and Amy inched ahead with the rest of the traffic. "Did you call the police?" she asked. "The FBI? Brad?"

"Yeah. Agent Fleming is on his way over. I had to leave a message for Brad. Amy, I'm scared."

So was Amy. She drove by the House of Flavors where she'd been transferred without a problem, past the National Guard armory — a big tank stood out front and she wondered if Charles had seen it.

"You don't have to stay there," she told her friend. "We can have you moved immediately."

"No!" Cara said. "I'm not scared for me, you idiot, I'm scared for *you*. Out there all alone. This isn't someone who's satisfied just to have Charles. Now they're coming after you, too!"

"Only to get me to quit looking. They must've been tipped off somehow that Brad and his men are still nosing around. Not to mention the FBI."

Amy pulled into the parking lot of the Manistee Water Works Historical Museum, a large structure of variegated brick that resembled an old school house. With the old-time hauling wagons on display, it looked like someplace Charles would've asked to visit.

"I really think it's time for you to come home. You can get protection here."

"Obviously, whoever this is thinks I *am* there," Amy told her friend. No amount of jitters or unease would make her stop now. "Out here is probably where I'm safest."

She'd tell Brad that, too, when he got the news and tried to call off her part of the search.

Just outside Manistee, in a heavily wooded area, a fox foraged in the softness of old fallen leaves, tossing an occasional branch with his nose, his tiny sharp teeth biting into anything that might be food. He moved slowly, deliberately, stopping occasionally to look around.

Apparently finding something of interest in a leaf-filled indentation, he shoved down his nose, digging.

And came up with a child-sized baseball mitt in his teeth.

Driven, at least in part, by the guilt and regret she felt over the aberrant affair with Josh, Amy discovered new energy to impel her in the search for Charles.

She hated herself for the damage she'd done to two innocent people, and she had to do whatever it took to make certain nothing of the kind ever happened again. She'd learned her lesson at Josh and Danny's expense, but she'd learned. She couldn't undo what she'd done to them, and the only way she could even hope to live with herself was to vow that from now on, she would remain completely focused on her son.

To that end she spent every free minute

that week among the people of Manistee, instigating conversations. She got to know several of the regulars at the city marina. She drove through the town's neighborhoods with their storybook bungalows, Tudor-style and aluminum-sided homes decorated with pink and red petunia-filled flower boxes. She took sandwiches she didn't eat to Douglas Park at Lake Michigan beach. Walked the pier and talked to people about the red-trimmed white lighthouse. And of course she visited the elementary school.

She struck up conversations with anyone and everyone.

And she watched her back.

She was staying at the Lake Shore Motel — a very inexpensive place located right in the town itself and, most importantly, a stone's throw from a huge grassy park with scattered picnic tables, grills, fenced areas and a ball field.

She spoke to Cara often, trying to keep herself informed of Wainscoat's current projects; she even flew home one afternoon for a special meeting of the board, but she didn't stay overnight.

And she spoke with Kristen late every evening. Those calls had become like a nightcap before bed. They always helped her sleep.

Her conversations with Brad were exactly the opposite. The shame of what she'd done with Josh was always at its worst when she heard Brad's voice. Which made her bitchier with him than he deserved.

It took her almost a week, but Amy finally found someone in Manistee who'd met Charles on the beach. Her son had been by himself, throwing a baseball up in the air and catching it. That was an activity someone in Ludington had reported, as well. The old man who'd seen Charles usually docked his boat at the beach. He'd talked to Charles for a couple of minutes one day until it was obvious he was making the boy uncomfortable.

"I asked him if he was lost or needed help," the almost toothless old man said, handing back the photo of Charles. "He said no, his mom was going to be right back."

He shifted on the seat of his boat — the place where he seemed to spend much of his time. He ate, drank coffee, read. And talked to Amy. The last two mornings she'd brought doughnuts to share with him.

"Yeah, that sounds like my nephew," Amy told him now. He'd been talking about fishing that morning and she'd bragged about her young nephew, who was already an expert fisherman. She'd shown him a picture.

And had finally hit paydirt.

"Well, someone ought to at least teach him his last name," the old man said. "He gave me his first name fine. Charles, he said. But when I asked for his last name, he just stared like he didn't have no idea what it was."

"I think I need to have a talk with my brother about that . . ."

Brad was relieved to get her call. He'd begun to conclude that they were chasing yet another dead end. That there was no connection — other than coincidence — between the Courts' presence in the various towns where Charles had also been seen.

"Bingo," he said when she reported her find.

"What now?"

"There's another name that's turned up more than once," Brad said, glad to finally have something to tell her. "Eliza Williams. Shortly after the Courts were in Manistee, she was in Beulah. It's just north of you on 131."

"I'll go there today."

If the situation hadn't been so god-damned serious, he would've grinned. He'd talked to Amy every day since she'd moved on to Manistee, and every day she was sounding more and more like her old feisty self. He had no idea what had happened in Ludington, but he was more than relieved to know that whatever it had been was behind them.

"Be careful."

She was always careful. Now more than ever. Those rocks at her house hadn't been an accident. As she drove past miles of trees and rolling hills, broken only by the occasional cattle farm, Amy thought about her conversation with Brad the day Cara had found those rocks at the mansion. He'd surprised her yet again.

He'd agreed that the message left by her door didn't pose any immediate danger to her.

"I'm not discounting it, mind you," he'd said clearly. "Someone's trying to apply pressure."

"Someone who wants us to stop looking for Charles," she'd said.

"Maybe." He'd paused for a moment. "Or it could be that we really *are* dealing with an extortion attempt due to that article in the papers. If so, these folks are total amateurs. As extortion goes, it's a damned lame attempt. . . ."

Amy drove through Bear Lake Village, past Bear Lake Foods and the Village Variety store, wondering, always wondering, whether Charles had been there. Trying to see the place through his eyes, to know what he'd thought.

Brad wasn't sure those rocks in her yard had been put there by the kidnapper or someone working for the kidnapper. He thought it just as likely that they'd been put there by someone trying to scare her into paying the ransom money.

According to Brad, real kidnappers would have asked for a lot more than $250,000 — unless, as they'd been supposing, whoever held Charles had used the ransom note just to scare her off.

It took only three days in the Beulah/Benzonia area to find someone who could confirm that her son had been there.

Not at Crystal Lake Elementary, though she spent as much time there as she could without raising suspicion. And not at the bowling alley or at Crystal Lake where a sign read, "Help Us Control Swimmer's Itch. Do Not Feed Those Birds on the Beach."

It was at the miniature golf course. Charles had been there twice. With a woman of average height, narrow shoulders and brown hair. He'd been holding his putter backward.

Both visits had been over the same weekend, seven or eight weeks earlier.

Just before Kathy killed herself.

Amy had made it as far as Traverse City on June first. Still following the Courts. There'd been no more appearances of Eliza Williams's name in hotel records after the one in Beulah two months previously. But as their search of records moved farther north, Brad's men had turned up a third recurring name, James Siddon.

Amy hadn't had a job since Manistee, but she was thinking about getting one in Traverse City. She had a lot of ground to cover and had found that a job tended to give her legitimacy, lend credibility to whatever story she concocted.

She was staying away from ice cream shops, though, her memories of Josh and Danny still too raw.

Her phone rang just as she was pulling into the Big Boy restaurant to put in an application on Sunday. With school out for the summer, she figured she'd focus on eating establishments that kids like to frequent.

"This one's hot."

Her foot on the brake nearly sent her through the windshield. "What?" she said, hands shaking.

"We've just had a call from someone who knew Charles in Chicago." Brad's voice wasn't even hinting at calm. "The family of a little girl he went to school with. Cissy Moore. She's on vacation with her parents near the Upper Peninsula and they recognized Charles in a line buying tickets to the circus."

"Oh, my God." Amy fell forward over the steering wheel. "Oh, my God."

She could barely hold on to the phone.

"He's alive. He's really alive." Tears streamed down her face and she hardly noticed. Her entire body shook so hard the phone kept bumping against her ear. She couldn't see. Couldn't think.

"I . . . okay," she said. Bless little Cissy. And then, "Oh, my Goooodddd." She tried to contain the sobs, to maintain some sense of control, but she'd been holding on for so long.

"It's not over yet."

Brad's voice steadied her. She wished he was there. More than ever before.

"I know."

"We're not even sure it's him. Remember, this is all based on the word of a five-year-old girl."

"But she . . . had a . . . crush on Charles in p-preschool."

"Her mother saw him, but only from behind. She said it looked like Charles, although he'd grown several inches. They tried to talk to him, but by the time they got close enough, he was gone."

He'd grown several inches. Without her.

But he was alive!

"Where are they? Where is he?" Suddenly Amy had a thousand questions, and the energy to fly to the moon if need be to get her son. It had been nine very, very long months.

"The circus is in Petoskey tomorrow. There isn't enough time for me to fly in and meet you for the drive up. I want you to call Kristen and see if she can go. You'll be on the road a good part of the night."

"Okay," Amy said, thankful for his advice. He was always rational, even if today he sounded far more urgent than she was used to.

One thing she'd learned over the past

months — besides the fact that she wasn't invincible — was that she could trust Brad Dorchester when she couldn't trust herself.

Kristen wished Amy had let her drive. Granted, she'd been up since five that morning, taking inventory at the store, but Amy had months worth of exhaustion on her.

It was pitch-black as they passed the Cherry Tree Orchards in Elk Rapids.

Amy was fidgeting. Turning the CD player on. And then off.

"Do you want to stop for anything before we hit farm country?" Kristen asked.

They'd loaded up with munchies and sodas in Traverse City. "No." Amy shifted in her seat, adjusting the tilt. Moved her purse to the floor behind her. Checked the display on her cell phone.

She was strung so tight, Kristen was afraid for her. Afraid that if this turned out to be another disappointment, it would be the one that put Amy in the hospital.

"I have something to tell you," Amy blurted into the silent darkness. Her face was eerily somber in the glow from the dash.

"What?" Kristen turned in her seat to face Amy. She felt relieved that Amy was talking.

"My name isn't Amy Wayne."

For a second, Kristen panicked. Had it already happened? Was this one stress too many for Amy to handle? She'd been alone a long time.

But then Amy turned her head, met Kristen's eyes briefly, and Kristen could read the lucidity there. Even in the darkened car.

Disoriented, she said, "What's your real name, then?"

The T-shirt and cut-off sweatpants she was wearing were too hot.

"Amelia Wainscoat."

Was that supposed to mean something to her? The only Wainscoat she'd ever heard of was the builder out of Chicago.

Not too long ago, there'd been an article in the Grand Rapids press about a woman who'd committed suicide. There'd been a sidebar about the Wainscoat heir, but . . .

"I need you, Kristen. More than you'll probably ever know. Please don't leave me now."

Kristen leaned forward, laying her hand over Amy's on the console, giving it a squeeze. "I'm right here, Amy," she said automatically. "I'm not going anywhere without you."

"The thing is, when I first met you, I had to lie. It was all part of the plan. You know, to find Charles."

The disjointed statements made no sense and Kristen thought about asking Amy to pull over and let her drive.

"Then, later, it was all so confusing. Amy Wayne, Amelia Wainscoat — I couldn't bring the two of them together. I know how you feel about rich people, but Amy Wayne wasn't rich. I was afraid that if you knew about Amelia, you'd treat me differently. Like someone I wasn't any-more."

"I know who you are."

"Do you?" Amy glanced at her again, the miles of farmland and cherry orchards rushing past without notice.

"Of course." Kristen smiled. "It hap-pened fast, but you're probably the closest friend I've ever had. I've never told anyone before about the baby I lost."

Amy paused. Frowned. "I can't be *just* Amy Wayne," she finally said.

"Okay."

"I promised myself when I left Ludington that I was going to face my

371

past, as well as my future, and I've been thinking about it a lot."

Kristen liked the sound of that.

"In some ways, I hate the money, but it's part of me, too, you know? Cara was right — I *am* a Wainscoat."

"Who's Cara?"

"My operations manager. And close friend. She's practically run the company single-handedly all this time. I've known her my whole life."

The company? Operations manager? Kristen frowned. She continued to study Amy. And reject the truth.

The Thunderbird slowed as they passed through the village of Central Lake. A sign said they could get prime rib at the Lamplight Inn. They drove past the high school and church, then the Chain o' Lakes Motel, which offered Internet access for ten dollars a month.

"What's your company?" Kristen asked, although she had a dreadful feeling she already knew. Amy had told her once she'd grown up in Chicago.

Kristen had pictured a nice but modest middle-income neighborhood in the suburbs.

"Wainscoat Construction." She said the words in a matter-of-fact tone, as though they'd both known what they were talking about.

"I thought a man owned Wainscoat."

"My father did until he died a few years ago."

"Now you do." Just to get things straight.

"Yes."

Kristen turned to the front. Nodded. Stared out into the darkness. She could sure use a good city right now. One with lots of lights and life.

She'd left Paw Paw and the Lawsons and rich people far behind.

She wished she hadn't been interrupted by a customer before she'd read much of that article about the Wainscoat kidnapping. She'd never gotten back to it. Never really even looked at the small grainy photos that accompanied the article.

Not the way she'd looked at Amy's photo of her son.

She felt like such a fool. Stupid, unremarkable Kristen, out of her league again.

She was quiet during the drive to the village of Ellsworth. Studied the Banks Township community hall and the Banks Township Historical Society building as if she was considering the real estate. Ellsworth had some upscale neighborhoods.

She wanted to hate the woman beside her.

"So what was all that about you and Johnny having problems because you had to work to support your family?" She knew she sounded a little disbelieving. Perhaps a little sarcastic. But Amy didn't seem to notice.

"When Daddy died, I'd fully expected Johnny to step into his shoes. He'd been in the construction business his whole life and he was next in line. The entire board expected the same. Johnny refused. He wouldn't even try."

Kristen didn't know what to think about that.

"So you took it on, instead," she murmured.

"I had to."

"And that's why your son had a sitter who thought she was his mother."

"Because, in essence, she was." Amy's words fell harshly through the darkness.

East Jordan, with its EZ Mart, elementary school and marina, came and went. And then all Kristen had to distract her was more dairy farms. Which weren't much of a distraction late at night.

She tried to conjure up some good, healthy anger. And all she could think about was how — in the midst of her own crisis — Amy had taken a job far beneath her and done it to the best of her ability. She'd even gone the extra mile to teach Kristen better business practices she'd never have had the opportunity to learn otherwise.

"I don't like rich people," she mumbled.

"I know."

"You're rich."

"Yeah."

"So how come I like you?"

"Because I'm a reformed rich person?"

The tension in Kristen's stomach subsided a bit.

"Just see you stay that way," she said.

They had a lot more to talk about; Kristen knew that. When Amy found her son, or even if she didn't, she'd stop living her life on the road. At some point, she was going to become Amelia again. And when that happened, Kristen would just have to pray that she didn't lose the good friend the Fates had sent her.

18

In the middle of the night, on a dark Michigan highway, the doubts started to attack Amy again. Cissy was a five-year-old girl. Amy was ludicrous to place her hopes on a child who was just learning to tie her own shoes.

"It's a comfort to know that whoever has Charles is listening to what he wants, trying to do things that please him," she said, grabbing on to whatever consolation she could.

"If we don't find him this time, Amy, we'll find him the next."

True to form, Kristen heard more of what Amy *hadn't* said than what she had.

"Do you think so, Kris? Really?"

Her chest tightened when Kristen didn't answer immediately.

"Be honest with me," she cried from the depths of her heart. She had to quit fooling herself. Even if the believing didn't stop, she still had to be realistic.

She couldn't risk Lowell and Ludington again.

"I honestly don't know," Kristen finally said. "I *want* him to be alive . . ."

"But it's been a long time," Amy finished for her.

"Yeah." Kristen drew the word out. "But we know for sure he was still around in April, so it's really only been two months, which isn't all that long."

That was why Amy loved Kristen so much. She always found a way to consider the truth, consider people's needs and somehow make everything sound okay.

"And don't forget," Kristen added, "this is probably the best lead we've ever had."

The circus outside Petoskey was crowded, especially for a Monday. With only an hour's sleep, grabbed in a room at the Holiday Inn, Amy and Kristen were there that morning before the gates opened. Amy stretched up as tall as she could, looking out over the crowd of people, and then ducked down to little-boy height, scrutinizing every child.

"I might not know him," she complained to Kristen. "Do you realize how awful it is that I might not recognize my own son?"

Kristen rubbed between Amy's shoulder

blades. "Cool it, Wainscoat," she said. "One step at a time. And this step is to find all the boys who look like they might be almost six years old and see if any of them have bright-blue eyes and glasses."

Amy nodded; Kristen was right.

"Brad's coming in this afternoon."

"Yeah, you told me," Kristen said.

"Do you think he's cute?" Amy had no idea where the question had come from. She'd been about to have a panic attack and had started babbling, instead.

"Cute?" Kristen echoed, watching carefully as they moved through the gates with the rest of the crowd. "No, I don't think he's cute. A forty-year-old private detective who's lived as hard as he has couldn't possibly be cute."

Okay. Amy pushed her way around an older woman blocking her view of a little boy up ahead.

The boy was shorter than Charles had been last year. And he had blond hair.

Damn.

"Sexy, then," she said. "Do you think he's sexy?"

"Unbelievably," Kristen replied.

If Amy hadn't been so preoccupied, she might have wondered about that more.

"How about you?" Kristen asked. They

were inside, walking around the perimeter of the circus, checking the bleachers. The washrooms. The game and concession stands. "Do *you* think he's sexy?"

"I guess," Amy admitted without really giving it much thought. "Who wouldn't? But it means nothing."

"You have feelings for him."

"Whatever I feel for him is all wrapped up in the fact that he's the man in charge of finding my son."

"I'm pretty sure he thinks you're sexy, too."

"You're nuts," Amy said, frowning at Kristen. "The man hates me. I'm nothing but a thorn in his ass."

"I don't —"

Amy cut Kristen off with a lethal grip on her forearm. "There he is!" she said in a hoarse whisper that hurt her throat.

She made a quarter turn to her right, weaving in between people, trying to get another glimpse of the little boy who'd been standing all alone, watching a machine pull taffy. She hoped Kristen was behind her, but didn't dare slow down to find out.

A three- or four-hundred-pound man cut in front of her, blocking her view. Amy swore, tried to swerve around him, but she was trapped by the bandstand wall on one side, and people coming in the opposite direction on the other.

"I can't see him!" she cried over the din of the crowd.

"Keep going," Kristen called back. "I'm right behind you."

Finally she was free of the obese man. Had a clear view of the taffy machine.

And no Charles.

"I won't lose him," she said between gritted teeth.

"Where was he?" Kristen asked, coming up beside her.

"There." Amy pointed. "I don't know which way he went."

"Let's split up." Kristen turned a full circle. "You go around the back and make your way to the exit so they can't escape. I'll take the inside and check all the stands again."

Nodding, Amy took off at a run, stumbling a time or two on a protruding root. Her eyes were on the space in front and beside her, not on the ground beneath her.

She looked behind and under the bleachers. Behind all the games and concessions and novelty booths. Studying cotton-candied kids, harried mothers, impatient fathers with backpacks over their shoulders and cameras around their necks. She circled the washroom facilities. Even went into the men's room, calling her son's name.

She saw a little more male skin than she needed to. And no Charles.

Half an hour later, she met Kristen at the gate.

"Any luck?"

"None."

The sympathy in Kristen's eyes was almost her undoing.

"Then let's keep looking," she said.

They did. Long past the time the circus acts started. And finished. They scoured inside the gates and out, patrolled the parking lot. Sat on a fence by the road. Only when the final guest had finally gone home, did Amy agree to leave and return to their room in town.

"I *know* it was him." Amy looked so small and lost sitting on the edge of the bed. She was hunched over with her arms on her knees.

Brad had a hard time sitting still in the too-small chair at the too-small table across from her. Kristen had left shortly after he'd arrived in Petoskey, needing to get at least partway back to Baldwin that night. She'd had to close the store on Monday.

"You said you didn't get a clear look at his face."

A small shake of her head was her only reply.

"It's been nine months since you've seen him, Amy. You can't be sure that boy was Charles."

The scowl she sent him left no doubt that he'd overstepped his bounds. "I know it was him, Brad."

He sat back. Unused to the inactivity. Frustrated that he couldn't solve this case.

For the sake of the boy. For his mother. And for himself. This woman was overshadowing every other part of his life.

He didn't know what to do when her shoulders started to shake. Uncomfortable, Brad pretended not to notice. He studied the pastel wallpaper. The folds in the curtains behind his head. His fingertips. And when none of that worked, he coughed.

She didn't make a sound. Didn't say a word. Just sat there, folding in on herself, her body jerking.

Brad couldn't stand to watch her.

He'd only seen her cry once before, and

it had been nothing like this. It had just been tears. This silent closing off was much worse.

Because he didn't have a glass of whiskey, he couldn't figure out what to do with his hands. Or any other part of him. Usually there was only one reason for him to be in a bedroom with a woman.

Somehow, without making any kind of conscious decision, Brad was on the bed beside Amelia Wainscoat, one hand lightly rubbing her back. It seemed to have helped once before.

To his relief, the silent sobbing came to an end. She straightened.

"Hold me?" Her tortured whisper froze him into immobility.

"Please?"

He knew better. She was his client.

He wanted to. Far too much.

He'd lost his objectivity.

She was just sitting there, needy and alone.

With an inner groan and a prayer that he'd be strong enough to act like the man his mother had raised him to be, Brad slowly slid his arms around her.

Amy awoke alone the next morning. She hadn't fallen asleep that way, but when she and Brad met just outside her room at six-thirty, neither of them mentioned the fact that she'd cried herself to sleep in his arms.

She didn't ask what time he'd left her room.

They spent the morning in her Thunder-bird, scouring Petoskey. Though the neighborhoods were filled with nicely kept older houses on quiet streets, just like so many of the smaller towns she'd been through in the past months, Petoskey was actually fairly large.

They strolled around the North Central Michigan College campus and then spent some time at Little Traverse Bay. A couple of hours at Sunset Park, walking the beach. Pretending to eat lunch at one of the picnic tables.

Or at least, Amy pretended. Brad ate all of his deli sandwich and part of hers. She tried not to think about the last time she'd had a picnic at the beach. And wondered how Josh and Danny were doing.

"What are you going to do when this is all over?" he asked as they sat there after lunch, watching people come and go. It was Tuesday, so the park wasn't very busy, but there were still a number of people around. No small boys with dark hair and glasses, though.

"I don't know," Amy said. "I guess that depends on how it ends."

With raised eyebrows he studied her. Stronger this morning, at least partially because of his support the night before, Amy met his eyes.

"Yeah, I'm finally starting to face the fact that I might not get him back," she said. How could she utter such words so calmly? she wondered. How could she utter them at all?

"Do you think you'll return to Wainscoat Construction?"

"I don't know. Maybe. But maybe not. I've actually been thinking about selling."

Once she'd finally dared give voice to it, the thought didn't sound nearly as shocking as she'd assumed.

"Might not be a bad idea."

She frowned. "You really think so?" Cara would probably have her committed if she could hear this conversation.

The men and women on the board, the people she'd grown up with, friends of her father's — they'd all be horrified.

"Yeah," Brad answered. "Might be the best thing."

His easy attitude toward such a momentous decision threw her.

"Why?"

"In all these months, you've never shown any sign of needing to go back. Of missing the job. Or even wanting it."

Oh.

"But it's . . . it's my birthright."

"Your life is your birthright," Brad said, his fingers rotating a twig on the table. "Anything else is up for grabs."

Amy smiled. "Why couldn't you be this nice to me eight months ago?" she asked him.

She'd expected a shrug and a flippant Brad remark. Not the almost introspective frown that crossed his face. "I didn't know you then. I've seen courage that most of my agents don't have. Stamina. Determination . . ."

He broke off. Looked away.

And when he turned back, gave her a flippant reply that, a month or two ago, she would have thought reflected the man.

Now she wasn't so sure.

They were at the winter-games park across the street from Sunset Park when Amy's phone rang.

It was Cara. And she didn't talk long.

"What?" Brad asked as soon as Amy had clicked off.

"There was a voice-mail message when

Cara got home tonight. She said it was Charles."

Though she felt slightly faint, Amy was mostly numb. Brad changed their direction, crossing immediately to the parking lot.

"On your house line?"

She shook her head. "No, the one I gave out during the initial interviews after the abduction."

Brad nodded. "So people could call if they didn't feel comfortable calling the police." His voice was dry. It had been a contentious issue between them at their first meeting, and it had set the tone for a relationship that had remained contentious.

He'd told her she was stupid for installing the line. She'd done it, anyway.

"We need to call in to listen to it."

"I already did."

So why wasn't Amy stricken with sorrow? Grief? Relief? Hope? Fear? *Something.*

"You heard it." He stopped with his hand on the car door, scrutinizing her.

She nodded. "Charles only said my name before he was cut off. His voice was muffled, but I'm fairly certain it was him."

"That was it? Just Charles saying your name?"

"No." She shook her head, trying to clear away her confusion. "Another voice, even more muffled than his, told me to have the money by next Friday. He said he'd be in touch with the drop-off specifics. And he warned me again to call off the search."

"The voice was male?" Brad's tension was unmistakable.

"Yes."

"Ray Court maybe?" He was frowning. "I wonder if you were seen at the circus."

She climbed into the car, intending to start it, except that she had no idea where to go. "What makes you think that?" she asked, forcing herself to hold her head up.

"The timing's pretty damned coincidental. If that really *was* Charles you saw . . ."

"But they called me in Chicago. That's where they think I am."

"Unless you *were* seen and they just used that number because they have no other way to contact you," he said slowly. "And if that's the case, you could be in a hell of a lot more danger than we thought."

No. No danger for her.

Charles was the one in danger.

Her son's voice had been filled with such stark fear, Amy didn't think she'd ever be able to get it out of her mind.

★ ★ ★

Though he hated like hell to do it, Brad had to warn Amy that the recording of Charles's voice did not necessarily mean her son was alive. It could easily have been made months before. Because it was so muffled, Brad suspected the abductors had merely been playing back a recording.

His suspicion was confirmed when Agent Fleming called him that night. They'd run tests on the voice-mail message and with enhancements had been able to pick up evidence of a tape recorder, and a cheap one at that. The call was traced to a cell phone registered to Kathy Stead.

Because she was so sure Charles was in the area, Amy insisted on spending the next couple of days in Petoskey. She knew Brad didn't like the idea, in light of the fact that her cover might be blown, but the timing of that call might have been coincidental and Petoskey was their most logical source of potential clues.

On Wednesday, the fourth of June, they drove up to Conway, exploring Crooked Lake. At Beach's Log Cabin Café, Brad made Amy smile when he nonchalantly pointed out that the building was made of brick. They saw the world's largest crucifix — a big cross in the woods.

But no sign of Charles.

And that evening, although she'd asked him to have a drink with her, Brad barely waited for Amy to unlock the door of her room before he said goodnight and strode off.

She was sorry her breakdown on Monday night had made him so uncomfortable.

Sorrier, still, to be alone. Since hearing her son's voice, she'd been running on automatic. Thinking and feeling as little as possible. She didn't know how long she was going to be able to keep reality at bay.

Kathy Stead had been unquestionably tied to Charles through that cell phone trace. Amy had no idea what that meant. Did someone who knew Kathy have Charles now? Had she turned Amy's son over to someone else for safekeeping? Or perhaps she'd killed him and someone she'd known was trying to make a quick buck.

Brad had suggested Kathy could have been working for someone else, perhaps one of her business rivals. But he didn't really seem to think so anymore.

What used to be nagging headaches were becoming more severe. Amy's neck ached all the time. She was dead tired and, if she slept at all, her dreams exhausted her.

And her emotional health was deserting her. She overreacted to everything. Panicked when she shouldn't. It was a wonder Dorchester could stand to be around her at all.

Of course, she *was* paying him well.

Thursday was spent going from McDonald's to McDonald's in a fifty-mile radius of Petoskey. Brad had asked for a turn at driving, and because Amy could see how hard it was for him to sit still all day, she gave him the keys. Truth be told, it was a relief to be able to invest her entire attention in watching for Charles. Not having to watch where she was going.

They passed Sweet's Kitchen Store. Drove by wooded areas, older neighborhoods and new ones, trees so tall they almost reached the sky, quaint old-fashioned downtowns.

"In my other life, I'd never have seen any of this," Amy commented as they drove through Alanson, Michigan, where there was a dentist's office next to a yarn shop, and not far beyond, an attractive middle-class neighborhood with a manicured hill of grass, a rock wall with blooming flowers in myriad colors and solid brick homes. "I missed out on so much living my sequestered, snobbish life."

Brad grunted. Even though it was summer, he was still wearing Dockers, navy today, a white polo shirt and loafers. Summer this far north in Michigan meant temperatures in the low seventies. Amy was glad. At least her jeans and sweaters were appropriate. There weren't many opportunities for clothes-washing — mostly in sinks at night. She generally wore the same pants two or three days in a row. But she'd long since relegated the parka to the trunk of her car.

"Don't be too hard on yourself," Brad said, breaking into her thoughts. It took her a second to realize he was replying to her comment about the things she'd missed. "Everyone lives his or her life in a pretty narrow context. I doubt the people you've been living among all these months have any idea what really goes on in the world you grew up in. And probably not much awareness of the pressures it brings, either."

The man who saw so much and shared so little had just given her a peek inside.

"Maybe not."

"I've been a lot of places in my life,

worked for all kinds of people, and I can tell you that every single one of them has his or her own cross to bear. I can also tell you that most people don't look beyond their own lives, their own problems."

Amy wasn't sure what that said about humanity, but she thought he was right just the same.

"I'd like to believe that everyone has the ability to come to that realization and to have — I don't know — a larger focus. To look outward at other lives."

He glanced over at her and, with a sardonic grin, made a flippant remark about naiveté that effectively ended the conversation.

Just two minutes from Bayview Inn — a big, elegant New England-style inn right on Little Traverse Bay — at a McDonald's they'd already visited once, Brad struck up a conversation with a young man who worked the night shift. The high schooler was taking out the trash and Brad commiserated, telling the kid about his first summer job. He'd been a janitor at a mountain resort in Colorado and spent the day going from bathroom to bathroom and back again.

Amy wondered if that was true.

And somehow hoped it was.

She promptly forgot all about any summer job Brad might have had when he started talking about baseball. He was describing the child of a friend of his, a little guy who could throw and catch a ball as well as any all-star Little Leaguer. As it turned out, the McDonald's employee, Jason, was an avid baseball fan himself. He played first base for Petoskey High School. The Petoskey Northmen were tournament winners, and Jason hoped to move on to the Detroit Tigers farm team when he graduated.

Amy was a little intimidated by Brad's smooth, natural approach, the subtlety of his interrogation. He made the thousands of conversations she'd instigated over the past many months seem paltry.

"Hey! I've seen that kid!" Head turning sharply, Amy saw that Brad had pulled out his wallet, presumably to get some money on his way to the counter, and one of Jason's co-workers, who'd joined the two men in their baseball discussion, noticed the picture of Charles, which Brad had stuck in the photo compartment.

"Yeah," Jason said. "He was in here the other night with some woman."

Amy saw stars in her peripheral vision.

Wondered if anyone could tell she wasn't breathing.

"Really?" Brad's voice came from far away. How odd, she thought. He sounds so calm. He looked at Jason. "That's my friend's kid I was telling you about. My godson. I knew they were heading up this way to do some fishing, but I didn't know when. What day did you see them?"

"Monday," both kids said at once.

The night of the circus. Amy *had* seen Charles.

Oh, my God. He's alive.

19

Amy started to shake.

"For guys who gotta have more important things on their minds than little kids, you two sound awfully sure about that."

"This kid kinda caught everyone's attention," David, the second kid said.

The two boys exchanged glances, as though checking with each other about what to say.

"You said he was the kid of a friend of yours?" Jason asked.

"Yeah, a guy I knew in college." Shoulders relaxed, feet apart, Brad looked like any guy on vacation with nothing more pressing on his mind than the hamburger he was about to order. "We e-mail, send pictures of the kids and Christmas cards, although I haven't seen him in a couple of years. But like I said, I'm the boy's godfather," he added. "Why?"

"Well —" Jason nodded at his friend "— it's just that the kid didn't look too happy."

"He was with a woman, though, so maybe your friend wasn't around," David said.

A woman. *WHAT WOMAN? He's MY son! He belongs with me!*

"She was kinda yelling at him, which is why we all noticed them," Jason said. "The kid didn't want anything to eat. She said something about him not eating all day and he was damn well going to have something."

"He didn't, though," David said. He was leaning on the broom he'd been sweeping with. "She got him a Happy Meal, and no matter how much she hissed at him to eat, he never took a bite."

Amy didn't think she could stand to hear anymore. And yet she couldn't walk away until she heard every single morsel of information they had about her son.

"Wow," Brad said, a concerned frown lining his brow. "I'm really surprised to hear that. Maybe I should give my friend a call. I wonder if he even knows . . ."

"The woman was complaining about some guy." David seemed eager to tell all he knew now that he thought something might be done to help the little boy who'd obviously been much talked about in the restaurant. "And every time she said anything, the kid would defend the guy. Maybe that was your friend."

"I hope so." Brad put his wallet away, folded his arms across his chest. "My friend and his wife are divorced," he said casually, and despite her emotional fog, Amy was impressed with that touch of realism.

She slid her hand between his arm and his side, grabbing hold. Hanging on. She was taking liberties she had no right to. But she had no choice.

"He was a tough little guy," Jason said, admiration in his tone. "His glasses were broken, kept sliding down his nose and he just kept pushing them back up —"

"And when the woman really started giving it to him for not minding her," David broke in, "he never backed down, no matter how much she threatened him."

On Friday, another warning with words clipped from a newspaper arrived at the mansion in Chicago. It told her to leave a black purse containing the money on a certain bench in the park near the estate. And it tersely warned that if Amy wanted her son to live, she had to let him go. If *she* wanted to live, she had to let him go. There was one more demand for her to call off her search.

Not the investigators. Or the investigation. Not Brad's search. But *hers.*

It ended with a plea to stop more deaths from occurring.

Agent Fleming read the note to Brad over the phone. And Brad relayed it to Amy minutes later when she picked him up after checking out of the hotel. She was still using her Amy Wayne alias, but he was beginning to suspect she no longer needed to. Whoever had her son knew she was in Michigan.

"What's that mean, let him go?" She was in the same state of unnatural calm she'd been in when she'd received the tape-recorded call from Charles.

She'd pulled onto highway 31, heading toward Mackinaw City. He'd had word that the Courts had stopped there two nights earlier.

The country through which the Courts were traveling was getting more and more remote. Before long, they were going to be in Canada. Police in northern Michigan and the Upper Peninsula were on the lookout for anyone trying to use Ray or Julie Court ID. And warnings had been placed at all the border crossings.

The precautions might be for nothing. Most of the positive accounts indicated

Charles was with a woman. But apparently he'd been defending a man. . . .

"It means stop looking for him." Brad was slow to answer her.

"They know I'm here."

"Seems that way."

"They must have seen me at the circus."

"Maybe. Not necessarily."

"At least we know Charles is still alive. And that we're getting close."

Brad wished those two possibilities were a safe assumption. He really detested the feeling that welled up in him, stifling his natural inclination to tell the truth. How could he protect her and be honest with her at the same time?

Because he had a job to do, and because he always did the job right, he chose honesty.

"If this is an extortion attempt, they could be warning you off so that we keep doing exactly what we're doing — looking for a live boy, instead of a dead one."

Amy coughed. The Thunderbird swerved and would have gone straight into a ditch if Brad hadn't grabbed the wheel.

"Pull over," he commanded.

Amy shook her head. "I'm fine." She

straightened the car and drove on. "The note said 'more deaths.' You think it was referring to Kathy?"

Or Charles. In which case the death prevented would be Amy's. "Probably."

And then, a few minutes later, "If it *was* an extortion attempt, why not ask for more money?"

"I still don't think it's about the money. Just doesn't make sense."

"What, then?"

"If Kathy gave Charles to someone else — a couple maybe, a man and a woman who want to keep him, to raise him, they'd certainly be getting desperate at the thought of losing him." Not to mention panicky about the prospect of being caught.

"So why ask for money at all?"

Brad didn't know. It was one of the elements that made the puzzle impossible to complete. He was missing a piece. Something that would bring all this together. And his instincts were telling him he'd better find it fast. Judging by his interview with the boys at that McDonald's, Charles's abductors weren't feeling kindly toward him. And as the pressure grew . . .

Precedent was pretty clear on this one.

Just because Charles Wainscoat was alive on Monday did not mean he would still be alive that Friday.

They were running out of time.

She was tired of being on the run. Instead of the life of luxury and class and respect she'd been promised, she was little more than a fugitive. All these towns, all these bars and clubs, and she could hardly ever go out because of the fucking kid. The few times she'd been able to ditch him and have some fun on her own hardly counted at all. But she'd take what she could get. And right now, that was a whole day and night to herself.

At least she was in a decent motel for a change, the most expensive one she could find.

Slinking down beneath the bedcovers, she let her hand slide down between her legs, making herself feel better.

But even that wasn't easy.

She was so tired of the brat whining for his precious mommy — the bitch — tired of pretending to be a goddamned mother to someone else's kid. She was tired of having to give in to the kid's whims. She was damned tired of being jealous of a five-year-old brat.

Giving in to her own whim for once, Cyndi pulled off her panties. She deserved more than just a tease. Eyes closed, a tiny grin on her face, she reached and squirmed, reached farther. This was the way sex had started out. Sometimes it was still her favorite way.

She knew exactly what she wanted. And how to give it to herself.

And when she was done, lying naked and hot under the covers, she plummeted right back to hell. *Look at me!* Lying there all alone, with no one to appreciate her.

That pissed her off all over again.

Nothing was going like she'd planned. The bitch was getting closer and everything was changing. Getting out of control. Those threats — she still wasn't sure about those.

Jumping out of bed, Cyndi crossed to the mini bar, unscrewed the top of a tiny bottle of whiskey and drained half of it in one gulp. Taking the rest and another couple of bottles, she grabbed her cigarettes and sat her naked ass in the chair at the small dining table. The cool silk felt rather nice against her heated skin.

Another little bottle down, and she still couldn't get the thoughts out of her head. Hell, she kept waking up in a cold sweat at night, thinking about that Stead woman, wondering if she could somehow be blamed.

The end was coming. She practically puked thinking about her own guilt. She could get thrown in jail, and no way in hell was she going back there. Period.

She'd been pushed into a goddamned corner and there was only one thing to do.

She picked up the phone.

Mackinac Bridge, the Western Hemisphere's largest suspension bridge, was just ahead. Crossing Lake Huron and Lake Michigan at the point where the two bodies of water met, the bridge was about five miles long. And according to a sign, it hosted 4.8 million vehicles a year.

To avoid losing her grip on sanity, Amy focused her energy on the world going on outside her.

They were approaching a long, two-lane mammoth metal structure that had no visible end. The speed limit was forty-five.

Driving onto the bridge, Amy could hear the hum of her tires. The water beneath her, on either side, was more than three hundred feet deep. It wouldn't be hard to get lost in there. To disappear and never be seen again.

Brad rode silently beside her. He'd been quiet a long time. Amy hoped he was figuring out who had Charles. And why.

Any second now, he'd tell her he had it all figured out.

She tried to concentrate on the beautiful purple hues of the water where it met a light-blue sky at the horizon. But all she could think about was getting off this bridge.

"There are thousands of acres of wilderness on the other side."

Amy nodded. "I'd heard the Upper Peninsula was popular for hunting and fishing."

"We've got to find Charles before they get too far in."

She'd still been trying to focus on the world outside.

"It's possible that he's going to be killed soon." The voice that said those words resembled hers. Sort of.

"Yes."

"Because we're putting pressure on them and the game's up."

"Maybe."

"But if we back off, we lose him."

He sighed, lifted his arm, laid it over the

back of her seat. His other hand rested along the window frame of his door. Strong hands.

Capable.

"Yes," he said.

She took a deep breath. And then, when a sob almost escaped, she took another breath. "What, um, do you think the chances are that he's dead already?"

She could feel his scrutiny. And kept her eyes trained on the car in front of her. They were almost across the massive bridge.

"Why does it matter?" he finally said. "We're going to proceed, regardless of what I think."

"What do you think?"

"Why torture yourself, Amy? It only weakens your ability to help him."

The Thunderbird rolled off the bridge. She felt only a slight lessening of the tension that gripped her.

"I'm through kidding myself," she told him. "I'm too close to the edge. If I'm going to do this, I have to face reality."

"Based on what we could tell of Charles's mental condition on Monday, something that obviously hadn't just come about that day, my guess is the chances are fifty/fifty."

"And they get smaller with every day that passes."

"That would be my guess."

"When did you become so damned tactful?"

He didn't say anything.

"It's stupid and irritating." She didn't mean those words.

And his lack of response drained the fight out of her. "I'm sorry."

His acknowledgment was a simple lift of his hand.

"You know, somehow over these past months, a man has emerged from behind the mask of Brad Dorchester." Any other time, Amy would never even have considered saying something like that to him. But these weren't ordinary times. She had to do whatever it took to keep her thoughts focused.

He grunted.

"I like him." On business loop 75, Amy sped past the series of hotels lining Lake Huron. Passed a rocky beach lined with restaurants and more hotels. And a Victorian village that could have looked interesting if she'd been in a different state of mind. "I like him a lot."

They were heading toward Sault Ste. Marie, a border city forty-three miles due north. Trees towered on either side of them in this barren country. There were few cars on the road even though it was Friday, the beginning of a weekend.

Tension tightened Amy's stomach. And spread.

"He likes you, too."

Too damn much uncontrolled space. Brad was surrounded by it. Miles and miles of territory in which a young boy could be held hostage. In which a body could be hidden.

He needed to pound something. To get out of this damn car and kick some ass.

He needed to drive.

"Even if we find him, we have no idea what atrocities he's suffered." Amy's voice, frightened and strong at once, cut into him.

"I've seen a lot of bad situations in my line of work, and I can tell you one thing for sure. Kids are resilient." He'd told her this before. It was the truth — but not all of it. "There'll be counseling available to him. And, most important, your love."

"How's he ever going to feel safe again? All the money in the world couldn't protect him."

It was a question Brad didn't even try to

answer. He'd learned a long time ago that no one was really safe. You just couldn't go through life worrying about it.

More trees sped past, so close to the car that he could make out the patterns in the bark.

"I wonder if he'll be glad to see his things again. Or if he'll have outgrown them."

"Probably a little of both." Wondering wasn't something Brad allowed himself to waste much time on. "But you might consider taking him away on some kind of extended vacation. Someplace he won't have to face familiar circumstances that'll only remind him how much he's changed."

"Yeah."

"There's going to be a lot of press."

If nothing else, he was distracting her. The lines around her mouth had loosened a bit. There was a break in the trees. A farm.

"Going away would be good," Amy said. "It would remove him from the paparazzi, too."

"Some of them, anyway. Chicago'll have the worst of them."

They stopped at the one rest area he saw. It was large, with a park, and he wanted to take a thorough look around.

He turned up nothing.

This time, back on the road, he was in the driver's seat.

The trees were still looming, still enormously tall, thick but —

Brad's cell rang.

And two seconds later, the Thunderbird was leaving skid marks in a grassy median and speeding south again.

"What's going on?"

A quick glance showed him Amy's stark-white face.

"That was Agent Averill. There was a call on your machine. A woman who knows where Charles is. It's only about ten miles from here. She wants to cut a deal."

One rush of breath was all the reaction she showed. Sitting up straight, her face a mask of strength and determination, Amy stared silently ahead.

One way or another, no matter what lay ahead, they were almost through.

Five miles down and Amy wanted to fly through the windshield. She called Kristen. Filled her in with brief, clipped words. They were almost there. Pulling off Interstate 75 at highway 123. Turning onto a dirt track in a heavily wooded area.

There was supposed to be a clearing a mile ahead of them.

All was quiet, as though she and Brad were the first of the troops to arrive.

Or maybe they were too late and they'd find nothing but empty acres of trees.

A turn, and she had a glimpse of the clearing. Caught a glint through the trees, like sun shining on the hood of a car.

She focused on that glint. Sending every bit of her energy up ahead, willing a car to be there. And people.

Not once did she think about seeing her son. There'd been too many disappointments. Too many false hopes. She didn't think she could survive another.

She had to be prepared to face anything. Even if it meant finally knowing that she'd never see Charles again. Never hear his dissertations on the life around him, never feel those arms clutching her neck.

Her heart beat so fiercely she could hardly breathe as they rounded the corner.

And then all coherent thought fled.

20

"Johnny!?"

Angling the Thunderbird to block the only way out through the thick mass of trees, Brad slammed it into park and stared at the woman next to him.

Amy was so pale she didn't even look like herself. The voice hadn't sounded like hers, either. Her eyes, when they caught Brad's gaze, were wild.

"It's Johnny." The words were little more than a hoarse whisper. They sent chills down his spine.

"And oh, my God — Charles!"

Fumbling with the car door, Amy flung herself out and stumbled toward the two figures just coming out of a tent in the clearing.

Stopping only long enough to grab the keys from the ignition, Brad followed her. Because he was steadier on his feet, he was able to catch up, placing his body slightly in front of hers as she ran forward.

"Mommy!" The scream was hysterical, almost inhuman-sounding, from a child who'd obviously withstood more than he could tolerate. "Mommy!" It came a second time. "Momm—" The third time he was cut off by a hand over his mouth.

Brad halted so fast Amy ran into him. With an arm behind him, he kept her there.

"Let me . . ." She was pummeling his back and Brad was hardly aware of it. Keeping her behind him, he focused his attention on the figures ahead.

The scared-out-of-his-wits grubby little boy with torn clothes, bare feet and glasses that were falling off his face, in the iron grip of a blank-eyed madman.

A madman with a gun.

Johnny Dunn saw nothing but the woman who'd stripped him of every bit of pride he'd ever had. He saw her money. Her answers to everything. That intimidating confidence that never once let her wonder if perhaps she was wrong. He saw the woman who had the ability to buy him out of anything he got himself into, who used that ability rather than letting him handle his own crises.

The woman who'd come close to destroying him.

413

Deaf to the leaves moving in the wind, the birds he'd listened to that morning, to everything but the rage roaring inside his own head, he grabbed the one thing his wife couldn't buy. The one thing she couldn't take from him. With his son held securely against him, he thrust out his gun.

"Stay back," he demanded in a voice grown harsh with tension that had built to desperation. "Get out of the way! Let my son and me past and no one gets hurt."

He was talking to Amelia, but the bitch was hiding behind some man with dark hair and a cold-looking face.

Johnny hated the man almost as much as he hated Amelia Wainscoat. But he didn't need to kill them. He didn't give a damn about them as long as they let him go.

He couldn't even feel the weight of his son against him. Caleb was a good boy. The best.

"All I want is my son!" he hollered. He'd be as good as his word. He wasn't out to hurt anybody. If they'd simply move out of the way while he and Caleb got in his truck and drove off to the life he had planned for them, no one would get hurt.

If not, then he'd start shooting.

He was not going to lose Caleb.

Over the man's shoulder, Johnny saw

other cars arriving. Official-looking cars. People were shouting at him. He could see their mouths moving, but he couldn't hear a word.

He started to back up.

Amy kept her eyes glued to Charles. Her son was alive. And he needed her. Nothing else registered.

Shouts, men moving, Brad conferring with arriving officers — it all happened around her. Charles's tear-filled, stricken eyes were begging her to save him. She was begging him to hold on. She wanted to tell him not to worry. To tell him Brad was the best money could buy.

But money wasn't going to buy them out of this one. They had to be strong.

That was what she told her son, over and over, with the look in her eyes. *They had to be strong.* She couldn't think beyond that.

"You're going to have to talk to him."

"What?" Amy continued to stare fixedly at her son.

"He's irrational, Amy. I don't think he even hears us. It looks like our only chance is you."

"Okay."

She was still staring at Charles.

"Amy!" Brad pulled her sideways,

breaking her eye contact with her son. He took her by both shoulders. "Listen to me."

"I'm listening." She tried to peer around him, to assure Charles she was still there, but the tight expression on Brad's face got through to her.

"What?"

"We need you to go out in front, as close to Johnny as you can. Get him talking while we move in around you. He's not going to surrender. We've got a negotiating team here, but he's not rational — they won't be able to reach him. The SWAT team's on the way, but I don't think he'll give them enough time to get here."

"Fine." She tried to move away. "I'll do it."

"Wait." He bit the word out. "The minute you step out there, you could die. So far, we've kept you shielded, but the minute he has a shot, he might take it."

"Okay, I'm ready." There was no question, no hesitation.

Brad's look was one she didn't recognize. Showing emotions she'd never seen before.

"Let me go, Brad. If he shoots me, it'll give one of you a chance to rush him and save Charles." She noticed that he was holding a gun and felt no reaction whatso-ever.

"Amy —"

"Let me go," she said harshly. "Before it's too late."

"If —"

"If I die and my son's life is saved, I won't be sorry to have died. If he's not saved, I'm better off dead, anyway. *Now let me go.*"

He started to argue, but when she jerked free this time, he didn't try to stop her.

With nerves she'd never had tested be-fore and without a single doubt, Amy stepped forward. Johnny, with Charles under his arm, was reaching for the door of his truck.

"Johnny?" she called.

The crazed man she'd once loved turned at the sound of her voice.

"You can't win this one, Amelia," Johnny said. His voice was flat. Emotionless. Charles flinched, and Amy was sidetracked for a second.

But only for a second. She made herself look at her husband.

"What's going on, Johnny?"

There hadn't been time for anyone to tell her how to do this, so she did the only thing she could. She asked him the question she needed answered.

And prayed the police were doing their job around her. Ready to grab her son as soon as Johnny aimed his gun.

"You're the one with all the answers," he said. "Except maybe this time. I'm taking him, Amelia, and you can't stop me."

"Why, Johnny?"

With a disgusted look, he started to turn away.

"I don't have any answers, Johnny. I honestly don't get this." She didn't know how the anguish got into that plea. She was so frozen she didn't think she'd ever feel again.

She hoped not.

Johnny had done this. These past nine months of hell . . .

And before that! It was testimony to her fatigued state that Amy had only just realized that there'd been no boating accident. Johnny had staged his own death.

She had a brief flash of the photo Kathy had been holding when they'd found her dead. A picture of Charles *and* Johnny. Had the nanny been trying to tell them something?

Charles turned so he could see her, and Johnny jerked him back.

"You want to know why? I'll tell you." His eyes were unfocused one minute, and fierce the next. Amy wanted them trained on her so they'd stay away from their son.

"Remember Cyndi? The woman I was living with when I met you? I ran into her one night a few years ago when you were working late. It felt damn good to be with her again — and you know why?"

The question was obviously rhetorical. Amy just shook her head.

"Because I was man enough for her. She never tried to make me into something I'm not. She loved me for the man I was." He was spitting out the words.

"You were having an affair?" It had never even occurred to Amy. Not once.

Dizzy, she forced herself to stand up straight and face her husband's gun. His ex-girlfriend. They'd never considered Johnny's ex-girlfriend in all their investigations.

"For more than two years!" he hollered at the top of his voice. "And you were so damn busy working you never suspected!"

She was willing to die.

"Cyndi and I wanted to get married, but I knew you'd never let me have Caleb."

"Charles," she said softly. "His name is Charles."

Her son's bare feet swung back and forth around his father's thigh when she said his name.

Hey, little buddy, hang on. Mommy's going to take care of this. Take care of you.

"No," Johnny said, taking a step closer to her, seemingly oblivious to his son's weight. "That's the name you and your father picked out for him. I wanted Caleb."

Amy didn't remember him ever telling her that.

"I could have proved in any court that Caleb belongs with me. I'm the one who walked the floor with him at night, who read to him, fed him, bathed him, played with him. But it wouldn't have mattered. You would've bought your way around that, too, just like you did everything else. But I wasn't leaving without him. He's mine."

Things were starting to make a horrible kind of sense. Amy's head throbbed so hard it was difficult to think.

But she hung on. Charles needed her. And for once in her life, she wasn't letting him down.

"It doesn't matter that she turned traitor on me," he snarled. "I know she did, because you're here and she's the only one who knew where we were. But it doesn't matter, you hear me?" He was screaming, rambling, holding Charles effortlessly while he pointed that gun.

"You women are all alike. I don't need her."

He was getting more agitated, and it was torture to stand there helplessly and watch this insane man threaten her son.

"So you faked the boating accident." Her voice was faint. She cleared her throat and tried again. "You faked the boating accident."

"Yeah," Johnny said, taking another small step in her direction as he barked a bitter laugh. "It was even easier than I thought it would be to get out of your life. And after we waited long enough to make it look good, I paid Kathy Stead to get Caleb away from you."

His eyes glazed over again. And then was back. "You helped me out there," he said. "I guess I should thank you for that. If you hadn't fired her, she might not have been so willing to help. But she wanted Caleb almost as badly as I did and I promised her she could see him. . . ."

Amy wasn't confused anymore. Just in shock. And certain that the world was never going to make sense again. She was in the clearing about halfway to the truck, and she could feel more than see agents and officers moving in around her, behind her. She didn't know where Brad was.

"The day you . . . died, you warned me about Kathy. That was all part of the plan, wasn't it?"

"Yes," he said, his lip curled in a sneer. "I just didn't expect it to work so well. I wanted to cast suspicion so that when he disappeared, you'd naturally think of her."

"You set her up to take the blame."

"Of course. Someone had to so Cyndi and I could live with our son. Besides, she believed Caleb was better off with me than you."

Amy's knees started to buckle.

"Oh," Johnny added, "and we had the money I'd been slowly siphoning from you since your father died."

"Kathy killed herself."

"Yeah." He backed up a step. "Stupid bitch got off scot-free, but she couldn't handle the guilt." He shook his head. "She was so convinced she had a right to take Caleb she passed two lie detector tests. Then she goes and lets the guilt eat her alive anyway."

She'd known Amy was on to her. Amy's heart went out to the woman whose only fault had been that she'd loved a small boy with all her soul.

All this unhappiness going on right under her nose while she'd moved blissfully, ignorantly, on with her life. Creating buildings that stood tall and strong while the people she cared about crumpled.

"I even let her see him, just like I promised," Johnny said. "She got him every other weekend when we were nearby."

"She watched one of his T-ball games in Ludington."

Charles's feet swung again. And she heard a sniffle. It was the first sound he'd made since his father had slapped a hand over his mouth.

"He was damn good," Johnny said. "Everything I taught him to be."

She was almost close enough to touch him. And Charles.

"How soon after she took Charles did you get him?"

"I was waiting right outside the park. You should've seen how glad he was to see me."

Amy could hardly breathe. "She had him in Lawrence, didn't she?"

"We met there," Johnny almost boasted. "She was late, said she'd had car trouble. I gave Kathy the truck and let her take

Caleb for a couple of days so Cyndi and I could hit some bars and have sex. She got a little loud in bed and I didn't like Caleb listening to that."

Amy might have retched if she'd been able to look away from her son.

Then, without warning, law-enforcement officers moved in, circling him, every one of them with a gun. They came from every direction.

"You'll never get away, Dunn." It was Brad's voice. Amy wasn't surprised, although she had an idea it wasn't normal protocol for a private investigator to take charge of an FBI arrest.

Except that Brad was very decorated ex-FBI. And not one to give up control of anything.

Johnny froze.

"Put the boy down and raise your hands above your head," Brad continued slowly.

"Back off!"

The circle tightened. Johnny's hand, pointing the gun straight at her, was steady.

"I said back off!"

Amy closed her eyes. Waited. And when she couldn't stand it any longer, opened them again. She would go in peace if she could just keep her gaze on Charles.

The little boy's bare feet were swinging furiously, his legs catching Johnny in the thigh again and again, though his father didn't seem to notice.

The circle grew steadily closer.

"You've always had everything you wanted, Amelia," Johnny said, his voice losing some of its harshness to desperation. "You didn't need me. And you didn't need Charles, either. You left him to be raised by a nanny."

Pretty soon he wasn't going to need the gun. She was just going to die on her own.

"Give it up, Dunn. We have you surrounded. You can't possibly win." The armed men were only yards away.

"You grew up with everything," Johnny accused Amy, completely ignoring the approaching band of trained detectives, agents and officers. "I grew up with nothing. Well, I have something now." He lifted his son higher, turned him so that Amy could see the little boy's tear-wet face.

She could feel tears filling her own eyes, sought and held Charles's frantic gaze in spite of those tears. But she didn't buckle. Instead, she took a step forward. It was time to end this. For Charles's sake.

"Caleb is all I ever really wanted," he said. "All I'll ever want. . . ."

She took the last step.

And Johnny's gun went off.

Epilogue

One Month Later

The room was buzzing, reporters from papers all over the country pressed so tightly together they could hardly move, everyone talking at once, exchanging stories, desperate to make sure no one knew anything they didn't all know.

They'd been that way for almost an hour, waiting for the press conference they'd been promised.

A hush fell immediately when a door opened near the front of the room. Hundreds of flashes went off, hundreds of photographs being taken all at once.

Men who were obviously bodyguards, entered the conference room first. A collective breath was taken and held when, moments later, the beautiful woman entered and stepped up to the dais. She was dressed in a soft-pink silk suit and matching shoes, with impeccable makeup, hair expertly cut in flowing dark waves around her shoulders and jewels glinting at her ears, neck and wrists. At her side was the man all the reporters knew to be her private investigator, Brad Dorchester.

There'd been very few suggestions that the two of them might be more than associates, but with him showing up like this — speculation was sure to be rampant.

On the woman's other side, dressed in a gray suit and white shirt with a soft-pink tie — a suit that, except for the tie, matched that of the intimidating-looking detective — stood a very subdued little boy. His face was hidden as he pressed against his mother's side. It was the only picture any of them got of him.

"Ladies and gentlemen, first I want to thank you for the privacy you've given my family and me this past month."

Recording devices whirred. Keyboards clicked.

"I don't want to take up a lot of your time, so I'll just say what I've come to say. As of nine o'clock this morning, I am no longer the owner or CEO of Wainscoat Construction."

There was a roar of questions, and the woman stepped back slightly, her gaze remaining steady. Who was the new owner of the multimillion dollar company? Had it gone public? What was she going to do now? And what about the boy? How was he? Had he . . .

She leaned toward the mike. "I'm turning you over now to the people who can answer those questions. . . ."

And just as quickly as she'd come, she was gone.

Rushed along by people who were paid to see that she wasn't bothered, Amy Wainscoat climbed into the back seat of her limo, an arm around her son, whose face was still buried in her side.

"That wasn't as bad as I thought it would be," she said.

Brad, sitting on her other side, squeezed her hand. "Piece of cake."

"Are we going now, Mommy? Are we going far away now?"

Heart lurching, Amy hugged the little body almost permanently attached to her these days. They had some hard months ahead of them, but the psychiatrists' reports had all been fairly encouraging. They expected a full recovery with time. It was just a question of how much time.

"Yes, Charles, after one more stop, we're going."

"Who's in here with us?" he asked, his voice muffled by her suit.

"You need to see for yourself." The hardest part of all of this was being firm with Charles. But if she was going to give him back his life. . . .

"Charles, look what I brought you."

Brad leaned over, tapping the little boy's foot. It was the most Charles would allow anyone to touch — except his mother.

"C'mon, buddy. You know you can trust me. Look."

Slowly, Charles raised his face, adjusted the new glasses that had gotten twisted and very carefully studied the soccer ball Brad was holding. His gaze never wavered. "Everyone plays soccer in Europe, and you and I are going to give it a try. That is, if you want to." He shoved the ball a little closer.

Slowly, Charles looked up, staring at Brad for a long time. And then over at Cara and Kristen, who sat in the seat across from them. His eyes skittered away from Kristen, the woman who'd become so important to his mother while he was gone, and back to Brad.

Slowly, his eyes never leaving Brad, he took the ball.

And, as she saw the small step forward, Amy blinked back tears that were never far from the surface these days. She had some recovery time ahead of her, too.

And probably years of counseling to deal with the guilt she suffered for her years of self-righteous oblivion. Two people were dead because of her. Kathy and Johnny. She had to accept that burden. Not all of it perhaps, but some. Her share.

"I'm glad you found me."

Amy gave a start. They were the first words Charles had spoken to anyone other than her and Cara since he'd been pulled from his dead father's arms.

"I'm glad I found you, too," Brad said.

Sitting back, he slid his arm around Amy's shoulders, and she knew that somehow, given time and the help of all the people who mattered to her, she was going to be happy again.

And healthy.

The limo pulled to a stop at the cemetery not far from the Wainscoat estate, and everyone piled out.

When Charles balked, Amy picked him up.

"Your father loved you very much," she told him softly, approaching Johnny's grave. He'd come here with her several times in the year after Johnny's feigned death.

Charles buried his face in her shoulder.

"He couldn't help it that he got sick, Charles," she said. "And in the end, he did the only thing he could do to free you from his sickness, to let you come back to me."

It wasn't something an almost six-year-old boy should have to hear, but then, he shouldn't have had to feel the shot reverberating through his father's body, shouldn't have had to see the blood that sprayed from Johnny's self-inflicted gunshot wound.

The Chicago sunshine was warm on their faces a few minutes later as they walked slowly back to the waiting limo. And while Amy had some very good memories of the city and knew she'd visit often, she didn't think she'd ever live here again.

"I've got the auctioneers set up to come tomorrow," Cara told her softly while Kristen and Brad talked together behind them.

Amy just nodded.

"Once everything's sold, I'll pack up your personal stuff and have it put in storage in Denver."

"Oh, Cara, I'm going to miss you."

"I'm going to miss you, too." Cara squeezed Amy's elbow. "So much."

"But we'll visit."

"As much as possible."

"When you've got the time, of course. You're going to be awfully busy as the new vice president of Wainscoat Construction."

"Yeah." Cara grinned. "Thanks for that. You didn't have to make my appointment a condition of the sale."

"You're right, I didn't," Amy said, eager to pass on her news. "Before I set forth my final demands this morning, they had a few of their own. The deal was only good as long as they got you."

"Really?" Cara's grin had grown even wider.

"Really."

Amy smiled, too. Cara was one person she'd treated right as Amelia Wainscoat. And, she believed, as Amy Wayne, too.

The small party talked among themselves on their way to the private Wainscoat airstrip. And then Amy, Brad and Charles were ready to board the craft they now owned privately, instead of corporately, for the overnight flight to Europe.

Charles was once again in Amy's arms. She figured she'd either have to take up weight training, or her son would have to recover rapidly.

"Be happy, Amy," Cara whispered, hugging them tightly. Cara's complete and unconditional acceptance of the person she'd become had been a big part of Amy's healing.

"You, too," Amy said, swallowing tears.

Cara stepped back and there was only Kristen's goodbye to get through.

"Dear, strong, loving Kristen, I'm going to miss you."

"Me, too. But with the move to Denver and getting the new store open and running, time will pass fast enough. And you, my friend, will be otherwise occupied, as well."

Kristen sent a meaningful glance to Brad, who was consulting with the pilot.

"Yeah." Amy couldn't believe she was blushing. "Well, we'll see."

"Okay, get out of here before I start to cry," Kristen said, giving Amy — and, by default, Charles — a hug.

"Hey!" The voice was indignant. "I'm here, too, you know." Charles was looking directly at Kristen. Glaring at her.

"I do know," Kristen said, her face breaking into a delighted smile as Amy's son finally acknowledged her.

"And when we come back, I'll still be here," Charles informed her.

"I can't wait. I have some great video games we can play."

Charles stared at her, his gaze behind the black-plastic-framed glasses intense. "Oh," he said after a brief pause.

That was all.

But for his mother, it was enough.

They'd only been in the air half an hour when Charles fell asleep.

"Poor little guy. This has been a rough month." Brad's voice took on that new note of tenderness every time he talked to or about Charles.

"Yeah. I hope that changes as of right now."

Brad, sitting in the armchair opposite her, his fingers steepled at his lips, studied her.

"I'm hoping that isn't the only thing that changes as of now," he said.

She knew that look. And felt the first stirrings of something warm and sweet.

"You've got three months, Dorchester," she retorted as well as Amy Wayne had ever done. "Do with them what you will."

"Is that a challenge?"

"Maybe."

"Be very sure, because I have to warn you, I never turn down a challenge." He raised his eyebrows. "And I rarely lose."

"Hey, I'm moving to Denver, aren't I?"

"You have to go someplace."

"True."

"I was thinking about retiring from the detective business. Raising a family."

"Oh?" she asked, having a hard time

meeting his gaze. Damned if she'd be the first to look away.

Reaching forward with one leg, he touched the tip of his shoe to hers. "Yeah. I'm forty-one years old. If I don't start now, it'll be too late."

"You have anyone in mind to start that family with, or you plan to be the first male mother?"

"I'll let you know in three months. . . ."

The engine hummed, cool air blew on her skin, and Amy settled back, her arms around her son, her eyes on the man who'd helped her define the person she wanted to become.

The person she was in his eyes.

She had a lot of hopes pinned on the next three months.

Three months in Europe with Brad and Charles.

A new environment. A different culture.

A new beginning.

About the Author

A certified high school teacher, **Tara Taylor Quinn** published several magazine articles before turning to writing as a full-time occupation. When she's not writing or fulfilling speaking engagements, Ms. Quinn spends her time with her husband, Kevin, and her daughter, Rachel.

The employees of Thorndike Press hope you have enjoyed this Large Print book. All our Thorndike and Wheeler Large Print titles are designed for easy reading, and all our books are made to last. Other Thorndike Press Large Print books are available at your library, through selected bookstores, or directly from us.

For information about titles, please call:

(800) 223-1244

or visit our Web site at:

www.gale.com/thorndike
www.gale.com/wheeler

To share your comments, please write:

Publisher
Thorndike Press
295 Kennedy Memorial Drive
Waterville, ME   04901